OUT OF THE DARKNESS & INTO THE LIGHT

Vanessa Matheny

Grey Wolfe Publishing, LLC
PO Box 1088
Birmingham, Michigan 48009
www.GreyWolfePublishing.com

© 2015 Vanessa Matheny
Published by Grey Wolfe Publishing, LLC
www.GreyWolfePublishing.com
All Rights Reserved

FIRST EDITION ISBN: 978-1628280722
SECOND EDITION ISBN: 978-1628281569
Library of Congress Control Number: 2015942429

Out of The Darkness and Into The Light

Vanessa Matheny

Dedication

I dedicate this book first to my Lord Jesus Christ who gave me the story and had me sit next to Him as we wrote it.

I would like to dedicate this book to Ann Howe, a special friend who God used to inspire me to write.

Thank you God and Ann! I certainly wouldn't be where I am today without you both.

Acknowledgements

I would like to give thanks to Karla Hawkins for taking her time out of her busy schedule for me to edit the "original" draft years ago.

I want to especially give thanks to Marj Hanes who did a lot of my editing along the way. I know it took many hours. Thank you for all your time and friendship.

I of course want to give a big thanks to my children. To Mikaela, you have been such an inspiration to me. Thank you for all the times I'd run to you with my thoughts and ideas and you would listen. You've certainly been my sounding board for many years. I love you Sisy-Lou. To my son Gabriel, thank you for always being excited for me and believing in me. It's greatly appreciated. To my eldest son Caleb, thank you for all your encouragement and for being proud of me. I love you all!

I especially want to thank my husband, Phillip for all of his support and for believing in me. I love you!

I want to give a very special thanks to my best friend, Sharolyn Coonrod, who had to endure many years of listening to all of my changes and ideas to the story. Thank you for being excited with me and being there for me through this long journey.

Last but certainly not the least, I want to say thank you to all of my friends and church family for all your encouragements, prayers and support.

PROLOGUE

It's hard to believe that one ultimate battle changed the course of every man's life; a heavenly war that would mark out a long road of deprivation, all because one celestial being, Lucifer, became prideful. Lucifer's violent descent to the earth unleashed a ruthless and relentless spirit called the Leviathan, who is king over all that are proud.

It is because of this ongoing war with pride that we face precarious times—the end times.

In 2020 our government shut down. We were told it was because they were indecisive about our nation's health care and since they were so divided, they felt it necessary to shut it down. It wasn't until twenty-four hours later we found out the truth behind the shutdown.

The announcement didn't come by way of television, or by radio or even the internet. It came by way of swarms of locusts. There were so many of them, that day instantly turned into night. Thousands upon thousands of people were stung by the locusts.

Thankfully, word of mouth spread like wildfire and people started to go underground. We learned very quickly that the locusts weren't able to eat through thick steel or cement. However; they ate most of the plant life, certain types of trees, most of the animals, and yet only stung humans.

In their stingers was a paralyzing agent that went straight to the nervous system leaving one in agony and torment. The searing pain was compared to that of shingles—and for most people that was putting it mildly. This excruciating torment lasted for six months. Many people wanted to find death, but it eluded them. As people made failed attempts on their lives, it wasn't until after the six months was over that they finally died.

Millions of people died over the course of two years, including the President of the United States and all the governmental officials. The Secretary of Defense is presumed dead. Only half of the U.S. military survived. And those of us that were lucky to survive stayed underground for a total of three years to ensure that the locusts were gone. But when we finally emerged, life was never the same. The earth was never the same. It was only the beginning of the end.

At the close of the third year of being underground, a radio broadcast came through exposing the truth behind the devastation.

A military man by the name of John Callaway introduced himself as the new leader of a group called the Idealists. He claimed that the President of the United States shut down the government because they were going to war on Korea by unleashing a new weapon. This new weapon—GMO animal bio-warfare, otherwise known as—The Locusts.

As an Idealist, John Callaway didn't agree that the U.S. should unleash the genetically modified organism on Korea. So on the very day the government shut down, he decided to take action against this war. As the commander and chief of the U.S. military,

Callaway, tried to negotiate with the President and the Secretary of Defense to keep peace with Korea. But during a full-fledged argument between the three men, a button to an underground vault was pushed unearthing the legions of locusts on the United States.

He explained his agenda to keep the peace and to help restore order. He encouraged us to help each other rebuild and carry on. But to enforce this peace, Callaway, felt he needed to create a group called the Elite, which were made up of doctors, law enforcement officers, scientists, and the like.

During this time of peace, small communities and towns were formed. Many people sought after the ones who we all called the "Doomsday Preppers," to help with food supplies and other survival necessities. Most of them helped after they gave us the "I told you so speech." The rest of them kept to themselves to show us that they weren't the crazy ones after all.

Life didn't seem too bad until another four years passed, Idealist John Callaway mysteriously died, and his son, Damion took over.

Damion Callaway became the new Idealist leader. He was not like his father, who was kind and sought out peace. Damion was prideful and wicked.

He kept the Elite group to continue to uphold his own laws and further organized his followers by adding three new groups. Below the Elites he established a group called the Bosses. The Bosses were made up of men and women who would oversee the next group, the Foremen's. The Bosses would determine to which town or community to send the Foremen. The Foremen's were sent to collect the community's prized commodities, such as seed, any type of food, clean water, money, and anything Damion deemed valuable to him.

Since the government shut down, the market collapsed and the value of our dollar is only worth what we the people say it is—which really is only worth what it's traded for. Trading has become our way of survival.

The Christians, and those who remain neutral, along with the "Doomsday Preppers" are what Damion calls the third group—the Misfits. He feels we are in rebellion to him.

I, on the other hand, feel he gave us Christians no choice. He's been sending Foremen's out to strip us of our Bibles. We are not allowed to preach the gospel of Jesus, let alone say His name. We are not to look any Elite in the eyes, and if we do, we are punished.

Damion has taken on the role of "Judge". He believes that God has sent him to be the judge and ruler over all of us. He has completely twisted the Word of God to best serve him and uses the Word against us Christians as a form of persecution.

And just like in the roll of the dice, Damion is slowly taking over the world. I'm not just living in the end times; I'm living in a horrifying true game of Risk.

Someone needs to take a stand. Someone needs to be the voice of reason. Someone needs to be the Truth, the Life, and the Way, and according to my dream, that someone just might be me.

God help us!

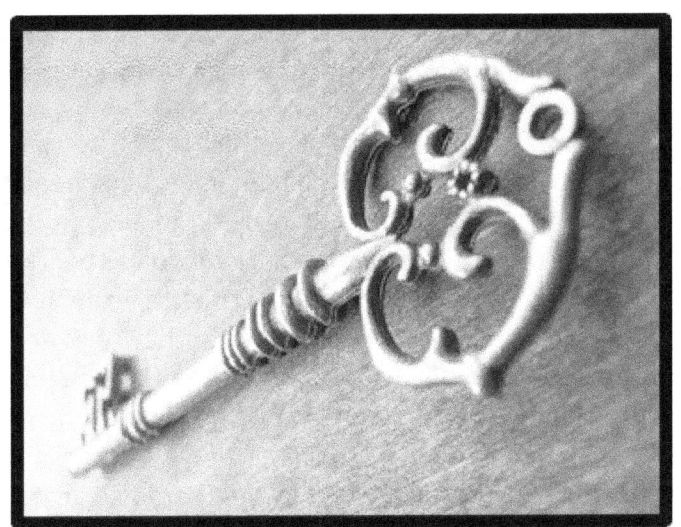

CHAPTER ONE
The Calling

Barefooted, I stepped outside into the moonlit night staring up at billions of stars that illuminated the sky. One particular star, however, shined brighter than all the others. As it glided through the Milky Way, its beauty and gracefulness captivated me. Awed by its splendor, I pretended to catch it with my hands. Just then, the star fell at an accelerating speed landing in the middle of the woods near my house. I ran after it in hopes of finding the falling star.

At the entrance of the woods, I stood fearful of what I might encounter, but something inside me was urging me forward. With each step deeper into the woods, the air grew colder and the silence overcame me. The crackling and snapping of twigs under my feet were the only sounds of comfort. Further into the woods, fierce creatures began to howl. Obviously the rustling of my feet had awakened them.

Up ahead I saw a beam of light shooting up into the sky. "The fallen star," I whispered, "I must be getting close."

In spite of my fears, I ran toward the light. After catching my feet in my nightgown and falling a few times, I managed to reach the fallen star. The star was so bright I shielded my eyes. When I stepped away from the star, a pack of wolves began to encamp around me. I started to panic. I tried to leave, but more wolves came. Their growls made it very clear that I was an intruder and their eyes spoke of hunger. In the midst of their growls, I faintly heard whining and yelping. To my right, I saw a small herd of lambs being watched by a smaller pack of wolves. The lambs were small in size and sickly looking. A couple of them had broken or maimed legs. Several of them appeared to be diseased, and the others looked like they'd been gnawed at.

One particularly large black wolf, who appeared to be the leader, had a small lamb dangling from its mouth. My heart immediately went out to the poor little thing as I saw blood oozing from the nape of its neck. I wanted to rush over there and rescue the lamb, but I was frozen with fear.

Out of sympathy for the lamb, I glared into the black wolf's red eyes. The black wolf raised its head to meet my gaze. He must have felt threatened by me because he dropped the little lamb and began circling a dead tree as if protecting it. Barely hanging on the tree's weak, withered branches were worm-infested fruit. It was obvious to me that no dog or person in its right mind would even consider eating one. So why on earth would the black wolf want to protect such a hideous tree?

While circling the dead tree, the large black wolf cocked his leg and marked his territory. He then turned his fierce eyes upon me. I looked around to see where I could escape, but the pack of wolves moved in and seemed to have grown in numbers. They were everywhere now—up on the hillside, behind me and on either side of me. All of them were foaming at the mouth, dripping and drooling as if they knew I would become their next meal. I wanted to run, but all I was capable of doing was whispering words of desperation, "Lord help me." My breathing intensified to the point of almost hyperventilating.

The weight of his glare announced he was ready to charge. In the most horrifying, demon like voice, it hissed, "It's you. Abigail Banderas. The wanna-be warrior of God." All the other wolves tossed their heads back in laughter and howls.

Their faces were distorted when they talked and laughed. "I'm going to eat you alive." The large black wolf laughed wickedly, showing his oversized fangs in an attempt to smile. Then he lunged toward me.

Out of natural instinct, I yelled, "In the name of Jesus Christ, I command you to flee from me!"

In midair, the wolf's body appeared to move in slow motion. Quickly the fallen star rolled amongst the lambs, gathering them together to become one huge bright light. So bright, it blinded the black wolf, caused him to miss me and hit a huge tree.

Frightened, I fell to the ground. I looked to see what was happening, but the brightness was blinding. When I was finally able to peer from behind my arm, I saw something so amazing—the star had formed into a huge blazing ball of the purest fire I'd ever seen. Then, within a fraction of a second the star dimmed to a flashlight's glow. I sat up and unshielded my eyes to see all the lambs standing around me. They were healed! The maimed stood perfect. The gnawed and diseased lambs were made whole and the weak, strong. Together they stood healthy and were whiter than snow. The one lamb, which once lay limply on the ground, stood at the top of the hill glowing with radiance. Astonished, I slowly looked about me. Scattered on the burnt ground were heaps of dry bones. That was all that was left of the wolves— nothing but piles of dead, dried bones!

I looked toward the hill where the illuminating lamb stood. It was good to see it was safe. Amazingly, I could sense its eyes motioning for me to follow. My heart began to pump wildly as I rose to my feet. When I took my first step toward the lamb, I heard an awful beeping sound as if the ground disapproved of me walking on it.

Beep... Beep... Beep... sang my alarm clock. I jolted up and slapped at the obnoxious contraption. I found myself breathing hard and dripping with sweat. I rubbed my eyes and realized I was in my room, in good ole' Tucson Arizona, not barefoot in the middle of the woods. On the contrary, my feet were still covered by an old pair of gray lumberjack socks that came up to my knees. The warm socks were my favorite pair that I always wore to bed. I took in a deep breath and slowly let it out to regulate my breathing.

"That dream," I said into the mindless air. "...has been haunting me since I was twelve. I've never heard of anyone suffering relentlessly from the same dream for thirteen years!"

I shook my head to rid the intentness of the dream and whipped off the covers to give my five-foot and two-inch body a nice hearty stretch. I casually walked over to the window and looked out at the desolation in my once thriving little suburb. It was both amazing and yet sickening to see just how much damage the locusts had done to the houses.

The few of us who survived, banned together as a small community, and helped one another to rebuild our homes. And with the loss of leadership, the community appointed my father, the pastor, to be their shepherd.

I was comforted in knowing that because of the extreme destruction, and the lack of manpower, Damion Callaway, the Idealist leader, was making only small strides in controlling each state. This meant, for the time being, we lived somewhat normal lives.

We didn't have to worry too much about his so-called rules. Here in Arizona we were still free to share the gospel, speak the name of Jesus, and control our trading. But I knew there was coming a day when Damion would send a Foreman to take charge over us and then we would be subject to his rules.

Daily reports of Damion had been coming in as to which states and cities were being controlled by him. He made his intentions known to all who are out there that he would one day rule the whole United States.

I whispered as I closed the curtain, "I miss the old days of only hearing the factious of the end times instead of living in them."

I stood for a moment in a daze knowing that I was about to have a really thorough discussion with my parents. I wasn't looking forward to it, but for me to expand my wings, I needed my parents to finally let go of their apron strings.

I plastered on a broad smile as I thought of my new prospects for leaving the nest. I then playfully slid across the hardwood floor over to my full-length mirror and was mortified at the sight. Apparently the dream had more of an effect on me than I thought. I looked like a twenty-five-year-old raging lunatic that had escaped from Alcatraz. My strawberry, blond hair was all matted up and wild and my face was covered with sticky drool. I must have tossed and turned in response to the terror of the dream.

I let out a deep sigh. As I started to walk away from the mirror, I hunched over, lifted only my left shoulder, and dragged my left foot behind me. I turned to face the mirror and in the voice of Igor, the mad scientist's assistant, said with an old English accent, "Yes, my master. Yes, my master. I'll go and fetch you your breakfast." I screwed up my face and laughed wickedly.

If my appearance didn't frighten anyone away, my wardrobe sure would have. Despite my age, I still favored the long flannel nightgown, which now stuck to me like glue. Yeah, definitely one would think I had escaped from the funny farm. It's a good thing I didn't have a boyfriend to see me like this. He probably would break up with me or at least convince me I needed to spend some serious time in a cocoon to finish my metamorphosis.

After spending thirty minutes detoxifying and exfoliating my body, my metamorphosis was complete. Once I was dressed and satisfied with my attire, I applied some light makeup and quickly dried my hair. I flapped my arms like a butterfly and said—again in an Old English accent— "And Voila! I've hatched! I am now a pretty butterfly—as if." I took my pointer finger and pretended to gag myself. "This is as good as it gets. Time for Igor to have her breakfast."

Happily, I jogged down the stairs greeting my mother at the bottom.

"There's my beautifully freckled, little button nosed, green-eyed angel. I was just about to see if you were awake. Sleep well?" My mother asked as she gave me a morning hug.

I stood there wide-eyed afraid to answer. If I told my mom that I didn't, she would know I had the dream again.

Shortly after my parents adopted me, I started having the dream. The first time I had it, I was so frightened I couldn't sleep for a week. The second time, my dad forced me to tell him. After I spilled my guts, his mouth hung open with disbelief. My dad has been a pastor for twenty-five years and not once has he heard a dream like that. The Lord specially gifted my dad with being able to interpret dreams. However, with this particular dream, God only shared with my dad that it had something to do with my calling and it was coded with symbolism—like I knew what he was talking about at the age of twelve. To me, it was a constant nightmare.

"Your silence," my mother interrupted, "Tells me you didn't sleep well, which means you had that dream again, didn't you?"

"Oh Mom, please let's not start this again. You know how Dad is going to start in on me about my calling and how he feels as though I've been running away from God."

"Well, you have." Mom said straightforwardly,

She walked with me into the kitchen where my dad was seated. He was holding up the newspaper so I couldn't see his shiny bald head and his big, brown puppy-dog eyes.

"Mom, I really don't want to get into that right now. Can't we just enjoy breakfast together for once without me being lectured about something? Let's talk about something else."

"Yes, like starting with that dream of yours. Stanford, Abigail had that dream again." She said interrupting his reading by pulling down the newspaper.

Frustrated I snapped, "Mom! Just drop it."

He neatly folded the newspaper and set it aside as he patiently waited for his breakfast.

I sat down and stared at the imitation bacon that lay limply across my plate. I so badly wanted to avoid the obvious question that I saw in my dad's eyes and knew an interrogation was about to come.

"They're getting stronger and more frequent, aren't they?"

I stuffed a strip of bacon in my mouth and mumbled, "Yes."

I avoided his eyes by watching my mother repeatedly flipping her long, salt-n-peppered hair out of the way as she bent over to retrieve a dish.

"Abigail," she said with her head inside a cupboard. "Your father and I are concerned about you."

Instantly, I felt like I was sixteen again. I squabbled out, "Don't be."

"Excuse me, young lady?" my mother said, surprised by the tone in my voice.

I quickly changed the subject. "Mom, Dad, I think it's time for me to start thinking about my future." Both of my parent's mouths dropped and instantly my mom's soft hazel eyes watered. "I know we don't have much of a future now that Satan has taken over the planet, but..."

Politically correcting me, my dad said, "You mean Damion."

"Yeah, whatever, my point is I have made arrangements to go live with my friends in Canada. They said their bunker is plenty big enough to share. I thought it would be fun and good for me to be out on my own. After all, I am twenty-five."

"What? You mean leave Arizona and go live in a doomsday bunker?" My mom's high pitch voice squealed with disapproval.

My dad crossed his arms and said as a matter of fact, "You mean hide?"

"What? No, I'm not going to go hide. What makes you think that?"

He pushed his plate aside, leaned on his elbows and folded his hands together as if to pray. I knew what was coming next. He takes a deep breath just before he gets serious. It's the same habit I hear him do right before he's giving a sermon.

He looked me in the eyes and said, "Because I believe you're running from God."

"Oh. So not only do you think I'm going into hiding, you think I'm running from God." I said. I shook my head angrily and added, "How do you even know that I'm running from God? I feel like you're constantly judging me of that."

"Your mother and I are very concerned for you. We've noticed…"

"Concerned? I'm an adult now, in case you haven't noticed."

"Physically yeah, but spiritually—I don't think so."

I put my hands on my boney hips and snapped, "You're a pastor. Should you even be judging me like that? I know Jesus wouldn't be."

My mother put her hand on my shoulder and said firmly, "I think you need to hear what your father has to say."

My dad straightened up in his chair, cleared his throat and said, "We've noticed that you've been spending most of your time watching movies, reading books other than your Bible, and hanging out with the two neighbor girls doing God knows what. You don't participate in our prayer times, you barely sing in chapel. I'm very concerned with your relationship with the Lord. As you already know, we are living in precarious times and we need to be stepping up our game of spreading the gospel and being ready for when Jesus returns. We shouldn't be wasting time with idol stuff." He paused and then continued, "I think I know why your dream is getting more frequent. God has been trying to get your attention and you've been ignoring him—thus running from God."

I twisted my mouth. It all sounded like a valid point, but as stubborn as I am, I preceded my argument.

"Based on all of that, you assume I'm running from God? You don't know my heart, Dad. I may not raise my hands or pray out loud, but I love God."

"I didn't say you didn't love God. I know you do. What I'm saying is for someone who has studied spiritual warfare and the end times, I'm surprised your view on life isn't different. I would think these tough and dangerous times would cause you to want to dive deep into a relationship with Christ and help save as many as you can instead of wasting your days on "your wants" by hiding out in an underground bunker."

I slouched down in my chair. When he put it that way, I did feel selfish and disconnected with God. I placed my hands on my head and breathed heavily.

"What's wrong my little kitten?" My dad asked as he stroked my hair.

I rolled my eyes and said, "Do you have to call me that. I'm not a little girl anymore."

"I know."

I let out a deep sigh and said, "I know what the Bible says and I know what we're experiencing is real, it just seems like Jesus is taking forever to come and until He does, I want to experience life on my own."

One of my mom's thinly plucked eyebrows rose up as she responded sarcastically, "Yeah, sure, why not live it up since Jesus is taking His sweet ole' time. Go, live wild and free to do as you please without any regard to anyone else and God's Kingdom. After all, life is all about you, right?"

My jaw dropped. I'd never heard my mother talk to me like that. I lowered my head and tears started to well up. "The truth is I know God has been trying to show me something about the dream. That's what bothers me. I'm not running from God, Dad. I'm running from the dream."

"Kitten, by running from the dream means you're running from your destiny and if you are running from your destiny, then you are running from God."

With tears streaming down my cheeks, I cried, "You don't understand,"

He stood up and asked my mother, "Opal, do I not understand?"

"Yes, Dear you do. Sit down before you have a stroke."

He turned to me and said, "Who told you that when he was a young man, younger than you, God called him to become a pastor?"

"You." I replied.

"Exactly, and I too, was scared. There's a lot of responsibility laid upon the shoulders of a shepherd for his flock. I didn't want that responsibility. Like you, I ran too until the Lord threw a mountain in my way to make me stop and think about my life. If I hadn't done it His way, I would have kept on living an empty, meaningless life. I would have never met your mother and we wouldn't have adopted you."

I gave my dad credit. He always did know how to reach me. I admired him for his truthfulness, even though the truth made my flesh crawl.

My mother sat next to me and asked, "Why are you scared? You know, fear doesn't come from the Lord. You know full well that the enemy is using that fear and the idol stuff as a distraction to keep you from your God-given purpose."

"I know," I said as I breathed heavily. "But there's just something about that dream that frightens me."

"What dear?" she said soothingly.

"I'm not sure. I can't explain it. But, whatever it is, it's keeping me from wanting to find out."

"Abigail, listen to me," my father began. "That fear is your flesh not wanting to submit to the authority of Jesus Christ. It means Abigail doesn't get to serve herself. It also means that Abigail's faith will be tested, having to trust in God, and not controlling her own life. And that, my Dear, bothers you. And to compensate for that fear, you have been running free doing whatever you want, and not what God wants. Therefore, you have become a wandering, restless disobedient spirit."

Ouch! Leave it to my dad to see right through me. Oh, how I hated that. How does he do it?

"Nothing like being dug at with a spoon here!" I cried.

My dad smiled and said, "Honey, the truth is what sets you free."

My mom added, "Well, you've always been a feisty, free-spirited child who never wanted anyone to tell her what to do."

I looked up at both of them through a veil of tears and said, "Are you guys done with your sermon now?"

"Abigail," my mother scolded.

"What?" I mouthed.

My mother reached over to straighten my blouse and whispered in my ear. "Regardless of your age, we are still your parents and we only want what's best."

My father sighed. "I only want you to be happy."

I stood my ground and said bravely, "And in order for me to be happy, Dad, I need to move out and experience life for myself. Who's to say that isn't my destiny?"

My dad's eyes began to water as he choked out his last words. "What if your destiny is here with us ministering to the community? Think about that?"

****

Later that evening, I laid awake meditating on my father's words. I thought with the conditions of the world the way they are, I would be more apt to make the most of my life for Christ, but my flesh was at war with it. The questioned remained—am I willing to give God control of my life? My freedom? In my spirit, I knew I loved God very much, but my flesh struggled with trust. Will God really be there for me, or will He leave me just like everybody else? What makes me so special that God would want to do anything through me?

My father was right; the fear was simply the fear of giving up control. For me, that was difficult. I never liked anyone giving me orders or telling me what I could and could not do. Growing up in an orphanage, I had only myself to rely on with few people really taking care of me. There were just too many kids, too many mouths to feed, and too many problems. I had to grow up quickly and take care of myself.

I swallowed back the painful memories and was grateful for the day Opal and Stanford adopted me.

I owed a lot to my parents. They taught me so much about the Love of Jesus Christ and just how much a person really does need Him. I enjoyed how my dad paints a beautiful picture of the love of a true Father.

The words from John 3:16 came suddenly to my mind, playing like a tragic love story. "For God so loved the world that He gave His one and only Son, that whoever believes in Him shall not perish but have eternal life." How much more can a Father love than to sacrifice His son, for me, for all mankind.   And if Jesus can sacrifice His will for me and all mankind, by dying on the cross, then why can't I lay down my selfish will and take a hold of His?

But what was God really asking me to do—this whole dream thing? I know God talks to me in my dreams, with His word and through people, but... It's one thing to have the knowledge of who God is, it's altogether different to step out and do what He commands. The question is—Can I do it?

I suddenly laughed at myself for thinking that. Whenever anything impossible came up with my parents, my mother would always say, "With God, all things are possible if you just believe."

She made it sound like an infomercial as she stood there with the pearly white smile and clapped her hands in happiness.

Suddenly I was flooded with many thoughts—thoughts about how cool it would be to live a sheltered life in a doomsday bunker and not have to worry about the Idealist finding me. It gave me great comfort to think of the peace I would have that if another bio-warfare broke out, I would be safe. I wouldn't have to worry about having enough items to trade.

As I thought about my possible new living arrangements, I suddenly became aware of my selfishness. What would I be doing for the Kingdom of heaven if I did hide away in a bunker?

With my face smothered into my pillow, I wailed as the battle of my flesh and spirit raged on.

****

Finally, the sun rose. The brightness of its rays shone through the thin white curtains into my room. Fear had gripped hold of me as soon as my foot touched the hardwood floor, and all I wanted to do was, run.

I felt a pit in my stomach. I knew it was from the decision that I had finally made. Instead of following through with what my spirit was telling me, staying home with my parents to fulfill my destiny, I decided to go live with my friends. I just wasn't ready to save the world. I wanted to experience life.

Both of my parents were heading in my direction as I was heading toward the bathroom.

"Have you thought about what we said to you last night?"

I looked at them. Both eager to hear the opposite of what I was about to say. "Mom, Dad, I..." I hesitated. When I looked at my dad, I knew what he was thinking by the way he twisted his mouth.

"You what, Dear?" my mother inquired.

"Two days ago, I was able to trade money for a plane ride. I want to go live with my friends. I think its time for me to move on and not live with my parents for the rest of my life." I took a deep breath and quietly said, "My plane leaves in two hours."

"But how? Commercial airlines have been grounded since the government shut down." My mom said with disappointment.

"People who privately own their planes are willing to trade for rides."

My mom's eyes grew large with anger as she asked, "And just what did you trade for this plane ride?"

I swallowed hard before answering, "I traded all of my college money."

"You what!" my dad snapped.

"I didn't see any harm in it since there's no schooling anymore. I didn't think the money would be useful."

"The money may not "technically" be useful, but we still use it to trade and that was a lot of money to trade, Honey." My dad said flatly as his mouth began to twist out of frustration.

He stood tall and sternly looked at me while his eyes spoke as if he was certain I was running from God. My mother only shook her head.

"Dad, I really did take to heart all you've said. I thought I was ready to give up my life to God, but now that the morning has come and knowing I've made a commitment to my friends... I... well... the truth is, Dad... I'm not ready yet." I said as I swallowed back some emotion.

I thought I was going to hear another one of his sermons the way he breathed deep.

"You've made your decision. This is between you and God now. Go in peace and be safe." He leaned in and kissed my forehead.

My mother hugged me and said, "Just be careful out there. I would hate for you to get trapped in one of Damion's cities and we'll never see you again. Being Misfits, we stick out like sore thumbs. I think Damion planned it that way; leaving us in our civilian clothes while the Elite are in military uniforms and the Idealist wear their tacky sports jackets with his face as a patch."

"Mom I'll be just fine. I'm flying out of an old, abandoned air strip. There will be others with me."

****

Go in peace. Yeah right! Those last words spoken by my father gnawed at me the whole half hour I waited to board the small aircraft. The war between my flesh and spirit made me break out into a sweat.

After being on the plane a few minutes, the conviction finally caused me to jump out of my seat. When I tried to get off, the so-called flight attendant informed me that the plane was now leaving and I had to buckle up.

It was too late. The plane headed down the runway and I couldn't be obedient to God. The pit in my stomach, the strong conviction, had turned into great sorrow. As we were flying over the towns, tears warmed my check. While wiping away the tears, I repeatedly asked for forgiveness.

The sorrow didn't go away until I heard the still small voice say, "You're forgiven." But I knew in my heart I was still only a wandering, restless, and disobedient spirit.

CHAPTER TWO
THE PROPHETESS

Carrying a tall glass of pomegranate lemonade in one hand, Bible in the other, Miriam headed outside to nestle into her favorite rocking chair. A sense of calmness swept over her as she soaked up the soft, warm breeze that blew through her wild, gray hair. A peaceful smile emerged from her lips as she admired the sun's display of radiance. Its iridescent rays encapsulated all of Bitterroot Forest, and to her, it looked as if God was sprinkling down glitter from heaven.

The display of beauty entranced Miriam, but the joy quickly faded once she looked past the rays, and over a small mountain range.

Miriam's eyes welled up with tears. "Father, please set the captives free and bind up the evil. Open the eyes of your children and bring revival into their hearts. Save the town of Chesterville."

The pain in her heart over the banishment, which had landed her in the midst of Bitterroot Forest, was almost too much to bear. She knew she wasn't going to allow the enemy a foothold by holding onto any bitterness.

"Bitterroot Forest, how ironic, of all places to be banished too," she spoke into the wind. "As if with that name they think they can place some kind of curse on me! I won't let bitterness enter, Lord. I have forgiven Foreman Lovit and his evil followers for what they've done to me and that town. For Your word says I need to 'Bear with each other and forgive whatever grievances you may have against one another. Forgive as the Lord forgave you.' So I command you—spirit of bitterness—to leave me at once, in the Name of the Lord Jesus Christ!"

Miriam then opened her Bible to the book of Exodus. For several months, the Lord had been talking to her in dreams and in visions about a young lady with red hair and the interpretations would always lead back to the story of Moses and the Israelites.

She was desperate to understand what God was trying to tell her. Even though Miriam had read the account of Moses delivering the Israelites out of Egypt many times before, she knew that God's answers were in there. When she began to read, she found that certain words or phrases jumped out at her. She knew what that meant. She quickly grabbed her notebook and started writing the verses that struck her.

God appeared to Moses in flames of fire from within a bush. The Lord said, "I have indeed seen the misery of my people in Egypt. I have heard them crying out because of their slave drivers, and I am concerned about their suffering. So I have come down to rescue them from the hand of the Egyptians and to bring them up out of that land into a good and spacious land, a land flowing with milk and honey... And now the cry of the Israelites has reached me... So now, go. I am sending you to Pharaoh to bring my people, the Israelites, out of Egypt."

But Moses said to God, "Who am I that I should go to Pharaoh and bring the Israelites out of Egypt?"

And God said, "I will be with you. And this will be the sign to you that it is I who have sent you..."

Miriam stopped writing and from within she heard the Lord's voice give revelation. Her eyes widened with surprise as she lifted up her concern to the Lord, "But she's so young?"

Miriam heard the Lord chuckle. "Who were you expecting, the eighty-year-old Moses?"

She giggled and then asked, "But how Lord? How will you save the town of Chesterville?"

"This is what I will do," the Lord said as He gave her verse six to read.

"Therefore, say to the Israelites: 'I am the Lord, and I will bring you out from under the yoke of the Egyptians. I will free you from being slaves to them, and I will redeem you with an outstretched arm and with mighty acts of judgment. I will be your God...'"

Miriam paused in her reading and whispered, "Thank you, dear Lord, for delivering the town of Chesterville. Lord, this is such a big task. Is she..." Miriam wasn't able to ask the question that was truly in her heart.

"The answer is yes, Miriam. She is ready. If I can use a man who stuttered, I can certainly use a young adult who is willing to be my servant. Trust me Miriam; I know what I'm doing."

"Of course, Lord. Forgive me for questioning and doubting you."

"Prepare yourself, Miriam, for there is much work to be done. I am bringing the young woman to you. I will give you instructions as to how to guide her and pray for her. You will be very instrumental; therefore, I need you to continue to seek after me." The Lord instructed.

"Yes, my Lord. Let the modern-day Moses come."

Miriam closed her eyes and began to declare the words the Lord gave her over Chesterville.

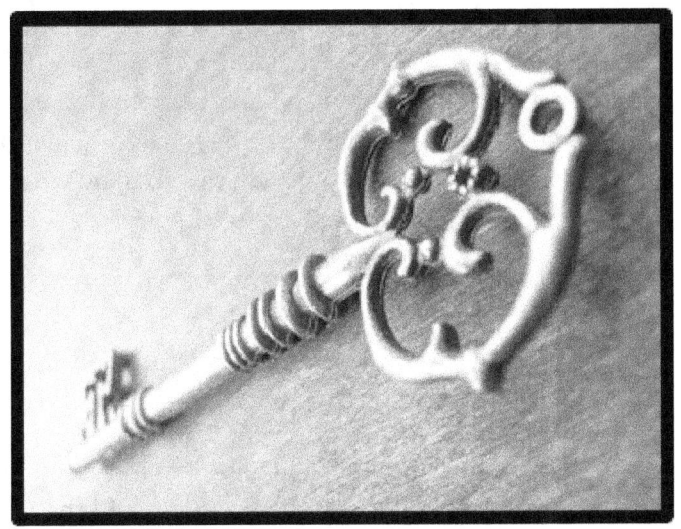

CHAPTER THREE
THE FALLEN STAR

I settled into my seat and was greeted by a rather unique looking person. To me, his large facial features resembled the famous wrestler, Andre the Giant. And he could certainly have won the ultimate award for a ski sloop nose.

"I'm Sam." The soft, gentle voice said.

"Abigail." I said, as I stretched out my hand.

When Sam smiled at me, I was captivated by the richness of the blue eyes. My face felt on fire out of embarrassment as I realized I must have been staring. I quickly looked away only to be spellbound by Sam's, silky, blond, shoulder-length hair. I wanted to stroke it, but what would I say?

"Oh excuse me? But could I touch your silky hair? It looks absolutely gorgeous. What shampoo do you use?" Sam would think I'm either nuts or invading his space.

Sam looked fascinating to me. I was tempted to ask if he belonged to a circus, but that would have been rude. He must have stood at least seven foot and I could only imagine what size shoes he wore. He barely fit in the plane's seat.

"Going on vacation?" he asked.

"Um, yeah, sure?" I said nervously as I fumbled over my words.

Sam leaned toward me and whispered, "That sounded really convincing. If one didn't know any better, one would think you're running away from something or someone."

I anxiously chuckled and wondered if the words "I am running away" were written on my forehead. I ran my hand across my brow in an unconscious attempt to wipe it clean. Was it really that obvious?

"No, I'm actually going to live with some friends," I confessed.

Sam shook his head and said, "Sure. If you say so."

What was up with this person anyway? I didn't owe anyone an explanation of what I'm doing or not doing. He was just some strange person who happened to be sitting next to me.

Sam made me feel uneasy and when I get super nervous, I have a bad habit of chewing on pen caps. I pulled a pen out of my bag and started going to town on a pen cap-twisting and flipping it round with my mouth. It just so happened when I flipped the cap around and accidentally shoved it up my nose, Sam looked my way.

"You're a very entertaining person," he said.

I quickly took the pen cap out of my nose and tried to respond. For the first time in my life, I went stupid. I couldn't think of a response and I'm usually quick to give one. I don't know what it was about Sam, but he made me feel out of sorts. I was beginning to feel as if he knew something or knew me.

To put an end to the awkward moment I said, "There's nothing like a good book to keep one's mind off a long flight."

Sam smiled, sat with his rather large hands in his lap, and didn't speak or move until...

We hit a quick jolt of turbulence which sent the airplane into a nose dive. The plane popped back up just as quickly, as if one's heart had skipped to an irregular heartbeat. In fact, I think my heart skipped a beat or two at that very moment. Instinctively, I quickly grabbed hold of Sam's left hand that was now resting on the arm of the seat.

Gripped with fear, I started to panic. I held my breath and squeezed Sam's left hand tightly. "Everything is going to be okay," Sam said, while patting my hand. Sam's hand was warm and soothing, not clammy or rough like some men's hands.

I slowly withdrew my hand as I nodded. I took a deep breath, rested my head back into the seat and closed my eyes. I couldn't wait until we landed.

Just as my heart went back to its normal rhythm, a screeching sound from the intercom pierced through the chatter of the passengers.

"This is your captain speaking. I regret to inform you that we will be experiencing severe turbulence due to inclement weather up ahead. I have turned on the seat belt sign and ask that all passengers remain seated until further notice. Please be patient with us as we fly through this storm. Try to stay calm and enjoy your flight. This is your captain."

I rolled my eyes and said, "Yeah, right. Enjoy your flight. Not when a sudden rush of seat belt lights simultaneously go on." *Bling, bling.*

No sooner did the captain turn on the lights that we hit several pockets of turbulence, one right after another. The chatter amongst the passengers grew louder and they became restless. Babies began to cry. Young children whined to be released from their belts and a man who appeared to be slightly intoxicated yelled for another drink. Apparently, flying didn't agree with him either.

I looked at Sam hoping for some sense of security. I think Sam sensed I was looking, for Sam met my eyes. There was nothing other than peace in Sam's eyes. How could he be so calm? We were headed right into a storm.

My breathing quickened and I swallowed hard. I looked out the window to a sky heavy with smoky gray clouds. They looked angry as they encamped around the plane. I couldn't even see past the tip of the wing.

I had never flown in a storm before. Sure, I experienced turbulence, but this was different. The turbulence came in pockets like a small boat getting slammed with three-foot waves.

All the passengers were getting more frightened with each burst of turbulence. One hard thrust into a pocket caused a couple overhead compartments to snap open, spilling luggage onto a few passengers.

The children were now crying. Women were screaming out while others were trying to soothe their little ones. Many people were yelling profanity and some, like a husband and a wife, were praying.

My immediate thoughts were with my parents. I should have listened to them. I should have never gotten on this plane. Why did I have to be so stubborn?   God, I'm so sorry. Please help.

I don't want to die. If this is some form of discipline for running away, I'm sorry! Just then, the story of Jonah flashed through my mind.

I bowed my head into my hands and prayed for the weather to clear and for us to reach our destination safely. I felt a warm hand rest on my shoulder. With tear stricken eyes, I looked up at Sam.

"Have no fear. God is here with you." Sam said. Sam's voice echoed in my ears as if my mother were speaking to me.

How can one not fear? The plane was bobbing up and down like a fish on a hook. People were screaming. Luggage was falling and as I looked back out the window, I was frightened at what I saw.

"Sam, look. A piece of the plane is peeling off. That can't be good."

Sam looked out the window. A piece of a panel on the left wing was peeling away and flopping in the wind. At any moment, it looked like it was about to rip right off.

Just then the plane hit an air pocket and began to descend at an accelerated speed. The aircraft shook violently causing the panel on the left wing to break off. The panel flew into a window creating quarter size holes. The plane suddenly began to lose cabin pressure. Instantly the oxygen masks burst out from above.

More people were screaming and yelling for help. "We're going to die!" yelled the intoxicated man.

"Oh God save us!" screamed another lady.

Little children screamed for their moms and dads. The heart-wrenching cries of the passengers were terrifying—a moment in time that will be forever engraved in my ears.

Suddenly an explosion occurred in the right engine causing it to come to a screeching halt. A small haze of smoke began to seep into the plane and then a fire broke out.

"The plane is on fire," yelled a man five rows in front of me. He carefully got out of his seat and took his jacket to stomp out the fire. Unfortunately, he burned himself.

The plane instantly veered off to the right as it continually shimmied violently downward. Engine particles were smashing into the plane like bullets shot from a gun.

I quickly looked out the window as best as I could. I was beginning to see land mass—more like a jungle of trees. I don't know what would be worse, crashing into the sea or a sea of trees.

Many people were being thrashed back and forth. Little children were tossed like rag dolls. An elderly man clenched at his heart as if sensing an oncoming heart attack. A young teenager lunged forward as the plane took more of a nose dive and smashed her face into the seat in front of her. Blood splattered everywhere as the blow broke her nose.

"This is your captain. I'm afraid we are going to have to prepare for a crash landing. I..." The intercom went silent.

The front half of the plane ripped apart. Chunks of debris flew everywhere, aiming at people like darts flung at a dart board. The gaping hole created a strong suction that ripped several people out of the plane.

Spiraling out of control, we landed belly down into a set of trees. The smashing sound of wood breaking plus metal twisting and ripping apart was unbearable. We hit so hard that it sent an intense thud right up my spine. Then, everything went black.

CHAPTER FOUR
The Dead Tree and
The Ill-Mannered Fruit

"Is it done?" Foreman Lovit demanded as he held the phone firmly to his ear.

"I'm sorry Foreman, we ran into a slight snag."

Foreman Lovit, who hated for things to go wrong, turned hot as he hissed back into the phone, "What do you mean a snag? The plan was simple.   Can't you carry out a simple plan?   How stupid can you be?   Tell me what went wrong."

The man breathed hard and shallow.   "Well, Foreman, it's done, but..."

"But, what? Don't leave me guessing!" Foreman Lovit yelled.

"We're not sure Maximus got on the plane."

There was a long pause as Lovit imagined pulling out a gun and shooting the man.   No one disappoints Foreman Lovit.

He rolled his eyes and sighed heavily.   "Well then, Jethro, where do you think he is?"

"We're not sure." Jethro's voice wavered.   He hesitated, knowing he was disappointing his boss.   "We saw Maximus at the terminal talking to some woman.   A group of people crowded our view and then they both disappeared.   Blake saw the woman board but couldn't see if Maximus got on the plane.   I'm sorry Foreman."

"Sorry, did you say?   Well sorry isn't good enough!   Sorry doesn't have Maximus out of the picture yet, now does it?   I can't have him running around and talking.   If he exposes what I'm doing, let's just say...   that is not an option!   I won't have him ruining everything I've worked so hard for.   That little weasel is not going to bring me down.   No one will bring me down.   Do you understand?   I will not have it!"

"Yes, Foreman," said Jethro.

"Now I want you and Blake to find him and find him now, or don't come back here!   Do I make myself clear?"

Jethro's hands shook as he said, "Yes, Foreman."

Foreman Lovit slammed down the phone.   "Incompetent fools!"   Lovit rummaged through his wavy, chestnut hair and sighed heavily.   At age forty-five, he felt too impatient to deal with armatures.

****

"It looks to be another scorcher of a day, Lisa Marie," Sheldon yelled from outside as he tapped on the temperature gauge. "Unless it's broken."

"Why? What's it reading?" Lisa Marie yelled from inside the house.

Sheldon slicked back his sweaty, thick, blonde hair and tapped on it and said, "A hundred and two degrees Fahrenheit."

"It sure feels like it. I'll make us some fresh lemonade. That should cool us down."

Sheldon's attention switched to watching the town's people walk aimlessly from one store to another. He looked toward the General Store, and as usual, it was busy, but not as busy as Lazy Days Saloon.

It didn't matter what time of day it was, that place was always hopping. He despised Lazy Days Saloon. Many people lost trading items in gambling, got into brawls, drank too much, or ran into the wrath of Sniper-Eyed Jones because they dared to share the faith. For Sheldon, that was the worst part.

Sheldon turned his glare to the place where all the trouble started eight years ago.

Set back on a very small hill, loomed the mansion of Foreman Lovit. The two-story mansion with a balcony was in great condition compared to the rest of the town. It was edged with intricate gingerbread framework. Each spindle was painted with the alternate colors of dark Maroon, forest green and vanilla cream. The window frames were trimmed in the forest green color and complemented with off white, lace curtains. The main part of the house was painted maroon.

A close second to the Foreman's mansion was the SunKissed Hotel. Though its grayish red and green exterior had weathered from thirty years of sun, it stood with great beauty in its all natural woods—from top of the line oak, pine and mahogany trimmings.

High above the only hotel in Chesterville, Idaho, in fancy lettering, was the sign.

The owners, Margo and Tony Sullivan kept the wooded hotel in its original condition. The hotel was very clean and Margo maintained the lavishly furnished, Victorian décor. As she put it, "It is like taking a step back in time to the Victorian age."

Even though the locusts damaged the area, the town was able to rebuild their homes and stores to the original structures due to the so-called kindness of the Idealist leader, Damion Callaway. But his kindness came with a price.

"Ice cold lemonade?" Lisa Marie held out a glass.

Startled, he returned to the moment. He paused to look into his dear friend's hazel eyes and said happily, "Oh, yes. Thank you."

"Busy day in the lives of Chesterville, hey?" Lisa Marie asked.

"Yeah, I guess you could say that. If gambling, drinking and causing trouble is being productive."

Lisa Marie sat down in a wooden rocking chair, twisted up her brown hair, and opened her Bible.

Sheldon almost choked on his lemonade. "What are you doing?" He snapped.

"What does it look like I'm doing? I'm reading my Bible." Lisa Marie said casually.

"Put that away before Foreman Lovit, or worse, his side-kick Sniper-Eyed Jones, see you."

Lisa Marie slammed her Bible shut and said, "I'm not afraid of Foreman Lovit or Sniper-Eyed Jones. And you shouldn't be either. It isn't like he's God!"

"I know he's not God. He's just the Foreman of this town, but rules are rules."

"Those are not rules, Sheldon, that's persecution. I'm so sick of his so-called rules."

"I just don't want anything to happen to you. You are like a sister to me and I would hate to see you burned at the stake or crucified."

Lisa Marie waved the Bible in Sheldon's face. "Don't you remember what God did for this town before the Foreman came? And what He did for Miriam. Foreman Lovit tried to have her burned at the stake, but it wouldn't catch on fire. Now that's a powerful God. It even frightens the Foreman and his little minions."

Sheldon grabbed the Bible and tucked it under his shirt. "Yes, I know what God did. But it doesn't change the fact that Foreman Lovit controls just about everyone in this town. And the only reason why the wood didn't catch on fire is because it was wet."

"Do you honestly believe that, Sheldon? That's the pathetic lie Foreman Lovit gave everyone, but I checked out the wood myself, and it was dry as a bone. It was God and even you can't deny that truth."

Sheldon lowered his eyes.

Lisa Marie placed her hands on his broad shoulders. "Where is the Eighteen-year-old I knew when God called him here thirteen years ago? The one who was on fire for God and believed he could move mountains? Where did that man go?"

Sheldon pulled away and walked inside. He hid and locked the Bible deep in a cupboard.

"Hey! What did you do that for?"

"For your own protection, Lisa Marie. Let's be wise as to when we should get it out and read it."

"I never see you read it anymore."

Sheldon walked to the door. Lisa Marie gently whispered, "The Foreman doesn't own everyone. He doesn't own me."

Sheldon paused for a moment and simply said, "I guess I need to get busy myself and get some supplies. I need to fix our sign over the door. The screws are coming loose."

Lisa Marie shrugged her shoulders. "What's the point? We haven't been a mission house in years."

"We still help people, Lisa Marie. That counts for something."

Sheldon walked out and looked up at the half-dangling sign over the door. "The Great Commission's House," he muttered. The sign was considerably gnawed on and the words were faded.

Sheldon opened the squeaky door to Trudy's General Store and was abruptly greeted by a middle-aged woman. "A good afternoon t'ya. Can I help ya find anythin' Sheldon?" Trudy asked with a wide inquisitive smile.

"I'm just in need of some screws and some white paint." replied Sheldon.

"Oh, whatcha needin' paint fer? Fixin' the ole' mission house up are ya?"

Sheldon knew she was hungry for juicy gossip, and he wasn't about to feed it. He placed a small box of screws and a pint of white paint on the counter and just smiled.

Trudy rang up his order as she babbled on, "Does the Foreman know that ya are fixin' up the place?"

Sheldon set his jaw straight and didn't say a word.

"It's mighty kind of Foreman Lovit ta help ya take care of that ole' run down place. Why, he's so generous with his access ta supplies, ain't he? Should I place this on ya account with him or do ya have the cash or somethin' ta trade ta pay fer it ya self?"

In an attempt to grin like a feline that was ready to eat a great big feast, Trudy's scarred face became disfigured. I think she truly enjoyed trapping people so she could run to Foreman Lovit with the juicy information. It was her way of "helping the community".

Sheldon looked at the total and wished he could trade or pay for it on his own without having to continue being owned by the Idealist's generosity. "Put it on Foreman Lovit's account please."

Trudy smiled with great satisfaction.

Before Sheldon walked out the door, he turned and said, "The Foreman would be happy to hear that I'm taking good care of his place."

"I'll be sure 'n tell em'." sang Trudy.

Before the locusts, the town was thriving. People gave generously to the mission house, which was Sheldon's and Lisa Marie's only source of income. They both enjoyed watching how God uniquely supplied their needs from week to week. But these days, the only way most of the town's people are able to receive any supplies to trade is through the Idealist group. In this way, Foreman Lovit controlled everyone. Sheldon hated to rely on the Idealist group to supply his every need, since the Foreman stripped him of everything.

Sheldon hated to be owned like that, but what else could he do? He was afraid for his life. He had nowhere to go and no family to be with since the locusts killed them. He had nothing to trade and no money.

The pain in his heart for the loss of his family and his fiancé Katie sank him deeper into a pit of despair. He wasn't sure God could pull him out. He felt trapped and alone.

Shortly after the Foreman came to the town, he shut down the Great Commission House. Sheldon, in his grief, gave up and did whatever Foreman Lovit said to do, even taking charity from a wicked man just to survive.

Sheldon left the General Store in deep thought and as he walked down the sidewalk, he about plowed into Isabella Thompson. "Oh goodness, I'm so sorry, Isabella. I wasn't watching where I was going. Are you okay?"

Isabella looked at her feet and said, "Yes. I'm okay." She held her package close to her as if it gave her comfort.

Sheldon tried to look her in the eyes, but she would not meet his gaze. Not very many people in the town met each other's eyes. That was one of the Idealist rules and Foreman Lovit, along with his partner, Sniper-Eyed Jones enforced. To them, looking anyone, especially an Idealist, in the eyes was a sign of disrespect that incurred severe punishment. On the contrary, by lowering your head to them it showed honor and respect.

One time, a local townsman, challenged the Foreman and looked him in the eyes. Shortly after that, according to Trudy, he read the passage from Matthew to the man just before he had

Sniper-Eyed Jones gouge out his eyes. "If your right eye causes you to sin, gouge it out and throw it away. It is better for you to lose one part of your body than for your whole body to be thrown into hell."

Sheldon shuttered at the thought of having one's eyes gouged out. Especially from an ex-marine who was a highly trained sniper and a personal hit man.

"Here let me get the door for you," Sheldon said as he opened the door for Isabella, the Foreman's housekeeper.

Sheepishly she said, "Thank you."

"Well a good day t'ya, Ms. Isabella. How are ya?" Trudy asked.

Isabella looking down said quietly, "Just fine. I need to return the shirt the Foreman ordered. He says it's too itchy and wants a softer fabric."

Trudy unwrapped the package and said, "This is the fourth one we've exchanged. I don't know any other dress shirt ta order. He's tried 'em all. Ya jes gonna have ta tell em' ta warsh it. That should sofen' the fabric."

Isabella's pale blue eyes widened with fear. "No. You don't understand. I have to bring back a softer shirt. He insisted it to be a softer fabric and If I don't bring him a new one..."

Her voice trailed off and tears welled up. "I just have to bring him a softer shirt. Please. Don't you have one on the shelf or something?"

Trudy came out from behind the counter and wrapped her arms around Isabella's thinly framed body.

"Now, now. Don't ya worry ya pretty little head of ya'lls. Trudy will fix everythin'."

Isabella slightly looked up at Trudy with hopeful eyes. "Really, you mean it? You'll help me?"

"Well, of course I will," Trudy said mischievously, as she headed toward the shelf that had a small handful of men's dress shirts. Trudy handed the new white dress shirt to Isabella. "This oughta work." Trudy said.

Isabella looked at the tag. "It's one hundred percent cotton. These are the ones that are too itchy for him. I can't give him this one either."

"Honey, they all one hundred percent cotton. Jes change the tag and he won't notice the difference."

"Yes, he will." Isabella said tearfully.

"Don't ya know anythin' about men? It's nothin' but a head game ta them. If he sees the tag ta be one hundred percent cotton, his mind automatically thinks he's gonna itch. But if he sees the tag differently than he won't. Git my drift?

"I-I guess so." Isabella stammered.

Trudy carefully cut off a tag to a woman's shirt that was forty percent cotton and sixty percent rayon. With tiny stitching, she sewed the woman's tag onto the men's white dress shirt.

"If ya don't tell em', he won't notice a thing."

"I won't. And you won't tell him either right?"

"Of course not. Yall's secret is safe with me."

"Thanks, Trudy. You've been so kind to me. You know, you're not as bad as everyone says you are."

Isabella left, leaving Trudy wide-eyed and stunned.

"Sure ya'lls secret is safe with me." She picked up the phone. "Hello, Foreman."

****

It was a record hot day in Chesterville, Idaho, so Lazy Days Saloon was busier than ever. Marco Deportenello couldn't keep up with his thirsty customers. He was almost tempted to pull Simona Simpson, the twelve-year-old orphan girl, off the streets to wash dishes. But with the rough company the saloon keeps, he wasn't sure if having her in there was such a good idea. Not that he cared about what the town folk say. He was just a man who tried to live with some sense of morals.

But as the crowd of men drank their fill, and the more glasses he went through, the more he looked at the light brown-haired girl sitting outside his steps.

"Hey, Marco," yelled Sniper-Eyed Jones, "How about another round for my friends and me? It's hotter than the devil's lair and I need some cooling off!"

Marco went to look at his glass rack and caught a glimpse of himself in the mirror. He didn't recall seeing the deep pitted wrinkles before and noticed the silver in his beard choking out the brown. He suspected the stress he was under was taking more of a toll on his body than he had thought.

Eight glasses left, and with everyone ordering food and other specialty drinks, he couldn't get back there to do the dishes.

"Hey Simona, how would you like to earn a little money?" Marco asked as he squatted next to her and dried his hands on a towel.

Simona turned her small, rounded, head in his direction, but didn't dare look him in the eyes.

"What did you have in mind, Mr. Deportenello?"

"How good are you at washing dishes?"

She smiled. "Real good, sir."

"Then you're hired."

Simona entered the smoke-filled saloon. It reeked with stale beer and heavy tobacco. The drunken men carried on loudly as she covered her ears and kept her eyes on Marco's shoes so she would know where she was heading.

Sniper-Eyed Jones clumsily made his way to the counter. "Hey, Marco! What are you doing bringing in a child in here for? Is she here to do your dirty work?" He laughed as he stumbled.

"Yeah, you could say that. Since I can't keep up with you thirsty men, I need someone to do my dishes—unless you're for hire?"

Sniper-Eyed Jones took a big swig of his beer as most of it went down his chin. Then he slammed it down on the counter and let out a huge belch. "I've got my eye on this one." He pointed a wobbly finger at her. "You know, she's a Misfit—them so-called Christians and whomever else."

Marco pulled the tiny girl behind him and told her to go into the kitchen to wash dishes.

"This here town is made up of mostly Misfits, Sniper." Marco said. "I promise she's not going to be any trouble. Those days have come and gone."

Sniper-Eyed Jones pushed his thick pointer finger into Marco's wrinkled forehead and spat his alcoholic breath on him. "That's right. So I better not hear anything about this Jesus or any gospel mumbo-jumbo stuff. Because you know what happens to any fool who disobeys the Idealist rules."

Sniper's voice grew louder. "They either get burned at the stake or crucified." He laughed and then looked into the kitchen at Simona, who at that very moment looked up into his dark piercing, brown eyes.

Simona quickly looked down.

Sniper tried to climb over the counter top. "Did you just look at me, Misfit?"

Marco tried to stop Sniper by wrapping his hand around his muscular arm. "I'm sure she wasn't looking directly at you. Why don't you go back and sit down, and I'll be right out with those drinks for you and your friends.

Sniper smiled wildly, as he formed his hand into the shape of a gun and pretended to shoot Simona. "Pow," he mouthed and blew on his finger.

"Yo, Snipe, catch any fool trying to preach lately?" Henry Slater asked.

Sniper got right in his face and pulled him by his tie. "Yo, my name isn't Snipe, its Sniper-Eyed Jones, you fool." He shoved Henry back into his seat. The chair wobbled, almost sending Henry backward.

Henry straightened his tie and swallowed hard. He looked at his watch and said, "Break time is over. I best be getting back to the trading post."

Sniper sat down, propped his feet up on the table and leaned back in his chair. "Yes, you should," he said and winked. Henry bolted out of the saloon.

Sniper shook his head and said, "Young fool. I can't believe the Foreman put him in charge of the trading post."

"Apparently the Foreman thought he would be the wisest choice since he used to be the banker. He's very good at determining the value of an item to be traded." Marco said flatly as he handed him his drink.

Sniper pushed his drink aside as he threw out his words to a bunch of drunken men. "Maybe it's time for a visit to the ole' mission house. I'm just burning to catch someone." He laughed as he stood up and staggered his way out of the saloon.

****

"Margo, I've been going over our figures. We're not going to have enough cash to pay the Foreman at collection day." Tony admitted. "I just don't understand why he insists on cash anyway. It has little value." His forehead creased in frustration.

"Maybe so, but you and I both know it's great for trading. I have suspicions about Foreman Lovit."

Tony walked over to the window and looked out. "I do too. I also think it is more than just about the cash because it's not typical for a Foreman to stay four years in one town. They normally stay long enough to strip a community of their resources and leave them to rot. Instead, Damion Callaway sends a Foreman to rebuild this town and blesses us with an abundance of supplies."

"Yeah, and we're all paying for that—at collection day."

"I just wish there was a way I could find out why Foreman Lovit and Sniper-Eyed Jones are really here.

"Me too." Margo said flatly.

Her slightly wrinkled hands shook as she looked around the beautiful hotel that she and Tony established years ago. It was her dream to manage an exquisite hotel. Her eyes fell on each piece of antique furniture and thought it was unfair how the Foreman could take whatever he wanted.

Margo studied her husband's face. She could tell the years of owing the Idealist group took its toll. The circles under his eyes protruded more and more. They both knew that if they didn't have enough, the Foreman would take one of their prize possessions or one day, take the hotel. Then where would they live? How would they survive? They needed the items to trade so they could eat and have clean water.

"What are we going to do since we don't have enough cash?" Margo asked.

"I don't know."

Margo cringed at the thought of the Foreman taking another one of her treasures. "Maybe we should pray. You know God is always faithful in taking care of our needs."

Tony quickly looked up at his wife of thirty-seven years and looked around to make sure no one heard what she said.

"Margo," he scolded. "You've got to be careful. What if someone had heard you and reported to the Foreman or Sniper-Eyed Jones?"

She ignored him. "He's always provided before. I know it's been awhile since He has, but if we just pray..."

"Enough. Let's drop this conversation right now. I will not lose you on account of us talking like this. If we have to give him another piece of our possessions then so be it. It's just stuff."

Margo covered her face and cried. "It's not just stuff. We've worked hard to collect each piece. We've traveled to many places to get these items and they're very special to me. Each time he takes one, it's like he's taking a piece of my heart. I can't bear it anymore. We've got to find another way."

"Well, it could be worse. We could be like Sheldon and have nothing to trade and fully relying on the Idealist. At least this way, the Foreman gets whatever cash I do have or one of our items. I mean it's not like I can just randomly pull people out of a hat and force them to stay here."

"I just won't see another piece go! I won't." Margo cried.

"What's the difference if the Foreman takes one of our possessions or we trade it?"

"Food and he gets nothing!" Margo ran out of the room and up the stairs.

****

Isabella held the white dress shirt firmly to her chest as she headed home. She took a moment to look up to get a sense of direction. When she looked up, she noticed Sniper-Eyed Jones headed her way. She quickened her steps.

Upon entering the stuffy home, she looked around for the Foreman. He must have been waiting for her because he stood at the office entrance with his arms crossed.

Isabella's heart pounded as she handed him the shirt. He looked as if he knew something. He took the shirt and leaned over to give her a light kiss on the cheek.

"Thank you for getting me a new shirt."

"You're welcome." She kept her eyes to the floor.

Foreman Lovit lifted up her chin and said, "You know, Isabella, you can call me Walter when you're home." She slowly nodded her head, still looking down. "And it's okay for you to look me in the eyes when you're home. I enjoy looking into those beautiful blue eyes of yours." He gave her another small kiss, this time on the lips. "Isabella, you don't have to be afraid of me either. You know I won't hurt you. Right?"

"Yes." she whispered, trembling under his hands.

"I love you, Isabella, and that's why I need to take care of something for you."

She looked at him with a puzzled expression. "What? You didn't think I'd find out? I know it's not your fault." Walter picked up the shirt and examined the tag.

Isabella's eyes widened. The adrenaline in her heart was pumping so fast, she thought she was going to faint. Her breathing quickened.

He just looked at her with his intense, piercing, dark brown eyes. "I just had the most interesting conversation with Trudy."

At first, Isabella was at a loss for words. She swallowed and spoke fast. "I tried to tell her that one-hundred-percent cotton makes you itch. She insisted that you had tried them all and that I should wash it to make it softer. She didn't have any other shirts. She thought it best to change tags so your mind wouldn't think you would itch."

Walter blinked his eyes to her exasperating speech. "I don't recall ever saying anything about one-hundred-percent cotton making me itch. I just don't like the name brands she carries."

"But you told me to make sure I get you ones that are not one-hundred-percent cotton."

"No, I said to make sure you don't keep getting those itchy off-brands. Anyway, that's beside the point. The point is, Trudy tried to make me and you out to be fools and I will not have that."

Walter moved closer to Isabella. She stiffened in his embrace. To any other woman, Walter was a very attractive man. He took great pride in keeping himself fit and muscular. He even dressed for success. It was his heart that made him ugly. His eyes contained a coiled dark shadow, which made the hairs on Isabella's arms pop up, plus she was always afraid of what he might do to her.

He whispered in her ear, "Relax. I told you, I will never hurt you. I'm not mad at you." He looked deeply into her eyes. "Don't you worry; I'll take care of Trudy. And I'll make sure she doesn't do this again to us."

Her voice quivered. "What do you plan to do?"

"Let's just say she won't feel like doing any sewing for a while."

The phone rang.

"I best be getting dinner started." Isabella said as she quickly left his office.

The doorbell rang.

Isabella opened the door to a wanna--be Popeye. Sniper-Eyed Jones stood with his legs apart and his arms crossed which made his muscles pop out even more. He even had the sailor's anchor tattooed on his left bicep. His military hair cut glistened with sweat as he lowered his head to give her a mischievous smile.

"Why, it's always a pleasure to see you, Isabella," he said as he winked at her. "Is the Foreman in?"

She pointed in the direction of Walter's office and shut the door behind him.

"Then it's official? Are you sure this time?" Walter said into the phone. "Good. Then you and Jethro are on your way home? Ah. Ah. Good." He hung up the phone and noticed Sniper standing in the room.

"Any word on Maximus?" Sniper inquired.

Walter smiled. "Blake talked with a stewardess who saw him get on the plane."

"So Maximus is dead?"

"Yes. That thorn is out of my flesh."

They both laughed wickedly. Walter abruptly stopped laughing and slammed his fist down on his desk.

Sniper jumped a little. "Now who's got your tail?"

"Trudy Capone."

Sniper sat down and gave Walter a big juicy smile to let him know that he was ready to do his bidding.

****

It was rather late when Trudy heard a knock on the General Store's door. She was surprised to see the Foreman Lovit and Sniper-Eyed Jones standing on the other side of it.

"Is there somethin' wrong, Foreman?" Trudy asked as she half opened the door. Trudy's heart awakened quickly as the Foreman pushed himself into the store.

"Why don't we take this matter into your house?" Foreman Lovit demanded as he was annoyed to have to pull back a curtain instead of opening a door.

Trudy's hands trembled. "I don't understand this intrusion at this late hour."

"Shut up!" snapped Foreman Lovit. "I came to tell you that I admired your handy-work. It must have taken years to learn how to sew tiny stitches like that."

Trudy started to get up. "I told ya, it was Isabella who switched the tags and stitched it." Sniper pushed Trudy back in her seat.

Foreman Lovit began to pace the room. "Now you see here is where the stories don't match. First of all, Isabella would never undermine me. In fact, she's so kind-hearted that she wouldn't even harm a fly. She throws them outside." He began to rub his chin. "Secondly, Isabella is a fine housekeeper." He got real close to Trudy's face. "But she doesn't know how to sew!"

Trudy's face paled. "I will not be made a fool of. And you know what I do to people who try to do that." He hissed.

Trudy's eyes watered with tears. "Luckily for you, I have found someone who knows how to sew just as well as you, if not better." He nodded in Sniper's direction.

Trudy's eyes flooded with fear when she saw Sniper pulling a tapestry needle and thread out of a bag.

"I'm tellin' ya. It was Isabella who changed the tag. She said she was tired of runnin' back and forth fer a shirt fer ya. I tried tellin' her not ta. That it would only anger ya if ya found out." Trudy cried.

Foreman Lovit ignored her lie and asked Sniper for the little, black Bible.

"No!" Trudy yelled. She knew what was coming. "I'm sorry. It won't happen again."

"You're right. And I'm here to make sure of it." Foreman Lovit said.

He opened up the Bible to Matthew and read out loud, "If your right hand causes you to sin, cut it off and throw it away. It is better for you to lose one part of your body than for your whole body to go into hell."

"No! Please don't." Trudy pleaded.

"Fine, since you pleaded. I'm not that completely ruthless." Foreman Lovit and Sniper laughed. "I'm willing to bend my rules a little."

Again, Foreman Lovit motioned Sniper to continue and headed out the door. As he closed the door behind him, he heard Trudy screaming.

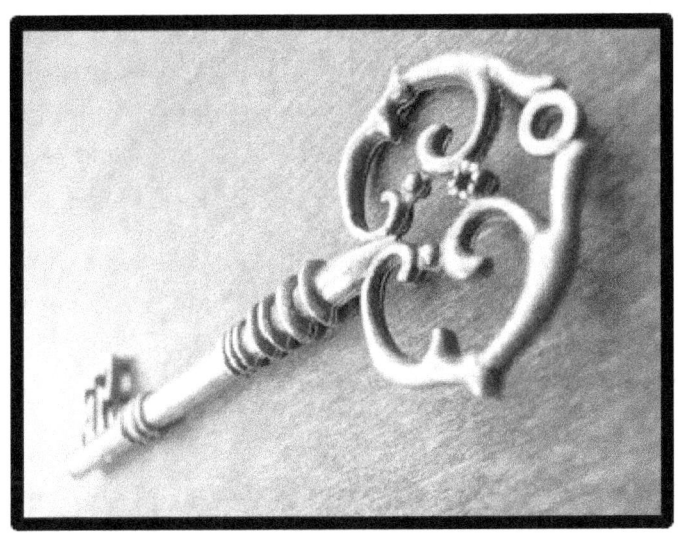

CHAPTER FIVE
The Bright Light

"Abigail, are you all right?" Sam's voice came through a mumbling haze.

"Mom, is that you?" I asked. Through blurred vision, I tried to focus on the face that stared back at me.

"No. It's me, Sam. Are you hurt?"

"My head hurts and so does my back."

I really had a hard time focusing on Sam's face. I felt tired and achy all over as if someone had beaten me.

Sam carefully unbuckled me. "Here, lean on me and I'll lift you out of the seat."

Getting out of the seat wasn't so bad. It was when I tried to stand up in what was left of the plane that was painful.

I slowly looked around and to my horror it looked as though we had been in a war zone and lost. Chunks of the plane were missing. Many seats were mangled on top of each other and tree limbs had punched through, killing so many people and wounding others. If help didn't come soon, they too would perish.

Sam slowly walked me out of the debris. I was surrounded by several fallen and broken trees. The ground was covered with wood splinters and chunks of bark. We had crash-landed in the midst of a thick forest and mountain ranges.

"Where exactly are we, Sam?" I asked as Sam helped me to sit up against a big tree trunk. Sam didn't reply he only sat next to me.

No matter what I did, I couldn't get comfortable. My head throbbed and my legs felt tingly as if a nerve was being pinched.

I looked over at Sam, who didn't appear to be injured, and asked, "Are you hurt? How do you feel?"

Awkward silence fell as Sam and I just stared at each other. Why Sam didn't answer was strange to me. I wondered if Sam's injuries could be internal.

Sam finally broke through the silence and said, "It's time."

"Time for what?" I moaned.

"Time for you to go."

I gave Sam a quizzical look. What on earth was he talking about? Sam must have hit his head really hard or I must have hit my head too hard because our conversation wasn't making any sense.

"Go where?" I said as I waved my hand at the obvious. "We're in the middle of one huge forest."

"It's time to trust God and lean not on your own understanding." Sam replied.

"You must have hit your head pretty hard. Quoting the Bible? Are you okay? Do you know your name and what year it is?"

I was very uncomfortable with the way Sam looked at me and the direction our conversation was heading. I tried to get up but the pain shot down my legs and I cried out.

"How can I go anywhere? I can barely walk."

"Do you believe that God can heal you, Abigail?"

It was the way Sam spoke that caused me to really look into those piercing blue eyes. It was as if scales fell from my eyes and I could truly see Sam for what he was.

"You're an angel?" I said as I touched his face with my finger and felt his smooth skin and his hair. Oh, how his hair shined and felt just as silky as it looked.

Sam's only reply was, "Abigail, do you believe God can heal you?"

"Um, yeah. I mean, sure I do."

"Well, that sounded pretty convincing. Just like you trust in God?"

I hocked a hair ball. "Of course I trust God."

Sam crouched down in front of me and said, "Then why are you here in the middle of the jungle."

"Um."

Sam's tone was like that of a loving father, firm yet gentle. "Abigail, we can do this the easy way or the hard way. Which is it?"

"What does this have to do with healing or trust?"

"You are about to find out. Now, which is it?"

"Well, of course, the easy way."

Sam stood up and looked toward the sky. "Lord she's your child." He squatted back down and said, "No, the Lord says you are to do it the hard way."

I narrowed my eyes. "What? What do you mean? Whoever wants to do it the hard way?"

"Abigail, all of your life you've been doing things the easy way. It's time to do it the hard way. Now get up."

I didn't know angels could be so tough. Even though Sam was being tough, it was as though he was my father trying to look out for me. He gave me tough love—the kick in the pants or as my dad would say, "The Good Lord placed a mountain in my way and I woke up." I believe this was my mountain.

I stood up and all the pain was gone. I couldn't believe it and yet, why should it have surprised me?

Sam gave me the biggest smile. "There. All better. Now it's time for you to go."

"I still don't understand, Sam. Where am I to go?"

Sam pointed straight, straight into the thicket of the jungle.

"Will you be with me?" I asked.

"It's not me that needs to be with you, Abigail, it's the Lord. Ask Him to go with you. I was only sent to protect you and to guide you in the direction you need to go. Once I have done that, it will be time for me to leave."

"How will I know where to go and when I get there?"

"Ask and it will be given to you; seek and you will find; knock and the door will be opened to you.   For everyone who asks receives; he who seeks finds; and to him who knocks, the door will be opened."

"Oh, boy," I breathed. "This can't possibly be happening." I looked quickly to where Sam was pointing and back at the crash site. "I suppose I should round up supplies?" I asked Sam.

He smiled and said, "That would be wise. One never knows how long their journey might be."

"Just how long will I be in the middle of nowhere?"

Sam's only response was, "I will help you gather supplies."

I was thankful for Sam's assistance. I felt sick to my stomach that I had to move the arm of a dead woman to reach for a blanket. But I knew it needed to be done. However, my thoughts were on the ones who were deeply wounded.

"Sam, what can we do for these few people? Will help come?"

"They will be okay. God is with them. You may not see what I see, but there are many angels around here to escort them home. However, the Lord is telling me that there is something He would like for you to do before you go."

"Yes, of course. What is it?"

Sam respectfully stated. "The Lord wants you to ask Him."

Looking the crash site over and at the few wounded people, I asked the Lord what He would like me to do. My eyes immediately went to a woman who was resting her head on a rock. Blood stained her hand as she tried to apply pressure on her wound. Her body was shaking from the pain and shock.

I instantly went to her. A medium-sized piece of metal protruded from her left rib. It looked deep and she was losing a lot of blood. Having no experience in the medical field, I left it alone. Her face was pale and I could tell she didn't have much time left.

The lady reached out and grabbed my arm. In a shallow breath she cried, "Please help me. I don't want to die. I'm scared."

"You don't have to be scared to go to heaven. God is with you." I reassured her.

"God? I haven't talked to God in years. Why would He be here with me and what makes you think I'll go to heaven?"

"Because, God's word is true. He will never leave you nor forsake you."

"But what if I'm the one who did the leaving?"

"Then all you have to do is ask for forgiveness and ask Him back into your heart."

Her breathing became shallower with each word. "You think it's that simple? I have spent most of my life living for myself. I used to have a relationship with Jesus, but after my husband died, I got angry with God. I left him right where I left my husband, in a grave yard."

I was stunned. I didn't know what to say. I didn't know how to soothe this woman of such deep sorrow—sorrow that was more than just a flesh wound. She was spiritually wounded, lost and feeling all alone. How could I get her to believe that Jesus still loved her?

In my mind I quickly prayed, "Lord, give me your words to say because only your words can soothe her."

She cried out in pain and squeezed my hand. "Please don't leave me, talk to me. It comforts me to hear your voice. "

I grabbed hold of her hand and looked intently into her eyes. I boldly took the Lord's words that were engraved in my own heart and spoke them to her.

"What is your name?"

"Meredith." She whispered in a weak voice.

"Meredith, have you ever heard the story of the prodigal son?"

Weakly she shook her head no and said, "I'm afraid to admit I didn't read the Bible very much."

I made myself comfortable and began to tell her the story of the prodigal son from the book of Luke.

"There was this man who had two sons. The younger son said to his father, '"Father give me my share of the inheritance.' So the father divided up his estate between the two sons. Soon after, the younger son gathered all his belongings and his half of the estate and headed off to a distant country. While there, he squandered all his wealth in wild living. After a famine had hit the land, he became in great need. So, he hired himself out to a citizen in that country to go work in his field feeding pigs. As he was feeding the pigs, he longed to eat. Even the pods he was feeding to the pigs looked good enough to eat, but no one gave him anything.

It was at that moment he came to his senses and he said, 'How many of my father's hired men have food to spare, and here I am starving to death! I will set out and go back to my father.'"

Meredith's eyes ran with tears as she squeezed my hand, "What if Jesus doesn't take me back? Did the boy's father take him back after living wildly?"

I smiled and said, "Oh, yes and so much more."

Meredith whispered, "Go on."

"So the younger son thought about what to say to his father. 'Father, I have sinned against you. I am no longer worthy to be called your son; make me like one of your hired men.' He got up and went to his father.

But while he was still a long way off, his father saw him. Filled with compassion for his son, the father ran to his son, threw his arms around him and kissed him. The son said to him exactly what he practiced. 'Father, I have sinned against heaven and against you. I am no longer worthy to be called your son.'"

I gently placed my hand on Meredith's face, looked into her eyes and continued. "But the father said to his servants, 'Quick! Bring the best robe and put it on him. Put a ring on his finger and sandals on his feet. Bring the fattened calf and kill it. Let's have a feast and celebrate. For this son of mine was dead and is alive again, he was lost and is found.' And so they celebrated his son's return."

I saw hope in Meredith's eyes.

"Meredith, you may have done the leaving, but God didn't. He is right here waiting to wrap His arms around you, to place a robe and sandals on your feet. To throw you a big welcoming home party—all because, He loves you.

Now, I don't know why your husband had to die, but I do know that we shouldn't blame God or be angry with Him when things don't go our way, or when we don't understand why things happen the way they do. That is where our trust and faith come into play. We have to have faith that God is in control and trust Him that everything will work out for those who love Him. I also believe that by asking for forgiveness for being angry with Him, He'll forgive you."

"You really think so?"

"I know so. I believe what His word says to be the absolute truth."

"I do wish to see Harold. I know he's in heaven." Meredith gasped. "It's been so long, I forgot how to pray. Will you help me?"

"Why not pray like the prodigal son did?"

Meredith wheezed, "Father, I'm sorry I sinned against you. Please forgive me. I need you. Be with me now." Tears stung my chapped face as I rejoiced as she gave her life over to Jesus Christ.

She winced in pain and whispered hoarsely, "I feel at peace and don't feel so afraid anymore."

"That's good, Meredith," I said as I pushed back a strand of her grey hair across her forehead.

Meredith struggled to take a breath as she said, "I have something in my pocket I need to give to you. Could you get it out for me?"

I reached into her left pants pocket and pulled out a small, metal rectangular pill box. She placed her hand on mine and tried to say more, but she was too weak to speak.

"It's okay, Meredith. Take your time."

"You must..." she gasped. "Give this to..." Meredith passed out.

"Give it to whom, Meredith? To whom am I to give this?" I asked, carefully trying to wake her.

In a low whispering voice she said, "The angel is coming." With a weak hand, she raised it as if to grab a hold of the angel's hand and closed her eyes. Her hand dropped and she breathed her last breath.

I sat there staring at her and the pill box wondering what this was all about. I opened the pill box and inside was a crumbled up Bible page and a skeleton key that was the size of the box. I unraveled the paper to read it, but I was startled when I felt Sam's hand rest on my shoulders.

"The Father says, thank you." Sam whispered down to me.

I got up and said, "No. Thank you Lord, for opening my eyes to see that You are truly in control and that everything does happen for a reason. I too, need to trust You. Up until now, I had forgotten that You do work out everything for the good of those who love You. Every situation has its purpose. My being alive instead of dead from this plane crash isn't just a miracle in itself. There is a greater purpose here." I looked over to the angel, "Isn't there Sam?"

"Yes, and this is just the beginning."

"I was afraid you were going to say that," I said with a little apprehensive laugh. In my mind, I thought, *this must be the hard way*.

"Come on, it's time to finish packing for your trip," Sam urged as he guided me through the rubble.

I shoved the small metal pill box into my pocket and continued collecting various items like food, a flashlight, and even a cigarette lighter. Then I thought how nice it would be to have my own belongings.

"Lord, it sure would be nice to find my luggage. There isn't much in there, but it would be great to have my own clothes." No sooner did the prayer come out of my mouth than, the Lord answered. Lying open-faced was my suitcase next to a mass of plane particles.

"Hey, Sam!" I squealed with delight, "I found my suitcase. It's a miracle." Finding one's luggage after a plane crash would be like trying to find a needle in a hay stack.

"Never underestimate the power of God," Sam said. "Ask and you shall receive."

I held up my suitcase and yelled, "I have found my needle! Go God! How cool is this?"

While I sorted through all the items I'd collected and placed them into one big backpack, I found a thick letter in a small pocket of my suitcase. I opened it up and went straight to the bottom. It was a letter from my dad. I wanted to read it right then, but I knew I needed to be on my way before night rolled in. I refolded it and tucked it away for later.

Sam and I walked and talked until we reached what appeared to be the beginnings of what Sam would call my wilderness experience. Standing before me was a thick forest and in the far distance you could faintly see the snow-capped mountain ranges.

"This is where I say good-bye. Trust that the Lord is here with you, for the angel of the Lord encamps around those who fear Him. Be strong and courageous." Sam placed his warm hand on the side of my head. "And do not be afraid."

I sighed heavily and said, "Well, I guess this means I won't be going to Canada." I drank in a long deep breath and headed into the forest. The only sounds I heard were the snapping of twigs under foot, and birds taking flight. A strange feeling came over me. Something felt too familiar about all of this, as if I had been here before.

CHAPTER SIX
The Lambs

Foreman Lovit slowly entered the house. He playfully looked for Isabella only to find her in the parlor putting away some dishes. He came up from behind and scooped her long golden locks in his hands.

Breathing in deep he said, "I love the smell of your hair." He wrapped all of her hair to one side, exposing the left side of her neck. Isabella jumped.

"I'm sorry; I didn't mean to frighten you."

"It's okay. I didn't hear you come in."

Walter wrapped his arms around her slender waist. Isabella's stomached turned sour at the thought of him touching her. She wished so badly to be free from his gilded cage.

"Marry me?" he asked happily.

Deep in thought, she didn't hear what he had asked. "I'm sorry, what did you say?"

He turned her around and repeated, "Marry me?"

She didn't know how to respond. Her heart forever belonged to Maximus and he knew it. She longed for Maximus' arms to be around her not his.

She hesitated. "I need some time to think it over."

"I understand. Still trying to get over Maximus? You know, he's the one who did the leaving. I mean, who in their right mind would leave his beautiful bride to be, three days before the wedding?"

Isabella struggled to hold back the tears. She didn't understand why Maximus thought it so important to leave just prior to them getting married. But he did, six months ago. He hadn't returned. She did not know where he went or if he was coming back.

"I'll give you a few days to think it over. But after that, I want my answer. And you know how I don't like disappointments." He kissed her forehead and said good night.

Isabella sat at her vanity table, grabbed her hair brush, and began to stroke her long hair. Her mind flooded with thoughts of Maximus. She reminisced back to the time they met four years ago. Walter had hired both of them to be his maid and butler. Each and every night after their duties were done, they would stay up and talk for hours. She fell deeply in love with him fast. He was a good man, full of pure love. There was something different and special about him. A few months prior to his leaving, he talked to her about a man named Jesus. She had never heard of him before and didn't understand why Maximus was so eager to talk about him. He tried to get her to read a book called the Bible. It was then that Walter noticed their relationship and he began to get jealous of Maximus.

Walter responded with rage when he saw Maximus reading the Bible in the parlor one day. He took it and ripped it up and told him never to read it again. He said that Maximus was breaking one of the Idealist rules, plus the book was nothing but a fairy tale full of lies anyway. Walter also warned him that if he was caught preaching or saying the name of Jesus again, Maximus would be punished.

Isabella noticed Walter keeping a close eye on her after that. He made advances toward her. She refused them until one day he threatened her. He threatened to have Maximus out of the way so they could be together. It was then, three days before their wedding that Maximus disappeared.

****

Simona barreled into the General Store. "My goodness, child, where is ya manners. Ya'lls recklessness is goin' ta break my door." Trudy grumbled.

Breathlessly, Simona slapped her list on the counter. "Mr. Deportenello needs to have these here items."

Trudy careful rested her left hand on the counter and picked up the list with her right.

"Whoa! Ms. Trudy. What happened to your hand?" Simona asked as she gawked at Trudy's bandaged hand.

"Nothin' that's any of ya'lls business." Trudy spat out as she hid her left hand behind the counter.

"Wow. That wound still looks fresh. It's bleeding right through the white bandage. Have you seen doc yet?"

"Like I said, it's none of ya'lls business.   But if ya intend on runnin' ya mouth about it, ya can tell people that I slammed it in the door."

Simona gave her a questionable look. Trudy glared down at her and said spitefully, "It's the honest t'gosh truth."

"Okay, if you say so."

Trudy glanced at the list and back at Simona.   "Since when did ya start runnin' errands fer Mr. Deportenello?"

"He just hired me yesterday."

"What? Hired ya. Ya only twelve. Ya shouldn't be in a place like that."

"I spent yesterday washing dishes."

Trudy shook her head at her.   "What is the world comin' ta that they allow a twelve-year-old girl in a saloon?" Simona just smiled.

"Tell Mr. Deportenello it's gonna cost a tradin' of three bottles of whisky fer his groceries."

"Sure thing."   Simona left the list on the counter and ran all the way back to the saloon.

"I've done what you've asked. I gave your grocery list to Ms. Trudy and she said it will come in by the end of the week. Oh, and Ms. Trudy slammed her left hand in a door. It's all bandaged up. It looks pretty bad. Gross actually. Blood is oozing out of the bandage. She did it yesterday." Simona rattled on breathlessly.

"Oh, okay, Simona. Thanks for the info. Run along now. I can't stick around and chat today. I have chili to make."

Marco turned around to head toward the kitchen. Simona followed. When Marco turned around, he almost tripped over her.

"Oh Simona, I didn't see you there. Can I help you?"

"I'm reporting for duty, Sir." She gave him a salute.

"Duty?"

"Yeah. You hired me yesterday." Simona cocked her head. "Don't you remember?"

"Of course I remember you doing the dishes. I just don't recall hiring you."

"You asked if I was good at washing dishes and I said yes. Then you said, hired."

Marco laughed. "Sweetie, I was just referring to that moment. Not a full time job. I can't truly hire a twelve-year-old. You have to be eighteen or older because I sell liquor. Besides, the Elite group would have my hide if they found out a twelve-year-old was working in a bar."

Simona nodded and slowly dragged herself out.

Marco felt bad. He wished he could do more for her and those other orphaned kids. It made his heart ache, seeing her in ratty old clothes sitting on his steps.

Simona sat limply and wondered how she was going to feed herself and the other children. Now what? She thought to herself; back to the run-down barn? She missed staying at the mission house, but the Foreman shut it down to all those who were in need of a home, which included the orphans.

Simona didn't have any parents to guide her. She missed being a part of a family. In her own special way, she had a family, except she was the parent.

Five other orphans crammed in a small, worn down barn that was a hundred feet behind the General Store. She cared for them as if she was their mother. They all looked up to her. At times, that was stressful, being a child herself. She didn't know how to take care of kids as well as real parents could.

On occasion, a few of the town's people would look out for the orphans, making sure they had the essentials, but Sniper-Eyed Jones made sure they didn't get too much help.

She was thankful for Mr. Deportenello. He helped out the kids by giving them leftovers. If the Foreman found out what Mr. Deportenello was doing, he would be in some serious trouble, so Simona kept his secret.

Sheldon supplied all of their beds, some homemade dressers, which were made from old book shelves and he hooked up electricity that connected to Trudy's General Store. It was nice to have lights.

Simona saw Sheldon as a father figure. She loved him dearly. She secretly prayed that he would adopt her. She told herself, that if he adopted her, she would be the best daughter ever, but there was always this nagging thought that plagued her. "Nobody wants to adopt a twelve-year-old. Everyone is looking to adopt babies or little children under seven."

One lonely tear slid down her dirty face. "Back to the barn."

Marco quickly squatted down next to her and said, "Here." He handed her an item that was in a brown paper bag.

She partly looked his way and said, "What's this?"

"I know I shouldn't being doing this and if I get caught I could get punished, but I won't let innocent children go hungry."

Simona looked inside. It was whisky. "I don't understand."

"Liquor is all I have to trade with and I have no leftovers today. Now, promise me that you will take this straight to the store and trade it for food. It's very valuable and I know you'll get a lot of food in exchange for it."

She stood up and hugged him. "Yes, of course. I don't drink."

"Quick, go before someone see's what I just did."

Simon ran as fast as she could to the barn and was greeted by four dirty, hungry little faces. All but one came running up to her in anticipation of something good to eat. Zack, a nine-year-old, was the second oldest of the six and he stood back and waited.

Zack was found on the steps of an orphanage in Montana when he was three. A small note was pinned to his blanket asking for the orphanage to take care of him until they could come back for him. When he turned seven, the orphanage placed him on a train to Chesterville, Idaho-to the mission's house.

According to their rules, once a child reached the age of seven, the hopes of being adopted were slim. They believed, by sending a child to another orphanage in a thriving town, their chances of being placed with a family was higher.

Prior to the locust's invasion, Chesterville was a thriving community, and many of the orphanages around Idaho and Montana would send older children to Chesterville in hopes of their being placed with families.

When Foreman Lovit came, he shut down the orphanage and would not allow the six remaining children to be adopted, which is how they ended up living in the barn and looking to the town's people to take care of them.

When Simona met Zack's saddened eyes, he knew. Once again, no one was coming for him. He quietly curled up on his lumpy bed and tried to be strong and not cry.

"Why don't you have food from Mr. Deportenello with you?" Lilly, who was seven, asked as she noticed Simona holding something other than food.

Simona looked down into a pair of big brown eyes and said, "I came home with something different today, Lilly." Due to the content of what was inside the bag, Simona decided not to show them. "I brought back something to trade and I thought we all could go to the grocery store and pick out what we want to eat for dinner."

All of them screamed with delight. Simona picked up little Anna who was the youngest, three. "How does that sound, Anna?" Simona asked, hoping to get a response out of her.

Anna was the one Simona worried about the most. She was way too undernourished and refused to say anything. Grunting noises and pointing were the only things Anna would do. Most of the time, Anna sat quietly in her own little world, and barely ate.

Anna pushed hard against Simona in protest—wanting down. She put Anna down only to see her run and sit in the middle of a worn-out carpet, which Margo Sullivan had so kindly given them.

Billy, who was five, and Carry, six, were very excited to take a trip to the General Store-anything to stop the constant growl pains. Billy hated going to bed every night with hunger pains. Carry always worried if this was going to be the day they were going to go without dinner.

Since Simona couldn't get Anna to budge from the carpet, she left Zack in charge of her.

****

By early evening, Lazy Days Saloon was hoppin' with the many townsmen. Several of them played poker. A few of them told tall tales of the good ole' days before the locusts came.

Foreman Lovit and Sniper-Eyed Jones walked into the loud, smoke-filled crowd. Suddenly the place grew quiet. All eyes looked to the floor. Even Marco stopped drying glasses and looked down at his dirty floor, which he noticed needed cleaning.

"I'll have my usual." said Sniper as he slapped his hand on the bar's counter.

"That goes for me as well." Foreman Lovit said wearily.

Sniper jokingly punched his arm and said. "Hey man, what's up with you? You sound as if you've lost your best friend today." He looked around at the silent men and said, "Back to business, boys." As if someone had released a bee hive, the buzzing of many voices came alive again.

Foreman Lovit leaned over to Sniper and said, "I suppose you could say that."

Sniper gave him a quizzical look. Other than Isabella, he was the only one who could get away with looking him in the eyes. Sniper nodded for them to go sit in their usual spot. "So are you going to tell me what's bothering you?"

Foreman Lovit leaned closer to Sniper so he could hear. "I can't find that stupid key. It's been missing ever since that day Maximus left."

"You think he's got it?" Sniper asked.

"I don't know who else would have it."

"Maybe Isabella took it."

"No. I don't believe so. She wouldn't do something like that. She's too afraid of me. Besides, she doesn't know anything. Half the time she walks around as if she's empty headed. She's too busy with cleaning to even concern herself with my business."

"So what are we going to do? Isn't your Boss putting pressure on you to give him the stuff?"

Foreman Lovit gave Sniper an agitated look. "Yes. That's because Damion is putting pressure on him, which makes him put pressure on me. I'm doing the best that I can. If I don't find that key, then I can't get the stuff."

"Can you somehow have another key made?"

"No, you fool. It's a rare key. And it's the only one that will work in my door."

Sniper thought a moment. "What if you picked the lock?"

Foreman Lovit shook his head. "Don't you know anything? The house was built in the late 1800's. You try picking the lock and you'll destroy the door. The door and the key were specially made. You can't find doors or keys like that anymore."

"So now what?"

"All I know, is my Boss is wanting the stuff and he and Damion aren't happy. I can sense he wants to meet with me soon."

"How do you know?" Sniper asked.

"He's been giving me dreams."

"Wow. That's cool that he can give you dreams."

Foreman Lovit put his arm around Sniper and smiled greedily. "The Boss can do more than just give dreams, my boy. Damion and him can give us power."

Sniper's eyes sparkled with excitement when he heard the word power. "I like power."

"Stick with me and you shall have it."

"You mean, power over people like Trudy Capone?"

Foreman Lovit threw his head back and laughed. "Power over her, this here town and wealth. Lots of wealth. The power is endless."

"Speaking of Trudy, having me sew her fingers together was your most brilliant idea yet." Sniper said, after he took a long swallow of his drink.

"Yes it was, wasn't it?" They both laughed.

Sniper held up his empty glass and yelled, "Another round! And keep them coming. We're thirsty men, Marco!" Foreman Lovit and Sniper drank themselves into oblivion.

"Oh, I've gots another idea." Slurred Foreman Lovit.

"Oh, yeah? What's that?" Sniper spit as he said his 'Ts'.

"The next person, who defiles us, gets stoned to death."

Sniper slammed his hand on the table in enjoyment, "I am just amazed on how you come up with this stuff." he laughed.

"I got that one from all those Bible thumpers. Since they believe in that stuff so much, why not use it to my benefit." Foreman Lovit laughed so hard that he about toppled over in his chair.

****

It was late into the evening and Isabella couldn't sleep. Her mind raced with many thoughts; the marriage proposal from Walter... where was Maximus... Maximus' last words about the man named Jesus...

She even pondered on the love Maximus had toward her and how different it was from Walter's. Walter's was demanding and selfish, while Maximus' was self-less.

She felt confused and didn't know what true love looked like. She knew the kind of love Maximus showed was the very kind she yearned for. Walter's love felt cold, dark and empty.

She remembered how Maximus' eyes lit up whenever he talked about this Jesus, as if they were best friends. He talked about him with such love and admiration. She had to admit, this Jesus person sounded like someone she would really like to meet. And from what Maximus said, one way to meet him was through reading the Bible. But Walter banned all Bible's, reading of the Bible and even talking about Jesus. No one was allowed to mention the name Jesus in front of him or they would be burned at the stake, crucified, or killed by other creative means. He even enjoyed having Sniper-Eyed Jones carry-out his punishments.

She just couldn't get Maximus' last words about Jesus out of her mind. To think God came down in the flesh, born of a virgin woman, crucified for her sins, died and buried, and rose again to give her eternal life. That amazed Isabella so much, that she wanted to read it for herself.

Suddenly her thoughts went to Walter's black Bible and wondered why he was the only one allowed to have one. She sat up in her cold, dark room and pictured the black Bible tucked away in Walter's desk drawer. Filled with curiosity, she flicked on a few lights and tip-toed downstairs. Cautiously she made her way into

Walter's office. She looked out the window toward Lazy Days Saloon to see if he was on his way home. As long as Marco kept the beer coming, Walter would be there.

Slowly, she opened the drawer. Her heart pounded in anticipation. She longed to read the beloved words Maximus so dearly spoke of, and she was curious as to why the Idealist had banned them.

Quickly she grabbed the black Bible and tucked it in her shirt. Like a bolt of lightning, she ran up the stairs as fast as her small feet could carry her. Turning off all but one light, Isabella opened up the book. Her heart fluttered with both excitement and fear.

For a few moments, she stared at the opened Bible. Many bad scenarios went through her mind as to what Walter was capable of doing to her for reading the Bible. Was reading it worth the risk? According to the passion Maximus had shown her, she thought it was.

She breathed deep, flipped through the pages and ended up in 1 Corinthians. Scanning over each chapter and reading the subtitles, she found them fascinating. An overwhelming sense of, "where do you even begin to read", came over her.

As she turned the page, her eyes immediately fell on chapter thirteen; for the subtitle read "Love."

When she read verse four, she began to weep. It was so powerful to her; she had to read the verse again. This time she read it quietly out loud.

"Love is patient, love is kind. It does not envy, it does not boast. It is not proud. It is not rude, it is not self-seeking, it is not easily angered, it keeps no record of wrongs. Love does not delight in evil but rejoices with the truth. It always protects; always trusts; always hopes; always perseveres. Love never fails...."

Isabella was speechless. This was the very kind of love Maximus showed her. Even though she knew he wasn't perfect, he worked hard to show himself to be an honorable man in everything he did, including his relationship with her. She was even surprised about how loving he was toward Walter. And Walter would be so cruel back to him. It was as if Maximus let Walter's words slide right off of him like water sliding off a duck's back. Walter's words never seemed to pierce his heart like they had hers.

Her heart felt like it was a target range for Walter's bullets. He would leave her heart bleeding and wounded, and walk away as if he didn't care. She wiped her runny nose and eyes on the sleeve of her pajamas.

Again, she thought of how different Walter's love was toward her. He definitely wasn't patient, especially when it came to dinner or having a clean, non-itchy shirt. He was defiantly boastful, a self-seeking man who obviously enjoyed evil. He liked to brag about the town's people he and Sniper-Eyed Jones punished. And when it came to anger, he could go down into the hall of fame. He angered easily and kept a tally of it to later spit out at his offenders.

"Come to think about it, Walter has never apologized for anything he has done to me." She whispered.

Where to next? She wondered. Then she quickly remembered a Bible verse Maximus would quote. She could almost hear his voice telling her.

Now where do you find this John 3:16? She looked in the very front of the Bible that listed the Old Testament and New Testament chapters. Carefully she turned the pages so as not to rip them. She was amazed at how thin and fragile the pages were.

She then read it aloud as well. "For God so loved the world that he gave his one and only Son, that whoever believes in Him shall not perish but have eternal life." She kept reading. "For God did not send His Son into the world to condemn the world, but to save the world through Him."

Even though she didn't quite understand it all, something about the words filled her heart with peace. She told herself to work hard to remember the precious words she'd read. She wasn't sure when she would be able to read the Bible again, but would work very hard to find a way.

She was hungry for more. Again, she randomly flipped the pages and feasted on the book of Psalms. "The Lord is compassionate and gracious; slow to anger, abounding in love. He will not always accuse, nor will He harbor His anger forever; He does not treat us as our sins deserve or repay us according to our iniquities. For as high as the heavens are above the earth, so great is His love for those who fear Him; as far as the east is from the west, so far has He removed our transgressions from us."

Isabella was astounded by what she read. The words painted a completely different picture of God than what she had heard Walter say to her. Suddenly, a cold chill ran down her spine.

She began to see Walter in a different light. She couldn't put her finger on it, but something was not right about what Walter believed. It didn't match up with what she read.

According to Walter, God doesn't care about problems. He's the one who creates them and lets bad things happen to good people. God is up there judging you for every sin you do and He will rightfully punish all those who break His commands.

Walter feels God appointed him to help carry out His punishments. For that reason, no one needs to read the Bible but him and the head leader, Damion Callaway.

The more she thought about it, the more it made sense to her. Seeing how Walter and Sniper-Eyed Jones would read the

Bible and then carried out what it said as a punishment.

Fear swooped down on her like a predator. It intensified as if it were feeding on her flesh.

What if Damion is God and Walter is one of his helpers? And they came down from heaven to punish everyone. And I'm committing a sin right now by reading the Bible that Walter told me never to read. He'll have me crucified or burned at the stake if he finds out I've done this horrible act.

The more she thought about it, the more confused and frightened she became. Fear would not leave her. It intensified to the point when she heard a noise, she'd jump. She hopped out of bed and opened her door to listen. Sure enough she heard right. Voices from downstairs drifted up to her.

"Hey Sniper!" Walter slured; "I gotts another good one. The next person who defies us, we should whip them with cattails."

Isabella looked at the Bible and trembled. "Cattails? What's that?" she whispered. "How am I going to place the Bible back in Walter's desk drawer without him seeing me?"

Securely, she placed the Bible under her pajama top and slowly headed down the stairs. Leaning over the bannister to get a better view, she saw Walter staggering toward the parlor.

"The parlor. That's good," she thought. "It's on the opposite side of his office. I can run quickly to it and sneak out before he realizes what's happened."

Isabella reached the bottom step, crossed over in the direction of the office when suddenly she heard Walter yell, "Sniper, I'm heading in the wrong room. I need to go into my office, not the parlor."

The parlor was right next to the dining hall behind the stairs. Isabella would have to pass the bathroom and the library first before she could reach his office.

The main floor wrapped in a circle, with the large winding staircase in the center. To the right of the staircase, in the main lobby was the office, a bathroom, and a huge library. The hall would then wrap around the stairwell that led to a huge mahogany door leading into the parlor. Next to the parlor were French mahogany doors that opened up to a very large dining room and then into the second smaller kitchen.

Her heart quickened. *Now what?* She wasn't even close to the office yet. She had to think quickly. She knew she wasn't going to make it to the office before him. Walter was closer to it than her. The closest room to her was either the bathroom or the library.

Quickly she ran into the library. Walter's voice was close. He must be in the office by now. She flicked on the light and looked around to try and figure out what to do with the Bible. He was coming down the hall toward the library. She tried not to panic.

"I thought you were going to your office, Walter?" Sniper asked.

"Somebody's in here. The library light is on and it shouldn't be."

Just as Walter twisted the door knob to the library, Isabella shoved the Bible in between two thick dictionaries. They both collided as he opened the door to walk in.

"Aw!" they both screamed out of fright.

Walter gripped her firmly, pulled her close and asked, "What on earth are you doing in here? And why are you up so late.

You're never up this late. I could have killed you. I thought you were an intruder."

She did not like being so close to him, especially when he reeked with alcohol. Her voice trembled. "I couldn't sleep so I came down to find a book to read."

"Really, I didn't take you to be a book lover. I've never seen you read."

Walter loosened his grip and she took a step back. "That's because I'm usually too busy to sit and read."

"So why start now?"

Oh, how she hated his probing questions. It always made her feel like she was under interrogation. Isabella mustered deep within her some courage and spoke real smooth and even keel. "I guess I'm just in one of those moods."

Walter looked awkwardly into her eyes. His eyes were bloodshot and glazed over. He grabbed her hand and put it close up to his face. "I don't see a book." He slurred and stammered his speech as he laughed and looked at Sniper.

"Do you see a book, Snip, cuz I don't." he held her empty hand out for Sniper to see.

Sniper laughed, "No. I don't see no book."

Walter dropped her hand and grabbed her arm and shouted, "I think you're lying! You're up to something! Tell me what you are really doing in here!"

Normally Isabella would be freaking out and panicking. But for some reason she was calm and not acting like herself. In a nice calm voice she said, "You caught me just as I got in here. I haven't had a chance to get a book yet. Now, if you don't mind, I would like to get a book and head up stairs."

She slowly pulled out of his grip and pulled a random book off the shelf. Thankfully it happened to be a fiction novel. Her random picking could have turned out badly. What would have happened if she grabbed a dictionary or worse, an atlas?

Isabella excused herself and started to head out the door. She could feel Walter's eyes heavily upon her.

"Are you still going to show me the cattailed part in that black Bible of yours?" asked Sniper.

Isabella froze half way down the hall. *Oh no,* she thought. Her heart started to pump hard.

Walter still had his eye on her. "Yes. It's in my office. " They both started to head toward his office.

"Think, Isabella, think," she whispered to herself. Isabella walked up to both of them and asked, "Since I'm up, is there anything I can get the both of you?"

Walter just stared. Sniper just shook his head no.

Isabella waited for Walter's response. He ignored her and went into the office toward his desk. His hand was on the knob of the top drawer where the black Bible was supposed to be.

He was just about to open it when she quickly asked again, "Walter, can I get you anything?"

The way he was looking at her, she knew she had to be convincing at everything she did or said. She had to keep telling herself to remain calm. All the while inside of her was jumping as if she had gotten jolted by a bolt of lightning. She had to clasp onto the book to keep her hands from trembling. Her very knuckles turned white.

He looked down at the closed drawer and then back at her. "What's wrong with you? You're not acting like your normal self. You're never this calm or anxious to serve me or my guest."

"Maybe because it's late in the hour," she said coldly.

"I don't believe you. I still think you're hiding something from me. And I do not like how you're acting. If I find out you've been lying to me, there will be..."

Sniper interrupted and added, "A cattail whipping? Or better yet, a stoning?" He laughed and about fell over.

"Well if there isn't anything I can get you, then I'll head up stairs," she said as she kept her eyes glued to Walter's hand on the drawer.

Walter began to open the drawer. Her heart pounded so hard she felt like she was close to passing out. The phone rang. She breathed a sigh of relief and stood in the darkness close enough for her to listen.

She heard Walter chit-chat for a brief moment than tell the person he would be there in a couple of minutes, and then there was a hard click of the receiver.

"The cattail story is going to have to wait. We've got business to attend to." Walter said.

Isabella ran quickly toward the library. She thought she would hide there until he left the house and then she would quickly return the black Bible, all would be well. She hoped.

CHAPTER SEVEN
The Wilderness Experience

I stood in the vastness of tall trees towering over me like sky scrapers and I instantly felt small as a grasshopper. As I looked around me, my breath was swept away, at the sight of the devastating wake the locusts had made. It was so sad for me to see God's handy-work turned into nothing but bareness. The pine trees were the only trees that had their needles. The scarce, brown grass was brittle to the touch and in small, scattered clusters were hodgepodges of flowers gently waving in the wind. The big oak trees looked like they had mange—chunks of bark were missing.

I circled around to get my bearings and figured I must have crashed in some kind of national forest range. If my flight took off in Arizona, heading toward Canada and we were in the air for approximately an hour and a half that would put me somewhere in... Idaho or Montana? If that's the case, then I should be able to find someone. The question is... when? Where? And how? And would this state be free from the clutches of Damion's Foremen's?

All I know is, Sam told me to go and that God is with me.

It must have been around noon, for the sun was at its hottest. I don't ever recall a time when I've sweat so much. I was wet in places I didn't know I had sweat glands. My T-shirt stuck to me like duct tape. My feet were slipping in my shoes because they were soaked with sweat. Thankfully there was a cool breeze to help cool me off.

I walked past a tree that was severally stripped of its bark and noticed something glassy sticking out. I tugged hard and finally retrieved it. I examined it closely and realized it was a wing off a locust. It was made out of a clear, fiberglass material, which confused me. But then again, I never really did see one to know what it looked like or what it was made of.

Instantly I froze. A horrible thought shot at me like an arrow. What if there were still some locusts lingering about burrowed in the brush or trees? I panicked.

"Run!" I yelled.

I ran so fast that my little legs couldn't keep up. My knees gave out, and I flew like Superman. I landed on my stomach, which knocked the wind right out of me. I slowly rolled over and stared up at the bright sky. I laid there contemplating whether I should laugh or cry.

Instead, one of my favorite songs came to mind. I started to bellow out the words, "La, la la, mmmmm, Lord save me... Yeah, help me, Lord."

I awkwardly got up and instantly felt the pain in my head and back. I was irritated and angry. I felt my eyes growing weary and then the voice in my head started picking at me like a crow feeding off a dead carcass. I began to wonder if I was having a heat stroke.

Well, Abigail, the voice inside my head said, *I guess I'm not healed after all. I knew it was too good to be true. I mean, what are the chances of coming out of a plane crash without any injures, unless you're an angel? And why wouldn't God allow Sam to come with me in this wilderness? He was there in the plane. Once again, I'm all alone. I'm always alone.*

I stopped and stood. "And why does everything look the same!" I yelled. My yelling must have frightened a group of birds away, for they took to flight out of protest.

God is leading me into the middle of nowhere, and for what? Why? He could easily have had Sam swoop me up and carry me to a town, or the plane didn't have to crash at all! I could be in Canada by now with my friends sipping on an ice cold cola with an umbrella and relaxing inside a really cool bunker!

But no! I'm out here sweating like a pig, suffering incorrigibly with a headache and back pain.

I sat down on an old rotted log for a break. My back was very tired which made it difficult to sit. I felt stiff and it was hard to turn my head to the left and to the right. Whenever I turned my head to the right, it would pull the left shoulder muscle and shoot a tingling sensation all the way into my head until I saw stars.

I closed my eyes and breathed in deep. The fresh air cleared my lungs and rejuvenated me a bit. I so badly craved to be pain-free and to have a homemade meal and a comfortable bed to lie in. Really, is that too much to ask?

Apparently so, for I am out here until God has me find someone or until my circumstances change. I was so discouraged that my mind went crazy.

So many awful thoughts played on like a broken record. What if I never find my way home? Would I find anyone? Would I wander out here for several days until I died of starvation? I even pictured locusts stinging me and becoming paralyzed for six months and then dying of starvation. After that thought, I suddenly became aware of my surroundings again. Even though we had been told that all the locusts were gone, I still had reservations about it. Am I truly safe out here?

I started to pray. "I hate doing things the hard way, Lord. Help me to understand what You are doing in this situation. I'm scared and I feel all alone. Help me to see and feel that You are with me. Please show me Your direction here, because I feel like I'm getting nowhere." I gave a deep sigh and continued.

"Lord, I'm sorry for constantly running away. I keep asking You to forgive me, but I never change. Something will happen, like stress or a difficult situation, and all I want to do is run. Well Lord, there is nowhere to run here. So You have my full attention. All I have is time and I wait on You. Please Father God, take this pain away. I ask for Your healing touch, in the name of Jesus Christ. Amen." I felt somewhat better even though I didn't hear His voice.

Well, I knew if I just sat there all day, nothing would happen. So I picked up a walking stick and told myself, get up and go!

After hours of walking, I was exhausted. My feet kept slipping on rocks, fallen branches, and uneven paths. The sun was starting to set and I desperately prayed to find shelter. Nothing was in sight.

I saw a huge boulder next to a tree and rested again. The boulder was cool to the backs of my legs. I set down my backpack and placed the walking stick against the tree. I tilted my head back and closed my eyes. In my head, so I thought, I heard the crashing sounds of a waterfall. My eyes popped opened and I painfully turned my head to the direction of the sound.

Did I imagine that? I was so tired; I imagined I heard a waterfall. I rubbed my face to get the circulation back and to help wakeup. I sat still for a second and heard the noise again. A waterfall! I jumped up with renewed energy and strength. The excitement and adrenaline overrode the pain in my back and head. I walked as fast as I could down the cobbled pathway. The sound of rushing water grew louder and louder as I drew nearer.

I threw my walking stick down and clapped my hands. "Oh! Praise the Lord! It's paradise. Thank you Lord, my own Eden!" Or so I thought.

Although the water fall sounded invigorating, the look of it wasn't. A gush of rusty, pee-colored water crashed down from two-hundred feet into a medium-sized pond. Around the pond's edges a yellow foamy substance discouraged any thoughts I had of bathing. I imagined what kinds of bacteria were living in there, plus the air smelled like sulfur.

I looked up to the right of the fall and noticed a huge cavern. The cavern looked picturesque, with layers of limestone stacked upon each other, etched and carved in such a way that it looked like a masterpiece. I knew that the cavern would be my shelter, at least for the night. I suddenly felt ashamed for my lack of faith in believing God wouldn't take care of me when in fact He had.

I grabbed my belongings and carefully started to climb the small boulders that lined the edge of the cavern's opening. The boulders were wet from the fall's mist, so I cautiously grabbed the partially, decomposed roots that poked out between the boulders and pulled myself up. Thankfully the cavern's opening wasn't as high as the waterfall. The boulder's shapes and spacing made it difficult to maintain my footing which shot pain up my neck and to my head.

I turned on my flashlight and entered the cavern. I prayed that it was unoccupied. My hands trembled as a horrifying childhood memory, flooded my mind.

"Abigail..." I told myself. "This isn't a dark alley and I pray to God that there aren't any surviving mice!"

I quickly scanned the cavern. Sure enough it was unoccupied. It wasn't too deep nor did it have any tunnels. It was spacious and big enough for me to stand in. Big boulders lined the walls that were perfect to use as chairs or tables to store my belongings. However, it had a musty smell from the dampness and the cold. Crystal mineral deposits hung from the roof like icicles. They sparkled like precious gems when I held the light to them. I could hear a light dripping sound, like that of a leaky faucet.

I threw my backpack on a boulder, moved closer to the back of the cavern and waved my light around. What I found was rather odd, but then again with God, anything is possible, right?

It was an old rusty lantern. Beside it was a smashed and dampened match box.

"I'm sure these matches are no good." I ripped opened what was left of the box, and sure enough, the matches were ruined. Thankfully I grabbed a lighter from the crash site. "Boy, I hope this lantern works."

I dug into my pack and found the lighter. "Okay, God. I see this lantern as a blessing. So I'm asking that it works. Obviously, someone had been here before me and left this behind." It took a few tries to open the rusted door, but with persistence I got it opened and lit.

After a while, I managed to bed down for the night. Nestled between two rocks, I curled up with the lantern, the plane's blanket, the metal pill box and my father's letter.

All day, I eagerly waited to read the crumbled Bible page and wondered what the skeleton key was for. And who was I to give it to? And, of course, there was my father's letter.

I took the small rectangular top off the pill box and unraveled the Bible page. Carefully I tried to flatten the Bible page over the rock and I noticed one particular verse was highlighted in yellow.

I leaned in closer to the light to read the highlighted verse. "See to it that no one takes you captive through hollow and deceptive philosophy, which depends on human traditions and the basic principles of this world rather than on Christ."

The page was ripped off at verse thirteen, but only verse eight was highlighted with philosophy and basic principles underlined in red ink.

I took the skeleton key out and examined it. It was a rusty, copper color and had two square teeth with a wide gap in between each. Its shape reminded me of a puzzle piece. At the opposite end of the key was a welded hoop with fancy scroll work around a red ruby. The size of the key was slightly smaller than the pill box.

What did all of this mean? I clasped onto the key and began to pray. I shivered when I felt a cold breeze blow through the cavern, as if someone walked in. I popped opened my eyes to look around. I saw no one.

My heart fluttered a bit. I thought maybe it was because I was cold, but then fear struck my heart. I felt claustrophobic. The damp smell was familiar. My heart raced faster and faster. I felt sick at the thoughts of something gnawing at my feet. I grabbed the lantern to check. There was nothing.

I panicked. Maybe it was a mistake to come in here. But where else would I go? I don't know what would be worse, sleeping outside in the elements or in here? What if there were still mountain lions and they came in here? I can't take this darkness. I can't take the smelly dampness.

I ran out of the cavern. It had quite a bit of a ledge to it so I knew I wouldn't fall off. But it was just as dark outside as it was inside. At least inside, with the lantern, it wasn't completely pitch-black. I turned slightly back to the entrance and wavered.

"I can't stay in there and I can't be out here. So which is it?" I slowly headed back in. My mind raced with so many scary and tormenting images. I wanted to unplug my mind to stop the scenarios that played on like a bad horror flick. Especially one particular one that once was real. I wedged myself, again, between the two rocks and curled up.

What makes me think there's any hope of me being rescued? Will I ever find someone to help me? I don't even know where I'm going. What if I'm stuck out here for weeks or worse, months? I only have enough food for a few days. It's not like I can easily find food considering the conditions outside. This is insane! What was that? I think I felt something tugging at my feet.

I again took the lantern and waved it around—nothing.

"I'm such a scaredy-cat. I am falling apart here. What was God thinking? He knows I'm afraid of dark, damp places. I think He was wrong in sending me to... oh I don't know where! Don't you care God, that I'm all alone, afraid and hurting! Oh, the pain. The shooting pain! It's traveling down my legs and my head hurts again. What was that? Mice! Get the mice off me!" I jumped up, stomped around and waved my arms in protest to what appeared to be nothing at my feet.

What is happening to me? I'm totally freaking out here. This isn't the dark alley and there aren't any rats in this cavern. I curled up closer to the light and cried. My mind went back to that dark, cold rainy night when I was five.

****

My real mother ordered me to wait by the front door while she put on her coat. She angrily yanked a ratty, old wool, coat off the hanger and hurriedly put it on me. She forcefully put my arms in each sleeve and turned me around by my hair to leave. I cried out in pain. She slapped the back of my head and told me to shut up. Being five years old, I didn't understand what was happening, but her cruelty wasn't anything new.

We walked out into the cold, dark, rainy night. She squeezed my hand and we walked fast-faster than my little legs could go. I don't know how many times I tripped over myself.

"Hurry up. You're slowing me down, kid," she said, as she tugged on my arm. My arm was already sore from her constant pulling to hurry me along. Most days it felt like she had pulled it out of its socket.

Her voice was still etched in my mind as I recalled her words. "We're almost there."

"Almost where, Mommy?"

She squatted down and shook me hard. And in a voice full of regret said, "Don't ever call me Mommy."

I began to cry hard. My nose ran and I was cold and confused. We turned the corner and headed down a damp, dark alley. Just after we passed a big trash bin, which smelled of rotten food, my mother pulled me aside.

"Look, kiddo, I'm just not cut out to be a mom. Okay? I can't keep living this lie. I can't bear the weight of this secret any more. I have a life to live and want to pursue my dreams. I can't afford another mouth to feed. I should have done this a long time ago. Stay here and someone will get you." She knelt down and whispered in my ear, "I should have never taken you."

She pushed me up against the brick wall and told me not to move until that someone came.   Then she walked away.

"Mommy, no! Don't go. I'm scared. Don't leave me!" I screamed and ran after her.

"Don't you get it? You'll be better off with someone else! Now get back there and stay!" She yelled.

I sat down on the wet and cold pavement not knowing what to do as I watched the darkness eat her up.   That was the last time I ever saw her.

I didn't know how long I had been sitting there, but it felt like forever.   I couldn't stop shivering and crying.   I was frozen with such fear because of the strange sounds that I wet myself.

There was only one street light that lit up half of the alley. It was just enough light for me to see a small area around me.   To my horror, several mice came scurrying out from behind a heap of garbage toward me.   I stood and squeezed myself closer to the wall.   They all surrounded me and began to chew on my boot laces.

"Ahh. Get away. Mommy! I want my mommy!" I screamed as I kicked and stomped my feet to scare them away.

I heard what sounded like horses hoofs coming my way. Faster and faster they came toward me.   The person abruptly grabbed hold of me. "Ahh. Let me go!"

"Get away from her." Came the voice of a woman as she scurried the mice away. "Are you alright? It's okay. You're gonna be okay. Oh my goodness. You feel half frozen. How long have you been out here?"

"I don't know."

The woman wrapped her warm arms around me and said, "Well, let's get you into some place warm."

"Who are you?" I asked.

"My name is Ms. Tabbatha and I run the orphanage around the corner," she said as we headed in that direction.

I looked up at her and asked, "What's an orphanage?"

That night, my life changed forever.

****

I sat up and said, "God, I know You're there, please help me. I feel like I'm five again. I need to know that You're there." Just then my father's letter came to mind. I quickly grabbed it and prayed that his letter would comfort me.

> *"My precious daughter,*
>
> *I know my words were tough when we last spoke. Please know that I mean everything in love. When I speak the truth, I show you that I love you. I never wish to hurt you. I adore you. You are my princess.*
>
> *The Lord laid it on my heart to write. I'm not sure why. I'm hoping that when you read this, it will be exactly what you need. That's just how God works.*
>
> *I sense that you'll be facing opposition from the enemy and I wanted to encourage you to fight!*
>
> *To put into practice all what you've learned about spiritual warfare. Because I believe that God puts situations in our paths so we can put that knowledge into use. God's timing is always perfect. He knew you were going to face the enemy and needed to train you to be His warrior! In*

your classes I'm sure you learned just how sly Satan can be. He's very crafty and deceitful at what he does. Watch out for his arrows and his tactics. He plays with the mind. Keep your wits about you and stand firm on the word of God. You know it's your sword. Use it against him. And by the name of Jesus Christ he must flee!

I know one of the tactics that Satan likes to use against you is the feeling that no one loves you. Tell fear and that unloving spirit to go in the Name of Jesus Christ! Use the authority that Christ gave you. Take back what Satan stole from you and call upon the God of peace and love. For Jesus truly does love you, Abigail. I love you!"

My father's words warmed my heart and gave me courage. I recalled what I had learned from my Bible classes. How could I have been so blind? Satan had blindsided me all day. First with the pain in my body, causing me to doubt God's healing. Then, I doubted I would find shelter. I felt like God forgot about me, leaving me here all alone, and I entertained the nagging thoughts about feeling rejected after Sam left me to travel in the wilderness by myself. And, to top it all off, this crazy fear and anxiety. That's the presence I felt. It was him! Satan!

I straightened up and said, "In the name of Jesus Christ, I command the spirit of fear and the unloving spirit to leave me. Satan, you have no authority over me and I plead the blood of Jesus Christ upon me. I ask, Lord, that you pour out your peace and your love."

Fear loosened its grip and peace flooded my heart. The only chill that I felt was from the Holy Spirit comforting me.

How quickly I had forgotten Satan's tactics. I should have recognized the negative thoughts as his way of causing me to focus on myself instead of Jesus.

After I finished reading my father's letter, hot tears ran like a river wetting the priceless pages in my hand.   For the first time, I truly felt my father's love and the love of my heavenly father.   Their love washed away the feelings of being unloved, rejected and abandoned.

I sensed a change.   My father's words from the Lord weaved through my broken heart as if He were sculpting it on a potter's wheel.

"My Jesus," I began softly.   "Thank you so much for showing me Your love, Your unfailing love for me.   Please forgive me for doubting You and for feeling like You've left me when You never really have."

A sudden rush of emotion came over me, as if it had lain dormant for years.   I felt it building up to a boiling point and I began to weep uncontrollably.

"Father," I cried.   "I forgive my real mom and dad for leaving me and I forgive her for abandoning me in that alley.   Forgive me Father for being so angry at them.   I let go of bitterness and resentment.   I no longer want to hold onto it.   I surrender my real parents to You.   I surrender myself to You!   Take me and mold me into the person You want me to be.   I thank You that You do love me and that You gave me new parents who love me like You do.   Thank You for Your forgiveness and for setting me free by dying on the cross for my sins."

I don't know how long I wept, but the more I cried, the more I confessed, the more I felt free! The presence of God encapsulated me.   I felt safe and so loved.   And when I finally fell asleep, it was the deepest sleep I'd had in a really long time.

****

I perched on a big boulder next to the waterfall and soaked up the early morning sun.   I rejoiced that I was completely pain free. I was also grateful for the renewed hope that helped me face the day with anticipation instead of fear.

While the cool mountain air danced around me, I sought the Lord. A revelation came over me about a mountain being placed in my path. Just like my dad had a mountain placed in his life. If I hadn't been in that plane crash, I wouldn't have faced one of my worst fears; one of many fears I was running from. Fear prevented me from moving forward. God set me free from my fears so He could accomplish His plans.

I looked toward the heavens and prayed, "Thank you Lord, for delivering me."

I saw life through a different set of eyes. I felt so close to the Lord, closer than I had in years. The weight that I had been carrying finally lifted. As soon as I thought that, I heard the Lord's voice. "Your burden has been lifted because you no longer need to carry it. You gave it to me. Now walk in freedom and in your Father's love."

I smiled in awe of the Lord. I also knew there were many more fears in me that needed to be set free. One in particular I kept hidden from my parents. I didn't wish to get married nor have any children. I was too afraid I'd inherited my biological mother's lack of parenting skills. I was afraid to love deeply only to be disappointed in a man leaving me. I couldn't take those failures or rejection, so I decided my relationship with the Lord was enough.

I sat for a while longer and sought direction. The Lord simply told me to stay another night.

I began to set up camp. I gathered fire wood and organized my belongings. I took stock of what food I had, which consisted of nuts, crackers, and granola bars. Airplane food! Yeah!

I thoroughly examined the cavern. I hadn't noticed the countless writings on the cavern's wall. I shined my light and began to read. "Finally, be strong in the Lord and in His mighty power. Put on the full armor of God so that you can take your stand against the devil's schemes."

The writing was somewhat difficult to read. It was smudged from the dampness and water streaks. I moved to a smoother section of the wall and read, "For our struggle is not against flesh and blood, but against the rulers, against the authorities, against the powers of this dark world and against the spiritual forces of evil in the heavenly realms."

The words "evil abounds" was scribbled all over, and there was a drawing of a person dressed up in armor with a large sword. Next to the man were the words, "Put on your armor and stand! Take up your shield of faith which extinguishes all the flaming arrows of the evil one. Pray! Pray to the God of the harvest. Send forth workers! Help us!"

I stepped back and processed it all. Obviously, the lantern and now the writings showed that someone had definitely been here and left a message. I began to laugh. I thought how awesome God was. Those scriptures were exactly what I needed to read. It fit perfectly for my situation, as if God had that person write them just for me. I felt empowered and encouraged.

However, as I stared at the writings, I sensed there's more to it than just a coincidence of encouragement. I believed I had stumbled onto something. I just wasn't for sure what it was or what it all meant. I took the metal pill box and sat on the cavern's ledge. I reread the crumbled up Bible page.

"What is going on Lord? Why would someone write those Bible verses on a cavern wall? Why would a dying lady give me a pill box that contained another important Bible passage and a skeleton key? Is there a correlation between Meredith, the cave writings, and this pill box? And what does all of this have to do with me?"

I admitted, the stranger my questions got with the Lord, the more curiosity grew within me. It was getting exciting, yet there was a slight fear of the unknown creeping in like a fog.

Again, I found myself waiting on God. I had to be patient, listen and look at everything through God's perspective. And pray!

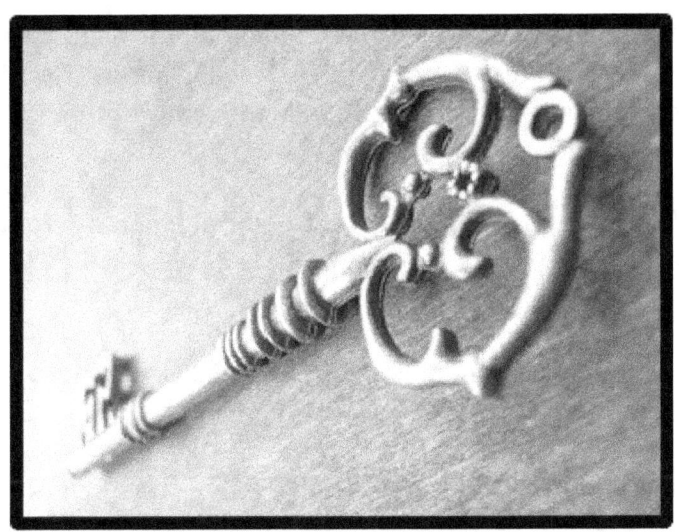

CHAPTER EIGHT
Collection Day

The front door of the Sunkissed Hotel swung wide open. It caught Margo off guard. She jumped and turned to see Foreman Lovit, Sniper-Eyed Jones, and Isabella standing in the doorway.

Her legs weakened and her heart about stopped. She wasn't ready. In fact, she knew Tony wasn't ready either. Last time she left him, he was still figuring out how much he owed Damion Callaway for all the hotel repair work and the year of living supplies.

Foreman Lovit slapped his greedy hands together. "It's collection time. Where's Tony and where's my money?"

Margo carefully kept her eyes down and managed to say, "He's in the office. I'll go get him."

Foreman Lovit walked around fingering the high class furnishings and batted at the chandelier's dangling crystals. Within minutes, both Tony and Margo stood in the lobby of the hotel. Tony had a small wad of money in his hand.

"This should cover what we owe for the month." Tony said as he handed him the cash.

"Well, well, well. I got to hand it to you, Tony. I didn't think you could pull it off." Foreman Lovit said as he waved the wad of cash and began counting it.

"I worked hard to trade. It's difficult to trade for money these days. Everyone wants food or water, not cash." Tony replied. "I just don't understand why you want money considering it's practically worthless."

Foreman Lovit crammed the money in his front pants pocket. He moved close to Tony's face and said, "I'll be the judge of that and besides, it's none of your business. I also decide if it's enough payment. And it's not! I want something else!"

Margo gasped. Tony reached out to her.

Foreman Lovit walked into the sitting room. He carefully examined each piece of furniture. His eyes came to a stop. Margo knew what he was eyeing. She casually stepped in front of her grandmother's china hutch that was passed down from generation to generation.

The hutch was solid oak, with the original hardware and glass. It was almost in perfect condition other than the one clawed foot that had been chewed on by her dog when she was a little girl. Several priceless items, collected by her mother and grandmother, lined the glass shelves, including a beautiful smoky-gray china set, and wine goblets that her father bought her mother during their first year in China. Several unique statues of couples made out of onyx, marble and crystal, were placed between various, vases and specialty pottery from all over the world.

Foreman Lovit moved forward toward Margo and the china hutch. Margo looked at Tony.

Isabella saw the desperation on Margo's face and it pained her. She knew that Walter was either after the cabinet or something inside. Margo's eyes pleaded with her husband's.

"You said all you wanted to collect is money. Surely the payment is sufficient." Tony said.

"Sufficient! I tell you if it is sufficient or not. And I'm saying it's not. I want the china hutch and everything in it." Foreman Lovit turned to Isabella, "Don't you think this would look great in the formal dining area, Dear?"

"No!" Margo yelled.

Sniper moved quickly toward Margo, but Tony stepped in between them. "If that will suit you for the payment then take it." Tony said as he avoided Sniper's glare.

Margo cried, "No. It's very special to me. It was my grandmother's. It's irreplaceable."

Foreman Lovit nodded for Sniper to move out of the way. He roughly grabbed Tony's arm and forcefully moved him aside. He then grabbed a hold of Margo's broad chin and squeezed it firmly.

Margo let out a squeal of pain. Tony wanted to go to her, but Sniper held him with a vice-like grip.

Tony feared for his wife. What was Foreman Lovit going to do to her? If he lost her, he wouldn't know what he would do. He loved Margo very much. Why did she always have to make a fuss over her stuff? Didn't she understand that he was only trying to protect her and save her life?

"No one says no to me! And since you are being defiant, maybe I should have you stoned to death." Foreman Lovit said happily.

Sniper pushed Tony and he fell to the ground at the Foreman's feet.

Head down and eyes staring at the foreman's shoes, Tony pleaded, "Please forgive my wife. Just take what you want and no one has to get hurt."

Foreman Lovit laughed, along with Sniper. He repeated what Tony had said, "No one has to get hurt. I think I'll do the deciding here." Isabella was almost in tears herself.

Foreman Lovit let go of Margo and grabbed the back of Tony's hair and pulled his head back, forcing him to look him in the eye. Margo looked at Isabella with pleading eyes, but what could she do?

Isabella watched Foreman Lovit. He had a pasty, satisfying smile as he puffed out his chest with pride, as if bullying people fed his ego. She looked around and saw a beautiful, mahogany six dresser curio cabinet.

"Walter." Isabella began. "May I make a suggestion? I think this lovely dresser cabinet would suit the dining area much better than that china hutch. I could put all the linens for the table settings in here. It would be more practical than just having extra stuff to dust."

Foreman Lovit let go of Tony and walked over to the dresser curio cabinet and Isabella. He stood in front of her and scowled at her.

Isabella took in a quick, deep breath, stood firmly and kept her voice strong. "I know how you like a well-presented, clean table and by having this cabinet in the dining area, I can have the linens organized and they wouldn't get wrinkled. It would also save me from not having to run to the linen closet all the time."

Silence fell. Margo looked to Tony. Sniper looked to the Foreman, who was rubbing his chin, as he examined the curio cabinet. He looked inside each drawer that was already full of table linens.

While Foreman Lovit talked to Isabella, he kept his eye on Margo. "So you think you would like this better, hey?"

Margo tried to keep her composure. At least that piece of furniture really didn't hold much value to her. She had gotten it at a yard sale and paid next to nothing for it. She knew Isabella was trying to help her. With that in mind, Margo tried to show some attachment to the cabinet so Foreman Lovit would think it valuable.

Foreman Lovit threw up his hands and said, "Fine. We'll take it." Sniper immediately emptied the drawers.

Walter walked up to Isabella and annoyingly said, "Now I am reminded why I don't bring you. You take the fun out of my shopping. And don't think I don't know what just happened here."

He looked back at Margo and Tony. "Next time I'll take the hutch." Margo bit her lip and Isabella looked at her with sorrowful eyes.

While the men loaded up the cabinet in the back of Sniper's truck, Margo reached for Isabella and quickly pulled her aside out of sight from the men.

"Thank you Isabella, for helping me. My grandmother's hutch means a lot to me. I don't understand how the foreman always has a knack for picking out my most prized possessions."

"I may have saved it this time, but I can't say for next. I would take out of it what means the most to you and hide it. He's good on his word. He will be back for it." Margo hugged Isabella and thanked her again.

"Isabella, let's go! I have lots of business to attend to." Walter yelled.

"So where to next, Foreman?" Sniper asked.

"Let's walk over to the Trading Post and see how our little buddy, Henry Slater, has done for us."

"I'm hoping someone doesn't do well. I have a hankering for a stoning." said Sniper. Walter looked at Sniper and shook his head in amusement.

"So Foreman, why are we collecting cash instead of priceless items?"

Walter glared at Sniper and said, "All I know is that Callaway wants it and I do what I'm told. Just like you, so drop the question."

Before entering the Trading post, Walter straightened his uniform jacket and smoothed out his tie. Sniper glimpsed Walter adjusting himself and attempted to adjust his own shirt, but it was too tight for it to be moved.

Foreman Lovit stopped shy of the door and whispered, "Sniper, just remember the real reason we're here."

"So why don't we start asking around to see who may have taken the key?" Sniper responded.

"Because you idiot, if we do that the people will start getting suspicious and start asking questions. Under no circumstance does Damion want these people to know why we're really here. So for now, let's just focus on getting payment for what these people owe him."

The Trading Post had limited activity considering it was an early Monday afternoon. Mondays and Fridays were usually busy for the post. Isabella knew why-it was collection day and everyone was either at home waiting to be visited or busy getting their finances in order.

Henry wasn't anywhere in sight. Foreman Lovit went up to a teller, casually leaned toward her and asked quietly, "Where is Henry?"

Nervously, the young girl of twenty, sheepishly replied, "He's still in his office. I'll tell him you're here."

Foreman Lovit smiled sweetly at the young girl and said, "That would be great. And since you were so kind to help me..." Foreman Lovit paused and pulled out a fifty dollar bill, and playfully handed her the money. "This is for you." He teasingly winked at her.

"Why thank you Foreman Lovit. I'll go right away," she said and playfully winked back.

Isabella watched as Walter was making a fool of himself. Had she been in love with him, she would have been furious with his flirting. But, still, it appalled her, yet she really didn't care. She knew he had a weakness for young women.

"Good morning, Foreman Lovit. It is still morning, right?" Henry asked as he nervously laughed and looked at his watch.

"No. It's just past twelve. Your watch must have stopped." Sniper corrected.

Henry looked at his watch and shrugged his shoulders and then held out his slender hand to shake Foreman Lovit's. He just looked at Henry's hand and said, "I'm kind of in a hurry. Let's just get down to business, shall we?"

"Yes, of course." Henry said as he pointed them in the direction of his office.

"Have a seat. I have all my receipts of the construction and the food supplies that were given to me and you'll find that everything is in order. At the bottom is the balance I owe Damion."

Walter looked the statements over and checked the last page; Balance due, $1,500. He looked at the balance. He thought that it should be more, but math wasn't his forte. Walter handed the statements to Isabella. He knew she was his mathematician. "Does this balance look right to you, Isabella?" He asked.

Isabella met Henry's frightened eyes. His eyes were trying to communicate something to her, but she wasn't quite sure yet. She assumed he must have done some calculations wrong, for he perspired profusely and his hands trembled.

She, at first, pretended to check the statements. She glanced at Henry then she looked on the last page and noticed that a few numbers had been added wrong. She realized he was trying to get out of owing Walter the full amount.

Henry noticed that Isabella figured it out and tried to plead with his eyes for her not to say a word.

Isabella caught on to his body language. She noticed sweat beading up next to his receding hair line. Her heart started to flutter. She didn't want to see another person die and she didn't want it to be by her doing either. What was she to do? Lie? Or tell Walter that this man is scamming him out of the money he owes. If she tells the truth, then there would be a stoning. If she lies, then she could end up saving a life.

"Well, is it the right amount? What's taking you so long? Need a calculator or something?" Foreman Lovit asked as he irritatingly shook the pages in Isabella's hand.

Isabella stared at Henry carefully as to not draw attention to Walter. Henry wiped his forehead with a handkerchief and nodded for her not to squeal on him.

After a moment of silence, Foreman Lovit sensed that something wasn't right. He looked up from the statements to Henry. Henry sat strait up in his chair, folded his hands and pasted on a convincing smile.

"I don't believe this is the right amount, Henry. What are you trying to do? Cheat the Idealist leader out of his money?" He snapped angrily. Henry's eyes widened and looked right at Isabella, who swallowed hard.

Foreman Lovit leaned over toward Henry's desk and slammed his hand down hard and yelled, "You are going to pay!"

Several of the Trading Post employee's turned their heads and shriveled back in their desk windows.

Sniper clapped his hands excitedly together like a child who had been waiting for ice cream all day. "Are we going to have ourselves a stoning?"

Isabella stalled so she could figure out the right thing to do. "I need a calculator!" she squealed loudly.

Foreman Lovit abruptly looked at her. "What? I've seen you do math in your sleep. You can't tell me you honestly need a calculator! I think he's holding out on me."

"There is a lot to these receipts, Walter. There's a whole months' worth and I need to make sure he's not trying to hold out on you. Now if you just give me a few moments to work these figures." Isabella squinted furiously at Henry for putting her in this awkward position. She grabbed Henry's calculator and began quickly typing the numbers from the receipts.

Henry continued to wipe his forehead. "Is it hot in here or is it just me?"

"I find it to be quite conformable." Foreman Lovit said as he kept an eye on him, which made Henry even more nervous.

After several moments, Isabella's hand stopped. She found that Henry not only added his totals wrong, but failed to add his past due amounts from the previous two months. His total that he really owed was $4,500. *This very moment,* Isabella thought, *could change this man's life.*

"Well?" Foreman Lovit asked impatiently.

Isabella put down the statements in front of Henry and slid them his way. She looked Walter right in the eyes and said, "He's cheating you out of the money he owes and from the previous months."

Henry stood up so fast that his seat rolled back and tipped over. "She's lying! I would never do that to you, Foreman Lovit." Henry glared at Isabella, "How could you do this to me? Why? What have I done to you to deserve this treatment?"

Isabella felt horrible, but she knew Walter only too well. He would drill her non-stop and force her to go over the statements with him at home with a calculator to make sure she added right. Either way, the truth of Henry's miscalculations would have come out. The selfish reasoning behind her logic was to save her own skin.

Sniper-Eyed Jones rushed to Henry's side and seized him. Foreman Lovit got in Henry's face. "Committing treason against the Idealist leader is punishable by death." He then looked at

Sniper, "Looks like we have a stoning."

Henry looked from Foreman Lovit to Isabella. "What? No! You've made a big mistake here. I promise I added up those figures right. Please Foreman, I beg you. I don't want to die!"

Sniper took Henry to the jail to hold him until the stoning. Isabella wanted to cry, knowing that his blood would be on her hands, but she couldn't risk being stoned to death too.

The dreadful day dragged on for Isabella. All she wanted to do was curl up in a hole until the day was over. But then again, living with Walter was like reliving a dreadful day every day; a never ending nightmare that she so desperately wanted to get out of.

The three of them crossed the street over to Trudy's General Store. *How was this to turn out?* She wondered.

Seated in her recliner, resting, Trudy heard the door to the store open and then slam shut. At first, she just sat there, frozen by fear. She recognized the footsteps. Only one man she knew who wore dress shoes on hot days—Walter Lovit. Knowing it was collection day; Trudy got up and walked over to a cupboard, and got an old cigar box. She pulled out all of the money she had traded for.

Trudy knew Foreman Lovit, Sniper-Eyed Jones and Isabella were standing on the other side of the curtain which separated the store from her house. Trudy lowered her eyes and said, "Good afternoon, Walter. Oh, I mean Foreman Lovit." Her voice shook after she corrected herself.

Isabella thought it odd that she had addressed him as Walter. Only those close to him called him Walter. "Please come in." Trudy invited.

Sniper and Isabella sat down, but Walter stood. His stance made Isabella nervous and by the look on Trudy's face, she was anxious as well. Isabella studied her. Trudy's eyes were puffy from lack of sleep, which made her look older. She noticed many bruises, cuts and a fresh wound on her left hand.

Trudy didn't look the same as when Isabella met her. Back then, Trudy was rather thin and somewhat attractive. Trudy dressed very modestly and kept to her traditions of keeping her hair long. She wore skirts or dresses instead of jeans. Her hazel eyes shone with life, but now appeared more gray than hazel. Isabella once envied Trudy's blemish-free skin. Now, her skin was covered with worry lines and scars-deep, altering scars. She looked as if she had packed-on forty pounds and didn't care that she wore a pair of old jeans. The only thing that resembled the young Trudy was her long, braided hair that now speckled with gray.

Isabella recalled that night that changed Trudy forever—the night Trudy's fiancé, Frank died. It was four years ago and around the time she and Maximus were hired to be Walter's maid and butler. Walter came home drunk and explained that Frank was rebelling against the Idealist group and called Walter the devil. Walter threw a hard punch and down the man went. He never got up.

Some say the man died because of the hard blow to the nose being pushed up into the skull. Others say he died of a heart attack. No one really knows for sure. After that, Walter stayed out late. Trudy wore more revealing clothes and acted weird around him, as if trying to get his attention. Things were starting to add up in Isabella's mind, especially with Trudy calling him by his first name.

No. It can't be what I'm thinking. Could it?

Trudy gave Isabella an odd stare. It was a jealous look as if Trudy resented Isabella's relationship with Walter.

"I have come to collect the money that's due Damion." Foreman Lovit said to Trudy.

His deep voice caused Trudy to come out of her stare. "Oh, yes. Here it is. It's all there."

"It better be. The last guy didn't have it all and now there will be a stoning," said Sniper.

Trudy handed Foreman Lovit the money and he counted it. All two thousand dollars were there. Foreman Lovit took half of the money and put it in his pocket and the rest; he threw at Trudy's feet.

Trudy panicked, Isabella was confused and Sniper said, "Foreman, what are you doing? I thought we're supposed to collect the cash."

Foreman Lovit ignored Sniper and arrogantly said, "I really don't want your money. I want something else."

Trudy's eyes welled up with tears. What more could she possible give him? She felt like he stripped her of everything else, what more could he want?

"Look around, what do I have that ya want, Foreman? I don't have much as is."

Foreman Lovit went to Trudy and grabbed a hold of her long braided hair. "I want your hair."

Trudy took her braid out of his hand and said, "No. I don't understand. I have the full payment. Ya know that my long hair means a lot ta me. I have not taken a pair of scissors ta my hair since..." She paused and looked at him.

Isabella thought Trudy would be punished for looking at him right in the eyes, but Walter didn't seem to care. This small allowance confirmed Isabella's suspicions of the two of them. *And why would he care to cut off her hair if it didn't mean anything to him. What is going on? What happened between the two?*

Trudy cried. Walter pulled out a pair of scissors from a drawer; obviously he knew where they were.

"Please, Walter." Trudy pleaded, with a voice just above a whisper. "I beg of ya, please!" She picked up the money and tried handing it to Walter.

Walter slapped the money out of her hands. "I said I don't want it! Sniper, you might have to help me hold her. As we both know, she can be feisty."

Isabella thought, *we both know she can be feisty. Is this not the first time he's done something to her? Is that where all the scars have come from?*

Trudy screamed and tried to protect her hair.

"Walter! Why on earth would you want Trudy's hair?" Isabella yelled above Trudy's screaming.

Walter stopped and quickly confronted Isabella. He was so close to her face that he spat when he talked. "What I do is none of your business. Get outside! I will deal with you later. Don't think I haven't been paying attention to how you have been treating me."

Isabella lowered her eyes and whispered, "And how have I been treating you?"

"With disrespect! Now go and wait for us outside, before I stone you with Henry!" Isabella quickly passed through Trudy's curtain and then out the General Store.

Trudy punched, and slapped at Sniper. Walter grabbed a hold of Trudy's braid again, but this time he tugged so hard, he pulled her down to her knees. And with one snip of the scissors, close to the scalp, her long braided hair now laid limply in his hand. Sniper pushed her head down and walked out of the house and out of the store.

With her hands covering her face, Trudy wept bitterly.

Walter knelt down and placed his mouth close to her ear. "It's a shame we didn't work out. But then again, you were never really my type. No one loves a Jesus freak!" He waved the long braided hair in her face and said, "So much for your covering and your glory!" and left.

The only noise in the house was the echo of Trudy's uncontrollable sobbing. She placed her hand on the back of her head. Her hair was so short. She felt some blood oozing from the nape of her neck where he had nicked her with the scissors.

She got up and placed a towel on her wound to stop the bleeding. It was a small wound, this time, from what she could tell. After the bleeding had stopped, Trudy stood in shock when she looked in the mirror. She felt almost bald. The tears dried up, her heart hardened and she clenched her fists.

Trudy walked into her bedroom and crouched under her bed. Hidden under a deep blanket of dust, were her Bible and an old worn-out jewelry box. She sat down at the edge of the bed, blew the dust off the Bible and took a cameo locket necklace from the jewelry box. She entwined the chain around her fingers.

She held the necklace close to her chest, "I'm so sorry, Daddy. I wish I would have listen' ta ya. I wish I would have never let Jesus out of my heart. Ever since I did, nothin' in my life has seemed ta go right. And I certainly wished I had never had the affair with Walter Lovit!"

Trudy got up and sat in her rocking chair with a view of the country side to where her father's, little, white church once was. Now a tall, charred stake and the town's cemetery were all that remained.

Oh, how she longed to be back in the little white church, wearing her favorite pink dress with velvety butterflies and sitting in the pew next to her daddy. During singing, her daddy used to play with her long hair. He said it reminded him of her mother's silky reddish hair.

After Trudy's mother passed, her father told her of the vow her mother had made to God. Her mother was strongly convicted by God never to cut her hair—said it was her head covering and her glory.

Since Trudy was about ten-years-old, she didn't quite understand, so her father read I Corinthians 11 where it talks about propriety in worship. When her father got to verse fifteen, she felt a nudge in her own spirit. "But that if a woman has long hair, it is her glory. For long hair is given to her as a covering."

After they had discussed the vow her mother had made, she too had decided to make that vow with God. To her, it would become a long lasting covenant, between her and her God. During her teenage years, she felt closeness with Jesus; an intimacy like no other. She loved Jesus very much and wanted to follow Him forever.

Trudy again reached up and felt her short hair. She felt stripped of her dignity and devastated over her broken covenant. A small tear slid down her cheek. Even though she wasn't walking with the Lord, the long-lasting covenant still meant something to her. It was also in memory of her dead father. He often told Trudy how beautiful her hair was and how special God had made her covering.

She truly believed that Walter enjoyed stripping people slowly of their souls, especially hers. Ever since the day she met him, he stripped her soul piece by piece. She felt he finally got the rest of her. She was empty, numb and full of hatred, so far from where she once was.

She opened the old Bible up to 1 Corinthians 11 and read verse fifteen over and over.

****

"Hey, why don't we make our next stop Lazy Days Saloon? I'm parched and I need a break. We'll sit in the back with Marco to discuss business while we sip on some cold ones." Walter said in a cheery mood.

Sniper smiled, "That sounds great! I'm thirsty too."

Isabella just rolled her eyes in disgust. She hated alcohol, and she hated what it did to people, especially Walter. Walter was a mean drunk and so was Sniper. She concluded that nothing good came out of drinking.

"Maybe this would be a good time for me to return home, Walter. It's four in the afternoon and I would like to get things done around the house and begin making dinner arrangements," Isabella said just before they entered Lazy Days Saloon.

She felt she had pushed him too far today. She kept her eyes glued to the ground and waited for his response.

Walter tightly squeezed her thin arm and harshly pulled her close to him. "Something has changed in you. I can't quite put my finger on it, but I can tell you thisss..." He hissed in her ear. "I don't like it or your actions today."

Isabella looked at him with questioning eyes.

"Yeah, don't think I didn't notice. You're lucky I don't stone you with Henry Slater! Go! I'm tired of you anyway. Dinner will be late tonight since there will be a stoning. And I expect you to be there tonight. I just might give you the honor of casting the first stone. After all, he who is without sin casts the first stone!" Walter laughed mockingly.

Walter gripped her hard before letting her go and then gave her a small shove off the porch. After a few stumbling steps, she got her footing and started for home.

Sniper was already inside waiting for him when he entered the noisy saloon. Marco looked up from wiping the counter and saw the Foreman enter.

"Marco, my man! Give Sniper and me a round of drinks and come join us." Walter showed all his white teeth as he smiled.

Marco hesitantly asked for one minute by holding up a finger. Marco quickly went into the back and grabbed the small stash of money he saved for this very day. In times past, he didn't quite have enough and Foreman Lovit didn't seem to mind. He would accept whatever amount Marco could pay. He felt as if he had favor with the Foreman since Lovit had access to the liquor twenty-four-seven. He believed that was the rest of his payment.

The three men sat, drinking and having a good time. At least Foreman Lovit and Sniper were. Even though Marco managed the saloon, he wasn't much of a drinker. He really wasn't the "let's get rowdy" type. He was more of a laid back, quiet kind of guy. But then again, he often attributed that to the loneliness in his heart for his deceased wife of six years. His wife was stung by the locusts within minutes of reaching shelter. The day after tomorrow would have been Elana's fifty-eighth birthday.

After many drinks and a couple of hours, Foreman Lovit told Marco his payment was enough and that it was time for them to go.

He had more places to visit before the big stoning later that night.

Marco swallowed back some emotions and asked, "Who's getting stoned tonight?" Sniper whooped and hollered as he excitedly revealed Henry Slater's name.

With both hands, the Foreman jokingly slapped Marco's cheeks and said, "I expect my ole' pal to be there for support. It promises to be a good time! And for this special occasion, I would like my usual drink to be set out for all to share."

Marco got up and went behind the counter and cleaned. Deep in thought, he processed the fact that tonight would be Henry's last night alive. He felt bad for Henry. No one deserved the punishments Foreman Lovit gave out. Marco knew that if it weren't for the liquor, he would be right out there with Henry.

"Oh, I forgot to ask if you have a loaf of bread?" Walter asked.

Marco shook his head to clear his thoughts and said, "Yes I do."

"Where to next, Foreman?" Sniper asked as he stumbled off the steps and out into the street.

Walter stood at the edge of the street and inhaled the cool mountain air. The sun seemed to have quickly ducked behind a cloud as the vast blue sky was slowly losing its light.

"I want to pop in on the little varmints and then..." he paused and gave Sniper a conniving smile, "as you know, I saved the best for last."

Sniper nodded, smiled back and said, "The mission's house."

As they approached the barn they could hear children playing, yelling and laughing. Walter screwed up his nose at Sniper and said, "What do they have to be happy about?" Sniper just shrugged.

Walter opened the door and stood in the doorway. At first, the children were unaware of his presence, until Walter cleared his throat.

Startled by the noise, Billy jumped and screamed. All heads turned to see Foreman Lovit and Sniper-Eyed Jones standing in the doorway. Not one of them moved, in fear of punishment. All eyes looked directly at Simona. She nodded for them to bow their heads to the floor.

"Foreman, Mr. Jones." Simona greeted them with a shaky voice while keeping her eyes glued to the floor. "What can we do for you today?" She asked, knowing full well they had nothing to give him.

Walter looked around at the thinly furnished barn and at all six, dirty children. He walked up to Simona and lifted her soiled face to meet his. Her eyes immediately looked off to the side and not directly into his.

"You know, Simona..." his voice seemed friendly. "I'm not a monster, as everyone says I am." His eyes darted around the room and met Zack's eyes, who quickly looked back to the ground.

"I actually have something for all of you." Walter said.

Before he let her face go, he gave it a firm squeeze. He opened the loaf of bread and grabbed several pieces. He gave some to Sniper and told him to tear them into crumb size pieces. Walter and Sniper threw the crumb pieces onto the floor.

"Enjoy." said Walter.

All five children, except Simona, made a mad dash for the crumbs. Anger burned within Simona. The Foreman made her feel as if they were nothing but dogs to him, eagerly awaiting their master's crumbs to fall from his table.

It was appalling for Walter to watch the children stuff the crumbs in their mouths. Some of them were even licking the floor to get all the crumbs. He had to look away.

Simona stood with clenched fists, wanting desperately to spit in his face. As she stood there fuming, she remembered what Sheldon taught her. "No matter how wrongly a person treats you, it's up to you to do what's right in the eyes of the Lord. We are called to love our neighbors, pray for those who persecute you and bless those who hate you. And most importantly, do not repay evil with evil."

Walter noticed Simona's fists and asked, "You don't plan on hitting the very person who is feeding you, do you?"

She quickly said a prayer in her mind, unclenched her hands, and said in her nicest voice, "Thank you, Foreman, for the bread. It was very kind of you. May the Lor..."

Foreman Lovit gasped harshly as Simona stopped herself. A brief silence fell as Walter stood staring at her. She wondered if he would punish her for almost speaking the name of the Lord. Instead, he wadded up the bread bag, threw it at her feet and they both left.

With a down-cast heart, she looked at the half-starved children with crumbs sticking to their faces, feeling like that was all they were going to get to eat. She picked up the bag that appeared to be empty and was happy to see several whole slices of bread left in the bag. For a second, she just starred at the slices of bread, and then she counted them, six. She was amazed to see that there were exactly six slices of bread left over. It was enough for everyone to have a whole slice of bread.

Carry asked, "Is there something wrong, Simona?"

Then it hit her. She fell to her knees and pulled out the six slices of bread and said with tears streaking her face. "No Carry. Something is very right! God has answered your prayers. Here is your bread you've asked for." She looked at each one and handed them each a piece of bread.

Carry carefully held the slice of bread in her dirty, tiny hands as if it were a rare piece of candy. Her jaw was hanging open in amazement that God answered her prayer. Excitedly, Carry asked, "Is there enough peanut butter to put on my bread?"

Simona quickly got up and opened her small trunk that was at the end of her bed. Deeply hidden under clothes and blankets was a small jar of homemade peanut butter that Margo Sullivan had given her. She held it up and saw that it looked to be enough to thinly spread on six slices of bread.

After she spread the peanut butter on each of their slices, Carry quickly asked if she could say the meal time prayer. Simona smiled. "Absolutely."

Carry quoted the Lord's Prayer. "Our Father in heaven, hallowed be Your name, Your kingdom come, Your will be done on earth as it is in heaven. Give us today our daily bread. Forgive us our debts, as we also have forgiven our debtors. And lead us not into temptation, but deliver us from the evil one."

Simona had a hard time focusing after Carry said 'forgive us our debts, as we also have forgiven our debtors.' Instead, she heard the Lord, "I can even use the wicked to provide for my children. I have provided your daily bread. And I will continue to do so, my beloved daughter."

Tears trickled down her flushed face. Hearing the Lord's voice were rare moments in her life and she held on to them dearly. A sudden rush of compassion filled her heart for the Foreman and Sniper-Eyed Jones that moved her to pray for them.

Even though the children became restless and anxious to eat their bread, they all knew they needed to give thanks and pray for Foreman Lovit.

Zack, on the other hand, wanted to speak evil of the Foreman, but Simona wouldn't allow it. She could tell that Zach was fighting to be obedient because of the stare down they were having.

"The Lord blesses those who are obedient, Zach. Remember that. So what will it be? Will you speak a blessing or curse upon them?" Simona asked.

Zach twisted his mouth before he whispered. "Lord, please bless Foreman Lovit and Mr. Jones for their kindness today. Give unto them what they have done unto us."

Simona looked up at Zach with wide eyes. She wasn't quite sure how to take that last statement. Zach looked at her and smiled. "Thank you Zach, for your kind prayer." Simona said hesitantly.

Just then there was a knock at the door. Trudy slowly opened the door to see the children on the floor sitting in a circle ready to eat.

"I'm sorry ta be bargin' in on ya, but fer some reason I felt like I needed ta git rid of these two loaves of bread before they spoil, along with a jar of peanut butter. Thought that ya'll youngen's might like ta have em'. Oh and I brought a gallon of milk that is in needen of drinkin'. I'm not much of a milk drinker."

"We don't have anything to trade for it." Simona said sadly.

"No need fer traden."

Simona closed her eyes and thanked the Lord. For she remembered that Sheldon had once told her, that God is a God of more than enough!

****

Walter and Sniper-Eyed Jones headed toward the old mission's house. Walter purposely saved seeing Sheldon for last. Out of the whole town, there were two people he enjoyed tormenting the most, Trudy and Sheldon.

From the very day Walter came into town back in 2027, Sheldon got on his nerves. Sheldon was way too energetic and reminded him of Tigger, from Winnie the Pooh. Walter hated Tigger. There was just too much bounce and too much double-g-errr'. The man never shut up about spreading the gospel of Jesus.

Sheldon grabbed a cold glass of lemonade and stepped outside for some fresh air. He could see Foreman Lovit and Sniper were a block away. The desire for fresh air suddenly left and the sweet, succulent taste of lemonade no longer appealed to him.

Sheldon opened the screen door and yelled, "Lisa Marie. The Foreman and Sniper are on their way."

"Oh, dear God help us!" Sheldon heard Lisa Marie yell from the top of the stairs. Then he heard a long hard thud. He turned back around, opened the door and saw that Lisa Marie had accidentally skidded down the stairs on her bottom.

He stepped inside the house. "Are you all right?"

"Yes, yes. Just in a hurry, I guess. I must have missed a step rushing to get down stairs to get the money. I'm fine, just a bruised toe."

"Thank you for holding the door open for us, Sheldon. I see you still hold to your Christian values." Foreman Lovit said as he pushed his way past Sheldon and into the house.

"What makes you think I would do that for you?" Sheldon snapped back, forgetting his once practiced values.

Sniper's eyes widened with anticipation to see what Walter would do in response to Sheldon's disrespectfulness.

Walter didn't seem too bothered by his comment. He said casually, "Now, now. I don't believe that's Christian-like. That's no way to talk to your neighbor." He slowly got right in Sheldon's face and arrogantly said, "I would watch it if I were you."

A strong, toxic, alcohol smell filled Sheldon's nose as Walter spoke. "You know what today is, don't you?" Walter asked.

Sheldon stood his ground and firmly responded, "Yeah, I know what today is. The day that you..."

Lisa Marie moved in front of Sheldon and cut him off before Walter took his anger out on him. Lisa Marie whispered, "Behave yourself before you get yourself killed. He's not worth it."

Sheldon moved away from Lisa Marie and stepped behind the kitchen table to grip the back of a chair.

Sniper kept his eye on Lisa Marie. His strong stare made her feel uneasy. It was as if the devil's eyes were piercing into the window of her very soul. The way his eyes scanned her face, it felt like he was taking inventory to see if there was an open door to come in. She quickly looked away and told herself that she belongs to Christ and she will not give the devil a foothold into her life. Many evil thoughts came at her like poisonous arrows. She began to pray and put on the full armor of God.

Lisa Marie looked to Sheldon and carefully downward toward the Foreman. They were having a stare down. If Sheldon wasn't careful of his eye contact, he would be punished. Lisa Marie tried to make eye contact with Sheldon advising him to be careful, but he didn't seem to care. She noticed that Sheldon was white knuckled and the chair was starting to lose some of its paint.

"We have the money, Foreman Lovit." Lisa Marie said, trying to interrupt the stare-down.

Lisa Marie went to a cupboard and pulled out an empty jar. She turned and looked at Sheldon, who kept his eye on Foreman Lovit. "I had to use the money to trade for food. I felt it was important that we eat." Sheldon said without batting an eye.

Lisa Marie's heart dropped, but she knew the rest of her money was hidden under the floor boards.

Neither of the two men moved their gaze off each other. She was surprised that the Foreman allowed Sheldon to look at him in his eyes. Or was he going to pay for it real soon. She was also deeply afraid of not having the money.

Finally someone spoke. "I have not come to collect anything today." Walter said as he too kept his eyes on Sheldon. "What I collected four years ago was more than enough to cover the cost of the both of you to keep living in the home. I just came to invite you to a stoning tonight. It seems that Henry Slater tried to pull a fast one on me and didn't pay his full wages."

Walter crossed his arms. Lisa Marie took a quick glance at him and noticed an evil glare overshadowed him. "However..." Walter continued. "With this stare-down we're having maybe there will be two people stoned."

Lisa Marie yelled out, "Stop Sheldon, please."

Sheldon still held his eyes firmly fixed on the Foreman's. "I have nothing to live for."

"Oh, is that so? Not living for your God anymore? Oh, that's right. Your God didn't come to your rescue did he? He let her die." Walter said.

Lisa Marie looked at Sheldon. She could tell that Walter struck a chord with him. Sheldon looked as if he was having a hard time containing himself from lashing out physically at Walter. A big, chunk of paint peeled off from the chair.

"He didn't save your fiancé Katie, like he supposedly saved Miriam." Walter laughed. "As you all think that God protected her, Miriam, the prophet!" He laughed again. "The stupid wood was wet, while your fiancé's wasn't. That is the only reason why that old woman is alive today." Walter uncrossed his arms and finally moved toward the door to leave. He placed his pointer finger on his closed lips before he spoke his next words, as if contemplating what to say. "On the other hand, I feel generous today. I think I'll let you live yet another day. For I know this is a very special day for you, Sheldon. "

Lisa Marie caught the deep pain in Sheldon's eyes. She knew that the Foreman chose to have his collection day, on the very same day he killed Sheldon's fiancé.

****

"If he thinks I'm going to his stoning, he has another thing coming." Sheldon snapped, slamming the screen porch door on his way out.

"Where are you going?" Lisa Marie yelled after him, but there was no response.

As Sheldon reached the top of the small hill behind the General Store, he looked up at the setting sun that radiated a deep, fiery, orange glow across the horizon.

He walked up to Katie's grave and knelt. He punched the ground. His small flow of tears watered the dry earth. "I'm so sorry, my love. I'm so sorry. I wish God would have saved you. I don't know why God let you die." Sheldon cried.

He looked off to the right of the cemetery at the charred stake where his Katie was burned alive. His heart burned with anger toward Foreman Lovit. He was so lost in anger that he didn't even know where God was anymore. The anger left no room for God.

Foreman Lovit caused such grief and heartache that Sheldon felt stripped of living. He had nowhere else to go. Where would he go if the Foreman did decide to put him out on the street? With the United States in ruins, he would become a wanderer until a community would accept him. He heard that it was difficult to join a new community due to trust issues, and living on your own is dangerous, not to mention foolish. He would starve to death without anything to trade.

The Foreman allowed them to live in the mission's house and gave them limited supplies. But in the end it would always come with a price at Collection Day. If Lisa Marie hadn't gotten her 401k out of the bank when she did, they would be starving. It was her money they traded for their essentials. But soon that money was coming to an end, and then what?

Sheldon stared at the sunset and imagined Katie sitting next to him. If she were here with him, she would comfort him with God's word. But he didn't want to hear it, for he didn't know if he even believed in His word anymore. Since Walter A. Lovit came into town, everything about God that he knew stopped. No prayers were answered. No feeling of His Holy Spirit. The town itself seemed just as lifeless as he was. Where was God anyway? Had He abandoned him, he wondered. Did God abandon the town to the devil and his son? What happened to crying out to the Lord for deliverance from troubles?

It was because of God's word that Katie was burned at the stake. Sheldon savagely pulled out a clump of dry, dead grass when he heard a commotion coming from down the hill. He saw people gathering near the town's old fountain. Several people were shouting and a man, who he believed to be Henry Slater, screaming out.

CHAPTER NINE
The Leviathan Spirit

I rolled over onto my side and pulled the blanket up to my nose and drifted off again. I saw myself standing on a stage wearing a beautiful, white, flowing gown. As I was singing a lovely worship song to the crowd, my voice changed into a high choking, pitch tweet. I began singing my name. "Aaabiiigaailll. Aaabiiigaailll."

I woke up abruptly to a sickly looking bird perched on a boulder next to me, just tweeting away. Its chirping sounded more like something was lodged in its throat, tempting to sing my name. I sat up and the bird fluttered its wings slowly as if it was trying to remember how to fly. I was surprised to see a bird. It was rare to see any forms of animal life, but then again, nature always has a way of surviving.

I walked out of the cavern and stretched. It was a blessing to still be pain-free—no headaches and no back pain. *Was today the day to move on or do I stay another day?* I closed my eyes and prayed. The Lord told me it's time to go.

After my slow descent down the cavern wall, I walked in the direction I had originally been heading. It was nice to be mobile again and I was very anxious to see if I was going to find somebody.

I thought of movies I had seen over the years—movies in which the main character was lost in the woods, or running for their life from a predator or a person. Lost in thought, I stumbled over a log and landed on my knees into a pile of dead wood and wet leaves.

I was face to face with an old, rotted sign that read, Bitterroot Forest six miles. Obviously, I was getting close to civilization. But, the question was, *which way do I go?* I noticed a worn path to my right. *This must be the way.*

"Well, Lord, I am heading this way and if this isn't the right way I pray that you'll let me know, a.s.a.p. That would certainly be great," I said looking up to the sky as I lifted my right foot onto the path.

At the end of six miles, I came upon an old, rustic cabin nestled amongst several tall pine trees. "Oh Hallelujah! Thank you, Jesus! Real sanctuary! Now let's hope somebody's home."

I was so excited I danced and clapped with joy. Oh, the prospects of a real bathroom, a comfortable bed, and a real meal. The musical tune "Over the hills and through the woods to grandmother's house we go" flooded into my head. I even thought of how Little Red Riding Hood must have felt when she finally made it to her grandmother's house. Excited!!

I balled up my fist and eagerly knocked on the door. The door creaked opened as an elderly lady greeted me, "Are you lost?"

I blinked my eyes several times in surprise. *What kind of greeting was that?* I chuckled and said, "Well, yeah."

We stood staring at each other. It was rather awkward. For some reason, my brain shut down and I couldn't think of a single response. Finally, the lady opened the door more and said, "Oh, of course. Won't you come in?"

"Thank you."

The elderly lady looked me up and down and said, "My, how many days have you've been lost? You are positively, filthy."

I winced out of embarrassment. I hadn't seen myself in the last couple of days and, therefore, wasn't too concerned about my hygiene. But now that it had been brought to my attention, I could only imagine what I must look like.

"It's been close to four days. I was in a horrible plane crash and I have been walking to find civilization."

The elderly lady smiled and said, "Well, you've found it." She paused and looked me over intently. "How did you manage to survive a plane crash? Are there more survivors? Does anyone else need help?"

"I'm afraid I'm the only survivor. And it was by the grace of God I survived-a miracle, no less. I did suffer from a back injury, but the Lord healed me."

As I was talking, the elderly lady kept tilting her head and staring at me. She reached out and touched my dirty hair. "Do you normally have red hair?"

Embarrassment rose up in my cheeks. I took a step back from her touch. Obviously, my hair was extremely dirty. "Yeah, why?"

The lady also stepped back and placed her right hand over her mouth. She almost stumbled to the floor, but a chair caught her which forced her to sit.

"Are you okay, Mam'?" I asked.

"Tell me your name, young lady."

"Abigail. Abigail Banderas." The old lady continued staring at me. It was so awkward that I wanted to flee back to the cavern.

I finally found my boisterous mind again and boldly asked, "Is there something wrong? I know I'm dirty. I haven't really slept well in days or eaten a decent meal, but if you could at least offer me a glass of water and call the authorities for help, you'd resemble a Good Samaritan."

"Oh, I beg your pardon, Abigail. I do seem to have lost my manners. It's just..."

"It's just what?"

"I'll get to that in a minute." She stretched out her hand. "My name is Miriam. And welcome to Bitterroot. I've been expecting you." I think she saw the blood drain from my face, for she quickly walked me over to a chair. "Here, let me get you a glass of water."

As I watched Miriam, I asked, "What do you mean you've been expecting me?"

"For several months I've been having dreams and visions of a visitor. A visitor that God himself would be sending my way for such a time as this."

"So you're a follower of Jesus Christ, a Misfit?"

Miriam met my eyes and said, "Oh yes, yes. I am also considered a prophetess. According to the dreams and visions, I knew God would be answering my prayers."

"Prayers for what?"

Miriam handed me the glass of water and paused for a moment. "I think you could use a hot shower and a hot meal, and then we'll talk."

The feeling of being clean invigorated me, but fatigue also set in. I didn't realize just how tired I was until I sat down at the table to eat. I had a hard time keeping my eyes open.

"I suppose I should let you rest awhile before we talk," Miriam smiled excitedly. "I have so many questions and much to say, but you don't look like you would comprehend a thing. You can sleep in my spare bedroom. You'll find the bed very comfortable."

As soon as my head hit the pillow, I was out. After several hours of deep sleep, I walked out to a coffee table covered with all kinds of books, Bibles, and papers.

"It looks like you slept well. Ready to talk?"

"Sure. Is this to help explain why I'm here?" I rummaged through the different notes she had spread out.

I noticed Miriam staring at me; studying me. Under the weight of her grayish-blues eyes, I felt as if I was standing in front of one of my old, college professors waiting to give an answer. In fact, she resembled one of my old, studious, professors. With her salt-n-pepper hair pulled back in a bun, small spectacles lying loosely at the end of her nose and a note pad in hand ready to give a lecture.

"Abigail, I don't think you realize the gravity of the current situation."

I sat back, crossed my legs and folded my arms. I didn't like being talked down to. I may not fully understand what was going on here, but I wasn't a dummy.

Once again Miriam tilted her head and said, "You don't really know why you're here do you?"

I took a deep sigh and said dryly, "No. I just assumed God led me here so I could get home."

After I spoke the words, the Lord convicted my rude attitude. "No, that's not true, Miriam. I do believe there is a reason why I'm here. I just don't know what that is yet. But I wonder if it has something to do with this..."

I got up and went into the spare bedroom to grab the pill box and held it out for her to see. "Have you seen this before?" Miriam wasn't sure how to answer.

"One of the passengers, a woman, gave it to me. She was just about to tell me who to give it to when she died." I opened it up and read the Bible page to her and showed her the key. "When I was out walking to find shelter, God led me to a cavern and inside was Bible scriptures written on the wall and drawings of people dressed in armor. Does any of this mean anything to you?"

Miriam looked off into the distance and her eyes glazed over as if she were going to cry. In a shaky voice Miriam said, "I think you should sit down. I have a lot to share with you. I know why God sent you here. You are Chesterville's modern day Moses that I have been praying for."

I stood up and said, "Whoa! Wait a minute here. I'm a what to whom? Who's Chesterville?"

"Chesterville is a town just over that small mountain you see outside my back window. It's about ninety miles south of here."

"What do you mean a 'modern day Moses'?"

"Chesterville is in grave danger, Abigail. The people of the town have been in captivity for a long time and I've asked the Lord to help save it."

"Well, we are all living in precarious times. We're all in captivity one way or another, thanks to the locusts and Damion Callaway."

"Yes. I understand that. However, Chesterville is special. It was my home and I've been asking the Lord for His mercy and saving grace to help." Miriam turned to me and smiled, "And now He has—he brought you."

"But what can I do? I mean, He's the all-powerful One and He can do all things with just a spoken word. Why does He need me? I'm just a simple girl from Arizona."

"I don't know." Miriam tilted her head again and said, "And so young too."

I widened my eyes and said, "What is that supposed to mean?"

"I thought the same thing when the Lord gave me a clearer vision of who He was sending to my door."

I folded my arms in defense and said, "Well, who did you want, the real Moses?"

Miriam laughed, "That's funny. The Lord basically said the same thing." She patted to the chair as a gesture for me to sit.

"Well, of course not the real Moses but the experience came to mind." Miriam said with an apprehensive smile.

"I may only be twenty-five, but I have plenty of experience."

"I guess we need to ask the Lord how you can help the town of Chesterville with the experience you do have."

I sat at the edge of the couch and asked, "You say the town is in captivity? What exactly do you mean by that?"

Miriam breathed out a long sigh and said, "Where do I start?" Miriam put down her note pad and told me the history of Chesterville. It was once a thriving community filled with God's people. The Holy Spirit moved freely in the town and many out-of-townies, she called them, were coming to know Jesus until the locusts came.

Tears began to fall from Miriam's wrinkle-circled eyes. "After Damion Callaway took over, he sent a Foreman to Chesterville. He blew into town like the big bad wolf in the "Three Little Pigs." He huffed and puffed his way into the community until all the houses were blown down, spiritually speaking. He immediately began to enforce Damion's laws.

He basically set himself up as god of the town. The Idealist ways and their philosophies slowly corrupted the minds of those who were new to the faith. Those of us who'd been Christians awhile knew that things weren't adding up according to scripture, but like an old hat, the idealist philosophies began to fit comfortably and some of us became deceived and lulled to sleep. It's just like the word of God says, the very elect will be deceived."

"So there's a Foreman. Damion's Boss group is sending out Foreman's right and left. I don't know what I'm to do about it. We're blessed not to have had a Foreman arrive in our town yet." I said.

Miriam looked down and was quiet. Then something she said about the big bad wolf triggered my mind. "So he came in like a big bad wolf?"

"Yes, why?"

Feeling a bit stressed, I began to rub my temples. It couldn't be, I thought. It was just a statement she used; it doesn't have anything to do with the dream.

"Perhaps this is where my experience comes in. Just prior to the locust's invasion, I was in college studying spiritual warfare. This big bad wolf sounds more like a demonic principality to me called, the leviathan spirit."

Miriam's eyes widened as she slapped her knee. "A few months ago when I was fasting on behalf of Chesterville, the Lord kept giving me scriptures to study on the leviathan but I didn't understand why. What is a leviathan spirit?"

"Well, I have learned that only God can remove it and it is not to be reckoned with, that's for sure. Even in the book of Job it talks about if you lay a hand on him, you will remember the struggle and never do it again."

"How does one deal with it then?" Miriam worried.

"First we need to understand how he got a foothold in the town in the first place and then we pray and ask God for His strategy on how to fight alongside Him."

"I have no idea how that demonic principality wormed its way into the town. God's presence was so thick and heavy and so many people were coming to know the Lord. God had me teach and disciple the ones who were new to the faith. God also revealed to me that He was going to take the leadership to a new and deeper level.

I saw a shift in the leadership over the beliefs when the Foreman took over our church. His way of speech was not in accordance with the word of God. It was as if he spoke half-truths and twisted the word just to suit his own beliefs. He wanted to be in control of everything. Oh, how the Foreman stood at the pulpit like a proud peacock, all puffed out showing off his ungodly feathers!" Miriam said as she shook her head in remembrance.

"The truly sad part is that this caused much strife amongst the congregation. We divided and then the Foreman announced there wouldn't be any more church services. Damion was shutting them down." Miriam looked away and down at the floor. Her voice was quivery as she continued. "The Foreman burned down the church. I believe it was his plan all along—to divide and conquer."

"What you have described definitely sounds like the work of the leviathan spirit." I let out a deep heavy sigh. I felt bad for Miriam. I could hear the deep sorrow she felt for the people. I could tell she truly loved and cared about the health and safety of the town.

I leaned forward and rested my elbows on my knees and said, "He's described to be like a crocodile with multiple heads. He coils around like a serpent, to cut off the spiritual flow of a person. His back has rows of shields tightly sealed together; each is so close to the next that no air can pass between them. Meaning, the flow of the Holy Spirit can't bring revelation, truth, and change to a person. He snorts out flashes of light, and his eyes are like the rays of dawn. Firebrands stream from his mouth and sparks of fire shoot out. His very breath sets coals ablaze. Nothing on earth is his equal—a creature without fear. He looks down on all that are haughty. He is king over all that are proud."

Captivated, Miriam said, "I believe you've just described Damion Callaway and the Foreman!"

"Miriam, pride is the main way this demonic principality gets in, especially when Christians begin to launch out into the deeper things of God. With the work of the Holy Spirit, obviously the town's people were getting closer to God and the enemy got angry and found an open door to unleash the Leviathan spirit on your town. His assignment was to block the spiritual development of people so that they cannot enter into the place where they can seek God, pray, or read the Bible. He works through deception, twisting and distorting communication, which severs once-healthy relationships. He comes to keep you from getting your inheritance, and we both know that our inheritance is everything that belongs to Jesus Christ!"

Miriam stood and paced around the cabin. "So, through pride it makes its way in..." Miriam stopped at a window and paused.

"Miriam, are you okay?" I asked as I got up and walked over to her. I looked out the window with her and noticed the mountain where Chesterville was located. "Miriam, did something happen? Do you know what caused the open door?" I saw a single tear slid down Miriam's wrinkled face. She swallowed, then licked her lips and wiped at her tear.

"No one ever said that being a prophet was easy." Miriam folded her arms as if trying to comfort herself at the memory. "I was close to Pastor Jacob. He was like a son to me. He always respected and received the words the Lord would give me to share with him. But something changed. After the locusts came and we all resurfaced, I discerned that Pastor Jacob was being secretive about something and when I asked, he pushed me away. He acted afraid and he didn't even try to rebuild the town like he told us he was going to. He really changed after the Foreman arrived."

Miriam looked at me and said, "The Lord had me give him a hard word telling him he would head down a wrong path if he didn't adjust his footsteps. The lamp of God would be blown out by a black olive tree. I wasn't sure what that meant. But now I think I do. The black olive tree represents bad oil... pride. Pastor Jacob must have opened the door to pride."

I nodded as we stared out the window at the mountain. "That is how I ended up here, you know?" Miriam said.

"What do you mean?" I asked.

"The Lord had me give the Foreman a hard word." Miriam's face screwed up in contempt when she mentioned his name.

"What did he say?"

Miriam chuckled sarcastically, "It's not what he said. It's what he tried to do." I went over to the chair, sat down, and waited for her to continue.

"He tried burning me at the stake for breaking the Idealist rules, but when it didn't work, he sent me packing to Bitterroot Forest. He told the people that if anyone tried to see me they would be punished. He told me that I was never to return. Abigail, this leviathan spirit must be taken down."

"You do realize this is bigger than the Foreman and Chesterville. We're talking about a whole network here. With Damion at the helm, we could possibly be dealing with the Anti-Christ. I can't just go off and fight this on my own."

Miriam smiled and patted my knee and said, "I know dear, one town at a time. Isn't it our job to fight on behalf of our God and help others? I believe you are a part of God's strategy. So tell me more of what you know about that principality."

I let out a heavy sigh and continued, "Well, in Matthew it tells us to first tie up the strong man so it won't carry away your possessions and continue to rob your house. The strong man refers to a demon, a higher-up principality. Just like ranks in God's army, Satan too has army ranks. In Ephesians 6 it talks about the ranks." We opened our Bibles to Ephesians. As I read, I stopped at verse twelve to explain the order of ranks to Miriam and when I got to verse thirteen, I stopped.

"What's the matter, Abigail?"

"This was one of the scriptures written on the cavern wall along with pictures of people dressed in armor. I believe God has been giving me strategy. We need to put on our armor and pray. Through my study, I learned that you need to handle the person who the demon is attached to with humility. For example, if the person is yelling in your face or cutting you down, you need to hold to peace and speak in love, but also in truth. If you fight fire with fire like it says in Job you will feel the battle. If the person repents from pride, the principality will no longer have the authority to stay."

"Well, hell would literally have to freeze over before the Foreman or Damion would repent from pride," Miriam snorted with laughter. I laughed with her.

"Abigail, can I ask you a personal question?"

"Sure."

"I'm just curious as to why you decided to study spiritual warfare?"

I looked to the floor in search of what to say. I inhaled a deep breath and let it out slowly to control the tears that wanted to escape. "I was so fixated on wanting to know why my real mother could leave me, her five-year-old daughter in a dark alley to be taken to an orphanage."

Miriam covered her mouth and mumbled, "Ooh, my."

"But it was my adopted father who sparked that interest. He shared with me that even though there is an enemy prowling around like a lion seeking whom he can destroy—we can't always place the blame on him. God has given us free will and He won't go against that. It's still our choice to make. However, the enemy does his best to influence that choice, whether it's through lies, circumstances or sin-ours or others. Unknowingly, we open that door of influence through those sins and invite in a demonic presence.

All of that intrigued me. I wanted to learn more about Satan's influence and how to overcome him. I wanted to know why people do evil things or do things they don't want to do. Just like what Paul says, 'I do the things I ought not to do and don't do the things I should do.'

I wanted to know why my real mother felt like the only option she had was to abandon me. I believe her to have been influenced by Satan because she didn't know Jesus Christ. It saddens me that she could have had freedom and the healing of her soul wounds. Plus, I wanted to forgive her." I looked to the floor. I was getting tired and I didn't want to talk any more.

"I can tell I hit a bruise by asking the question." Miriam paused to look at me and then continued, "How about we continue this in the morning? I can sense the Lord is close in sending you to the town. I want to make sure you're well-rested and prepared."

****

The call of a rooster signaled morning too early. I got up, showered and quickly joined Miriam for breakfast.

"Sleep well?" Miriam asked. I smiled and nodded as I yawned.

"Sorry about ole' Rupert. Somehow that foolish rooster survived the locusts. I believe he still thinks he's living on a farm and needs to wake up everyone bright and early for chores. Several times I've tried taking him into the wild to be free, but that crazy bird always finds its way back here."

I chuckled and then changed the subject rather abruptly. "Miriam, I believe today is the day that I'm to leave for the town."

"What about more strategy?"

"I believe the strategy is listening and obeying God's direction. I kept hearing those words all night. I know it's not going to be easy, in fact, I wanted to run back to the cavern, but I finally submitted to God's plan and peace settled in my heart."

Miriam filled a small pack with food and said, "In case you get hungry." She tossed a fruit bar over to me. "Here's one for the road. And if you come with me, I'll show you the four-wheeler you can borrow." She paused and looked at me, "Abigail, that key, I believe has something to do with the town's captivity. I pray you find whatever it is that opens it so God can set the people free."

After we prepared the four-wheeler that Miriam offered to me, we held hands to pray. Miriam's hands were warm and soft.

"Lord," Miriam began. "I thank you for this beautiful child. She is an answer to my prayers. So I ask Father that you will go before her into this battle that lies ahead of us all. Please give her the strategy to take down the evil one and to help the town's people. Give her the right words to say when it's needed. I plead the blood of Jesus Christ over her and ask for a hedge of protection, Father God. And Lord, give this child peace! In the name of Jesus Christ, amen."

"Most importantly, Lord, let Your will be done through me," I chimed in.

Miriam then pointed and said, "If you stay on the path that runs along the creek you end up in Chesterville."

"Thanks, Miriam, for everything. After I complete the Lords work, I'll be heading back home. So I guess this is good-bye," I said and hugged her.

Miriam giggled in my neck as we hugged. We pulled arm's length away and I asked, "What's so funny?"

"The Lord wants you to know that this is only the beginning," Miriam placed her hand on my belly and prophesied, "Soon you will have a fire starter."

I backed up and said, "Well, that's funny, considering I would have to be married and I don't want to get married."

Miriam just smiled and said, "Abigail, it sounds like it's going to be a tough battle. But just know that I will keep you covered in prayer. I know God will be with you, too, but there are some dangerous men there.   Please be careful."

"I will. Thank you."

Miriam hugged me again and said, "I will see you again."

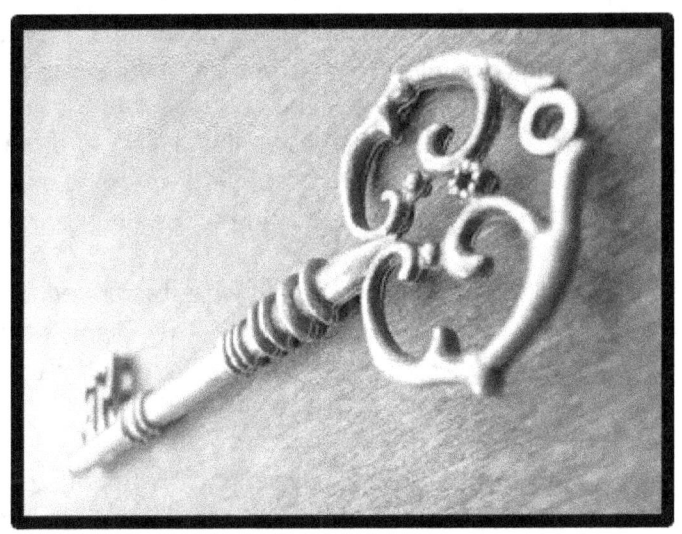

CHAPTER TEN
The Stoning

The radiant, fiery orange glow faded as the moon marked off a new season. The night sky was lowly lit by a few visible stars that were masked under swirls of smoky, gray clouds setting an eerie tone for the stoning. The bone-chilling breeze didn't help much either, for it swept across the dry land, making the evening a haunting place to be.

Wrapped in a knitted shawl, Isabella dreaded being out in the cold, dark night, preparing to stone a human being. She watched Henry standing in the center of the people, grievously awaiting his death sentence.

Lisa Marie couldn't stomach being there since it was the anniversary of Katie's death four years ago. Margo and Tony Sullivan, Trudy Capone, and Marco Deportenello didn't want to be there either. They were only there out of obedience and fear. The Foreman threatened punishment if they didn't help stone Henry.

They knew Foreman Lovit always punished a disobedient person on Collection Day as an example to the others.

They didn't believe the charges against Henry and feared murdering an innocent man.   They all knew Henry to be a wonderful tradesman, friend and all around good neighbor.

Those who belonged to the Idealist group enjoyed seeing justice given to a person who broke the law.   They highly respected their foreman and believed that he had done well for the town of Chesterville.

Spider-Eyed Jones pushed a wheel barrow full of stones to each Misfit and Idealist and demanded that they take a handful. Jethro and Blake, who finally arrived, walked up to the crowd of people.

Walter announced, "Good evening my friends and neighbors.   I'm glad you could come out tonight.   Please, also welcome home, my other two comrades, Jethro and Blake.   They have been away on business.   Now, you all know why you are here."

"Yeah! To stone Henry, that crook," said one man.

"And you call yourself a tradesman!" A woman yelled.

Tony and Margo lowered their eyes in shame, as they loosely held medium size stones in their hands.

"I say we stone him now!   He deserves what's coming to him," said Jethro.

Marco desperately wanted to stand up for Henry.   These people had no clue of the true person Henry was.   He wouldn't have cheated with his numbers if Foreman Lovit hadn't put so much pressure on him to come up with such a huge amount of money. Not that it was right to lie, but times were difficult.   Henry had helped Marco out financially before the destruction of the locusts. Marco wished he could help Henry now, but it would be to his death if he did.

Marco closed his eyes for a brief moment and furiously squeezed a stone. He replayed a message he had once heard from Pastor Jacob Capone, at the Little White Chapel Church about loving one another. It was the only service he attended with his wife, Elana. "We should love one another. Don't be like Cain, who belonged to the evil one and murdered his brother, and why did he murder his brother? Because his own actions were evil and his brothers were righteous. Don't be surprised, my brothers, if the world hates you. We know that we have passed from death to life, because we love our brothers. Anyone who does not love remains in death. Anyone who hates his brother is a murderer, and you know that no murderer has eternal life in him. This is how we know what love is. Jesus Christ laid down His life for us. And we ought to lay down our lives for our brothers."

Marco took the sleeve of his shirt and wiped away tears that were flowing fast, but he couldn't wipe away his thoughts. *I love Henry like a brother. I should take his place,* but fear was holding him back. *Does that make me a coward? Or maybe it really isn't my place. After all, I believe in God, but I don't truly feel like I belong to God. Does that make me belong to the evil one? Does this mean I truly don't love Henry enough to want to die for him? If that was the case, then he did not love at all. What kind of man does that make me?* He felt worthless.

His whole body began to shake. He felt ashamed and selfish that he couldn't take Henry's place. This was a moment of truth like the one Pastor Jacob talked about. The question was, when the moment came, could he, would he, lay down his life for another?

Marco opened up his eyes and whispered, "I can't." And he dropped the stone. "And I can't stone my brother either." He turned to leave. Walter scanned the crowd and saw that Marco was walking away.

"Hey, my good buddy!" Walter yelled across the sea of people and walked toward him. Walter put his arm around him, "And just where do you think you're going? I think I will have you throw the first stone." Marco froze. There was no way he could be the first to throw a stone at Henry.

Walter calmed the noisy crowd with the raising of his hand. "I hereby declare on this Collection Day, that Henry Slater is guilty of cheating the Idealist leader, Damion Callaway out of the full payment of his debt.   Therefore, the charges against him result in payment with his life.   Let this be an example to anyone who thinks he can get away with breaking the laws! My good buddy here will do me the honor of casting the first stone!"

Marco paled and thought he was going to lose his supper on Walter's best patent-leather shoes.

"Hand me my black Bible, will you Sniper?" Walter asked.

Walter opened up the Bible to John 8:7 and simply read, "If any one of you is without sin let him be the first to throw a stone." He looked at Marco and said, "I know you to be an honorable man. You're definitely a man without sin."

Margo was livid at the misquoting of scripture. She poked at Tony for his response and whispered, "That is not what that scripture means. We all have fallen short of God's glory. We're all sinners and we should all drop these stones and walk away and let Henry live!"

"Honey, please keep your voice down. We don't want to stir up trouble for ourselves."

"Yes, I know, but God's word says that if we claim to be without sin, we deceive ourselves and the truth is not in us.

Foreman Lovit is truly a man who is wicked and deceived. I don't want any part of this. Besides, what do you think God would have us do?"

Tony gave Margo an authoritative look that told her she crossed the line with him. He quickly looked over to the Foreman, who was too busy with Marco to even notice their conversation.

"For the last time, Margo, if you don't be quiet, we'll be the ones out there with Henry. Is that what you want?"

"Well of course not, but I can't stone an innocent man and I am definitely not a person without sin, either!" Tears streamed down her face.

Tony moved closer to her and whispered, "I have an idea. Just throw the stone at the ground a few inches away from his feet. That way, to the Foreman, it will look like we are participating, but we will purposely be missing so we won't harm him."

Margo wiped at her tears and said, "Good plan."

Tony wished his wife hadn't spoken her concerns, for now his conscience talked to him. He didn't want to throw a stone either. But, he needed to protect himself and his wife, so what other option was there? The pit in his stomach started to go away the more he thought about his plan. He would only throw a couple nearby Henry, and carefully try not to hit him.

Walter picked up Marco's stone that he dropped and handed it back to him.

Marco's eyes met Henry's. The look in Marco's eyes told Henry he was torn and unsure of what to do. Henry saw Marco fumbling the stone in his hand as if he was contemplating throwing it elsewhere.

Henry stood tall and brave, "It's okay, Marco. I will not hold this against you." Henry looked toward Foreman Lovit's direction, but continued to talk to Marco. "I know why you have to do this. It's okay. You can throw the stone."

Marco's pupils dilated as he shook his head, "No I can't. You don't deserve to die. I don't want to have to live with your blood on my hands." He dropped the stone.

Walter furiously picked it up and said, "You will throw this stone, and you will do it now!" With his own hand, he grabbed Marco's in his and together they threw the stone. The stone hit Henry right in the forehead and dropped him to his knees. "I want the rest of you to start throwing stones, now!" Walter demanded.

While the town's people began throwing their stones, Trudy took a step back from the chaos. She caressed her short hair while putting her thoughts in order. Knowing how Walter and Sniper made her feel, stripped of all her dignity, she couldn't bear the thought of doing it to someone else. Between the stress and fear, her mind immediately played back her late father's words to her as a child.

"Now, sweetheart, I know there are times when you will face bullies, but the good Lord says we are to 'treat others as you would want to be treated,' because you'll reap what you sow."

Nobody deserved the kind of treatment Walter gave. Not even Henry. She figured if she helped stone him, then it would come back on her, and she didn't want that.

What had happened to Walter for him to do such horrible acts to others? She wondered. Was he treated like this, and this was his way of retaliation?

There were so many people stoning Henry, she felt she could slip away unnoticed. She tossed the stones in the busy crowd to make it look as though she was throwing them, and then walked home. Thankfully, a few of the side street lights were burned out and she could walk mostly in the dark without being seen.

Walter slowly wrapped his arms around Isabella's waist and said, "Are you having a good time?"

Isabella didn't want to answer such a question. She kept quiet with her arms folded firmly to keep warm.

"I didn't see you throw a stone." Walter said as he picked up a rather jagged rock. "Here, let me see you throw a stone."

"I threw my share. And now I want to go home. I'm freezing out here." Isabella said, seeing her breath in the brisk, cold air.

"Don't you lie to me, woman. Throw this stone, or we will throw it together like Marco and I did. And if I have to do that with you, then I'll find a punishment for you come morning!"

Walter handed her the jagged stone. Thankfully it was dark and Walter didn't see her eyes red, and full of tears. To appease him, she tossed the rock and it missed Henry by a foot.

Walter grabbed another one from the wheelbarrow and frustratingly said, "You missed on purpose. The more you miss, the longer you're going to stay out here until you hit him."

Gripped with deep sorrow and remorse for Henry, Isabella didn't have the strength to throw.   Her stomach was in a knot and she felt queasy.

By this time, Henry was so beaten by the many blows from the rocks, his breathing was shallow. Lying in a pool of blood, in the fetal position, Henry was close to death. Under her breath, she said, "Forgive me, Henry." She threw the stone and hit him right on top of his head. Knowing it was her rock that killed Henry, Isabella wanted to turn and run. *What have I done?* She thought.

Walter scooped her up in his arms and said, "That's my girl!" He set her down on her feet and asked, "Since this is a time of celebration, how about you give me your answer?"

Isabella had to think. *Answer? A time of celebration? Since when is a stoning, or burning at the stake or a crucifixion, a celebration?* She rubbed her temples to rid of the pulsation pain. In a weak voice she asked, "Answer?"

"Tell me my love didn't forget my marriage proposal already?"

She couldn't believe his timing. This man was truly insane! And there was no way she wanted to marry him.

She stood there speechless with her mouth in the position of wanting to say no. Standing near a few lamp posts that were softly aglow, Isabella, could see that Walter was not going to take no for an answer.

Before she could say anything, Walter said, "Then its official. We are to be married in two weeks."

She tried to respond, but he had quieted the crowd and announced their engagement. The town's people cheered and hollered for them.

From Katie's gravesite, Sheldon could hear everything. The reverberating moans from Henry, the tormenting words of the people, and the confusing sounds of excitement that now echoed all the way up the hill.

Sheldon turned to look up at the scorched stake. He could still picture Katie ruthlessly tied to it and Foreman Lovit enjoying setting her on fire. With tears streaking his hot face, he whispered, "I'll never love again."

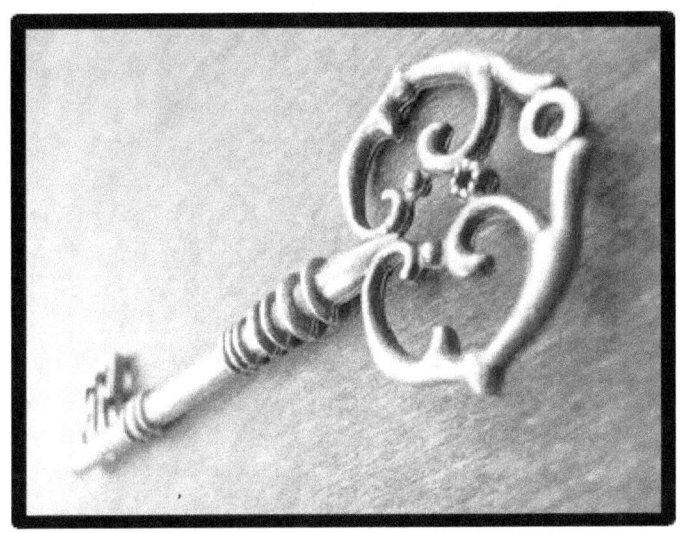

CHAPTER ELEVEN
The Big Black Wolf

Walter returned home from the stoning and sat on the edge of his bed. He remembered how this all began...

The train whistle blew and the conductor announced the upcoming stop. Three more stops and Walter would be stepping out into a phase he hoped would lead to power, riches and prestige.

Walter put the pill box into his uniform jacket and got himself ready for his stop A young gentleman, who sat across from Walter, got up and sat next to him. He offered his hand and said, "So how's it going? My name is Maximus Rodrigo."

Walter assessed the man dressed in street clothes. "You are a brave Misfit for looking into my eyes and wanting to shake a Foreman's hand."

Maximus nervously lowered his eyes and said, "Please forgive me, Foreman. I've seemed to have lost my manners."

"Where are you traveling from, Misfit?"

Maximus swallowed hard and said with his head slightly down, "New York City. I lost all my family to the locusts and wanted to move back to my native land."

"Well, Misfit, since I will be the Foreman of this town, I just might need a strong man to help me. Can I call on you some time?"

"I don't mean any disrespect Foreman, but being a Misfit 'n-all, I don't like what you Idealist stand for. So how can I be of much use to you?"

Instead of getting enraged with the Misfit, Walter smiled. He liked his feistiness. He could use a man like Maximus. "I'll be calling on you. You just might not have a choice, Misfit."

"Last stop, Chesterville," the conductor announced.

Maximus moved to his seat pleased with himself, knowing his plan just might work.

The whistle blew a couple of times, signifying the stop and the train came to a halt.

Walter picked up his belongings and stepped off the train. The fresh mountain air greeted him and so did the busy street of Chesterville. Walter looked around and saw the SunKissed Hotel. In spite of its damages, the hotel looked quite exquisite. "I guess this will do for now."

Walter looked to his left and a huge all wood, gingerbread house stood out from the rest of the town. All of the buildings were like a time capsule from the old west. It was a shame to see such damage.

A sweet, flowery scent greeted Walter as he entered the Sunkissed Hotel. He propped his bags against the counter and rang the bell. A tall brunette with a beaming smile and a bouncy voice came to the counter. "Good afternoon, I'm Margo Sullivan. Welcome to the Sunkissed Hotel. Would you like a room?"

"No, actually I'm looking to move into a home. Do you know where I may find one?"

Margo noticed the man's sports jacket with Damion Callaway's patch on it. *Is he a Foreman or just another Idealist passing through?* Her heart started to beat fast at the thought of him being a Foreman. They had been free to do as they pleased for the past couple of years. *Is our freedom going to be taken away?*

"You would need to see Pastor, Mayor Jacob. He and his family have owned this town for several generations and still own several pieces of property."

"Mayor? You do realize that our new government doesn't have mayors anymore?"

"Yes, but he's been the mayor of this town for years. So we continue to call him Mayor."

Walter smiled and said, "Not for long. Where might I find Pastor, Mayor Jacob?"

Margo nervously pointed and said, "He owns the General Store. It's right across the street. You can't miss it. It has a great big sign on top of the building."

Walter saluted a thank you and proceeded out the door. With his hand on the door knob, he turned back and asked, "Does anyone live in that big gingerbread house?"

Margo came around the counter and looked out the door window with Walter and pointed, "Oh, you mean the Capone's mansion? Yeah, Pastor, Mayor Jacob and his daughter, Trudy, live there. Pastor, Mayor Jacob spends most of his time at the store, so he lives in the adjacent part. If he's not at the church, that is. If you're looking to stay close to town, then renting a room from me would be what you need. Pastor, Mayor Jacob only has property on the outskirts of town which is several miles away."

"Then I guess I'll be in need of a room."

"Perfect. What will be the trade?"

Walter smiled sweetly and said, "I'm a Foreman. I don't need to trade."

Margo's heart dropped. *A Foreman has arrived. What will become of our town now?* She fearfully handed him a room key and said nervously, "Hope you enjoy your stay."

Walter grinned and said, "Oh I will. Thank you."

After Walter settled in and unpacked, he sat on the bed and pulled out the small yellow piece of paper his boss gave him. Staring at the name written on the paper he contemplated his next move.

"Too soon," he said and put the piece of paper back into his uniform jacket.

On his way down the stairs, an older gentleman was jogging up the steps. The man stopped and said timidly, "Hi, I'm Tony, Margo's husband. She said we have a new guest. Welcome. I apologize for the disarray of our place. We are trying to trade our way to restoration."

"Well, now that I'm here, our Idealist leader has made it my mission to help rebuild the community."

Tony smiled with relief. "That is mighty kind of Damion to help us."

Walter smiled wickedly. If only they knew just how much. Tony jogged up the stairs. Walter stopped halfway and turned back and asked, "Excuse me, maybe you can help me with something."

Tony jogged back down. "What could I do for you?"

"Could you tell me where I might find a doctor?"

"Yes, he's right around the corner from the hotel."

"Thank you. You're a kind man, Tony," Walter said.

Without thinking, Tony's words flew out of his mouth before he realized what he had said, "Margo and I like to spread the kindness of Jesus around."

Walter set his mouth straight and said firmly, "Since I just arrived and you Misfits are not use to the new rules yet, I will let this one slide, but let it be your last!"

Tony slowly shrunk back into the wall as Walter continued to head down the stairs.

Walter stepped onto the wooded sidewalk and turned the corner to the doctor's office. The bell above the door chimed as he opened it. "I'll be with you in just a minute." A deep voice sang out.

He looked about. The office was small. Only a few hard chairs lined the walls, and a small, chewed-up reception desk was placed next to a door with a sign that read, 'Patients Only'.

A man opened the door to see Walter standing near the desk. "Can I help you?" The man asked.

Walter looked up to see a short, stocky man in a white lab coat, wiping his hands. Walter smiled. The man smiled.

"Just arrived?" The man asked.

"Yes." Walter looked around and raised his eye brows. "An Elite, doctor hey?"

He smiled and said, "Yes. A doctor comes in handy. You just never know when someone is in need of a prescription, and it pays well."

Walter walked up to the framed doctor's license on the wall. "I thought it was revoked?"

"No one needs to know that." Walter gave the doctor a crooked smile.

"What ails you?" The doctor asked.

"Bad headaches." Walter teased and then spoke seriously. "Do you have that specially formulated prescription I'm here to collect on behalf of the Boss?"

The doctor irritatingly said, "I was hoping to get a shipment of it through the General Store, but no such luck. The owner said he retired from the pharmaceutical business. I think he may need some heavy persuasion that we are in need of it." Walter shook his head in agreement.

"Seen Jethro yet?"

"No. I stopped here first."

"He hasn't had any luck either. The owner's daughter's lips are just as sealed. Neither of them are talking. If you want to see Jethro he lives across the street."

"We'll be in touch," Walter said. The doctor nodded and escorted Walter out.

Walter balled up his fist and knocked hardily on the door. A very large man, with a mustache that curled up tight at the ends, met him at the door.

"Having difficulties, I hear, getting our prescriptions?" Walter said as he entered the home.

"They're not cooperating. I didn't want to push too hard and blow your cover before you got here."

"Good call. By the sounds of things, I guess it's time for me to do some shaking up around here."

When Jethro smiled, the tips of his mustache touched his eyes. "Thought you might like to know because of our questioning with, Trudy. She called the Elite group on us. I'm talking about the ones who are no longer for Damion."

Walter's mouth twisted in frustration as he rubbed his fingers through his hair.

Jethro smiled again and said, "Don't worry. The Boss has an inside man and will be sending him."

"What's his name?"

"Sniper. The Boss calls him Sniper-Eyed Jones."

"He must be the third man the Boss said he would send over in case of a snag."

"Well, we have run into a snag. Its name is Trudy."

Walter patted his uniform jacket and said, "Got it covered."

"So we were right?"

"Yes, she's a part of the plan." Walter plastered a wicked smile and said, "I think being Foreman is going to be fun."

"I hear the old man is dying."

"Not before I get my hands on him."

****

Walter entered the General Store. "Good mornin' ta ya Sir. What can I do fer ya?"

"I'm looking for a man named Pastor, Mayor Jacob Capone."

"It's just Pastor Jacob, if ya don't mind. That'll be me. Is there somethin' wrong?"

"No. I heard you're the Mayor of the town and I wanted to meet you and offer you Damion Callaway's services."

Pastor Jacob paled. "Ya'll be a Foreman?"

"Yes. That would be correct."

"What does Damion want frum us? We've lost jes about everythin' in the locusts' invasion."

Walter leaned over the counter and said, "We need to have ourselves a chat, privately."

"Trudy! I need ya ta cover the counter fer me." Pastor Jacob yelled. Trudy quickly came through the curtain door that separated the store and the house. Trudy's eyes lit up as she saw Walter standing at the counter. Walter smiled back and played with the yellow piece of paper that was in his pants pocket.

"I have business with this gentleman. I won't be long." Pastor Jacob said.

Walter took his hand out and offered it to Trudy. "I'm Walter Lovit, the Foreman." Trudy smiled shyly and took his hand.

Walter lightly kissed the top of her hand, winked and said, "It's a pleasure to meet you. I'm sure we will be seeing a lot of each other."

Trudy put her hand to her chest bashfully and said, "The pleasure was all mine," and winked back.

Walter let her hand go gently and followed Pastor Jacob into the house. "Before ya git ta excited about my daughter, I should let ya know she's engaged ta be married."

"Then we shall be good friends. We can never have too many friends, right?"

Pastor Jacob sat down and studied the Foreman's face. "So what services are ya offerin'?

Walter adjusted his tie and sat up straighter. "Damion wants to help rebuild your community."

Pastor Jacob narrowed his eyes and said, "In trade fer what? I'm assumin' it's gotta cost somethin'. Damion doesn't do anythin' fer free, I hear. But I'm tellin' ya, I ain't got nothin' ta trade. We're lucky that a few local farmers jes happen' ta be doomsday preppers and have been willin' ta trade fer their crops and other necessities. This town relies on their crops ta help feed us. Is that what ya want is their seed? Their food? What?"

Pastor Jacob glanced toward his window and stared at his little white church. A quick remembrance of Miriam, the prophetess, who gave him a word from the Lord, came flooding back to him. 'Do not take the fruit from a dead olive tree.' He pushed the prophetic word aside, too weak and tiered to heed it.

"We don't want the seed or anything else other than this..." Walter said and pulled out the pill box. Pastor Jacob's jaw lowered as he paled and gripped the arms of his chair.

Walter waved the pill box and the key in the air and said, "How about trading with your so-called prescriptions."

"Don't know what ya talkin' about."

Walter shook his head and said, "Now, Pastor, if that's what you really want to call yourself, you know exactly what I'm talking about. Let's not play this game shall we? I am a very powerful man with friends in very high places, so let's cut to the chase. Why not use those prescription pills of yours to help me to help you."

"Because, I'm no longer in that business. And where did ya ever git that key and pill box?"

"An old friend. Let's just say he's of Royalty." Pastor Jacob slouched in his chair speechless.

"Now this is how it's going to go. You are going to tell me where the prescriptions are—your diamonds and in trade, Damion will help you rebuild the town and help ship what food or supplies the people need. No diamonds—no help. In fact, I will strip this town of what they do have and leave it to rot."

Pastor Jacob was indignant. He stood and said, "Look, I don't know what ya heard, but I ain't got no diamonds. I got out of that prescription business a long time ago. I'm an honest man who loves preachin' God's word and holds ta em.'" Pastor Jacob started to head toward the curtain.

Walter got up, aggressively grabbed Jacob's arm and said, "Oh, we're not done!" Walter clenched his teeth and continued, "I hear you are a dying man. So why don't you just hand the diamonds to us so Damion can get on with his project."

Pastor Jacob tried to pull his arm out of Walters's vice-like grip. Walter grabbed Pastor Jacob by the throat and said, "If you breathe a word to anyone about this, I will tell the towns people how you once smuggled so-called "prescription pills" and kept all the money, and left the town to rot. And your daughter... well, I have plans for her unless you do everything I say."

"Ya leave my daughter out of this. She has nothin' ta do with this."

Walter inhaled deeply and said, "Oh, on the contrary. She's very much involved."

Pastor Jacob clenched his fist and said, "If ya hurt my daughter, I will come after ya."

Walter laughed. "I'm not afraid of you. But you need to be afraid of me. Now, as far as your daughter is concerned, I know how attached she is to a certain family heirloom that would lead me to your diamonds."

Pastor Jacob looked away and said, "There is no family heirloom. It was destroyed by the locusts."

"We'll see about that. I'm sure Trudy will be happy to show it to me." Walter mischievously smiled and laughed.

"Ya'll are a crazy man. And ya'll never git it."

Harshly, Walter released Pastor Jacob and said, "And, oh, by the way, I will be living in your house."

Pastor Jacob's face was red hot and sweaty. Angrily he said, "Fine, but ya'll neva git ya paws on those diamonds."

"Yes I will, and your lovely daughter will help me do it." Walter said directly in his face.

****

Walter stood and walked into the bathroom mirror straightening his tie. Suddenly he smelled the sweet scent of a cigar, and out of the corner of his eye he saw a puff of smoke form into a ring. His heart pounded.   There was only one person he knew that could make a smoke ring and that was, the Boss.

"I wasn't aware that you were in town."

"I had to come. Damion is breathing down my neck and now I'm breathing down yours. Where's the diamonds? Time is ticking and he is anxious to start working on his project."

"The Capone family—your cousins are making things difficult."

"How so?"

"They won't tell me where the diamonds are hidden, but I have an idea."

The Boss puffed out a ring of smoke and sighed with great irritation. "An idea? What are we, in third grade? Put pressure on them, torment them, do what you need to do and get me those diamonds."

The Boss studied Walter and noticed he was perspiring. "Something is making you nervous or you're not telling me everything. You are going through with this aren't you? We had a deal."

Walter swallowed hard and said, "Like I've told you before, Boss, I finish my jobs.   It's just…"

Irritated, the Boss said, "It's just what?"

"Something doesn't feel right."

The Boss puffed out another ring and mimicked Walter, "Something doesn't feel right." His voice switched to anger, "It doesn't have to feel right. Just do it! If you feel like you can't, I'll find someone who can!"

"I can do it. It's just... I sense something's off." Walter loosened his tie and looked down at the sink in apprehension. Not only did something feel off, but he didn't want to tell his boss that he lost the key, either. "Maybe it has something to do with a dream I had when I was on the train the first day I arrived."

The Boss coiled back further so Walter could barely see him in the mirror. "Dream? What dream?" The Boss' voice seemed strained at the mention of a dream.

Walter, deep in thought in remembrance of his dream, was interrupted by the Boss' deep raspy voice.

"Well don't just stand there in silence. Speak boy! What was the dream?"

If Walter hadn't known any better, he would assume the Boss seemed afraid, but afraid of what? It was just a stupid dream. It couldn't possible mean anything.

Walter retold the dream of how he found a ruby in the desert. How a flame of fire burned within it and it turned into an enormous eagle; and ended with him dangling from the human-like claws of the eagle only to be placed in its nest to be eaten by its babies.

Walter found himself breathing heavily as he recalled how real the dream felt. He looked up from the sink into the mirror in search of the silhouette, but only saw a haze of smoke.

"Oh, that dream. It's j-just a silly dream that's all. I-I-It means nothing." The Boss stuttered nervously as he lied. "Just keep your wits about yourself and don't let anyone get in your way. That's what that dream means. Someone will try to keep you from getting what belongs to me!" His voice became hoarser. "It's time for you to go."

The Boss shrunk back out of his own fear. It was confirmed. Walter receiving the dream meant his own enemy was close on his tail. His only hope for his plan to succeed would be based on Walter's seeing it through. The problem was... What if his enemy were to get in the way-the One who sits on the heavenly throne?

CHAPTER TWELVE
The Modern Day Moses

It certainly was a bumpy and noisy ride. The crazy four-wheeler sounded like it was about to explode. Every few feet it would kick back, followed by a slight popping sound. And then there was the black smoldering smoke oozing out of its engine. I wasn't sure if this baby had much life, and I wanted to get to Chesterville as fast as I could before the possibilities of being stranded. I already had to sleep one night in the rough; I certainly didn't want another one. At least it was another pleasant day if I were to get stranded.

The so-called luxurious ride was rudely interrupted when I heard a loud screeching sound. The four-wheeler came to a seizing halt and the handle bars locked up toward the left. I wasn't at all ready for the sudden stop. Before I could brace myself, I shot off the four-wheeler like a cannon and flew like an airplane. I did a face-plant, half in the creek and half on the dirt trail.

I slapped at the water, looked toward the sky and whined, "Seriously, Lord, I can't even have the luxury of riding a four-wheeler?"

I slapped at the water one last time for good measure. It still didn't change my situation, but I felt better inside. Well almost, I decided to kick the ole' mule. Unfortunately, I kicked it too hard bruising my pinky toe. The shooting pain caused me to lose my balance and I fell into a cluster of dead brush.

Fortunately for me, the four-wheeler puked just at the right time. Chesterville was straight ahead. My jaw dropped as I overlooked Chesterville. I thought for sure I had stepped onto a movie set of the old, Wild-West but without the horse and buggies.

I saw the large General Store sign and headed toward it in hopes of finding a place to stay. "Excuse me, but are you new to our town? Cuz I've never seen you before."

I looked down to a filthy, young girl wearing ratty, old clothes. I squatted down a bit and said, "Yeah, arrived ten minutes ago."

"Who might you be?" I noticed the young girl kept her eyes on the ground.

"I'm Simona. I live behind the General Store." The young girl motioned me to lend her my ear and whispered, as if it were a secret, "I'm an orphan."

"Oh." I whispered back. "I used to be an orphan too, until God sent me some wonderful parents."

"I'm still waiting for those," she said sadly. Simona leaned into my ear again and whispered, "We're not supposed to talk about God or you'll get in trouble."

"Gotcha."

"Do you have a dollar or some food? Of course, I don't have anything to trade for it. I'm poor you know." Simona asked as she held out her hand.

I stood and dug deep into my pocket for some money.

"Well, well, well, what do we have here?" Foreman Lovit said with a boisterous voice.

Simona's eyes widened with fear. She quickly withdrew her hand and said, "Gotta go." The girl took off like a speeding bullet and darted behind the General Store.

"Simona!" The Foreman yelled. "You'd better not have gotten a dime from that lady. I'll deal with you later!"

So, the infamous Foreman is heading my way. This ought to be interesting, I thought. The Foreman walked tall and proud with his chest puffed out. He narrowed his eyes at me as if to warn me of his coming wrath.

"Abigail Banderas is the name." I said as I held out my hand and looked into his eyes. My heart was pumping wildly, hoping I hadn't committed a serious offence.

The Foreman stared at my hand and then looked at me. "Being new and all, I'll forgive your ignorance of not knowing my rules. You see, I find it disrespectful for one to make eye contact with me. As Foreman, you should honor me with lowering your eyes, but then again, don't you know about Damion's rules?"

"You mean bow down and worship," I said under my breath.

"Did you say something?"

"No," I responded.

"My name is Foreman Lovit." He paused and then asked, "You plan on staying long?"

I shrugged my shoulders. "Not sure yet. At least a few days." I felt a strong itch across the skin on my stomach.

The Foreman looked me up and down and said, "Being a Misfit, I strongly suggest you learn my rules quickly, for those who break the rules reap consequences. I don't take to kindly to Misfits. As you know, they like to cause trouble." He moved in closer to my face and continued, "I will not tolerate trouble, you here?"

"Foreman Lovit, I don't mean disrespect. Where I'm from, good eye contact and a hardy hand-shake is a gesture of confidence and respect."

"Well, you're not in Kansas anymore, Dorothy. Welcome to my territory."

Even though I wasn't scared of Foreman Lovit, the way he said territory gave me the chills. Walking in humility with the Foreman wasn't going to be easy. And, what was this itch?

"Well, if we are through here, I have some unfinished business to attend to." I said as I did an about-face almost colliding with an older, blonde woman.

"Isabella, good, there you are. I would like you to keep an eye on this here lady. She's new in town and she's going to need to be taught my rules. Also, I still have plenty of questions about her visit," the Foreman glared at me. "Bring her to my office as soon as she's done with her unfinished business."

Isabella cautiously looked over at me. I smiled and said with desperation, "I'm Abigail by the way. If you don't mind, I seriously need to get something to stop the itching. It's progressing down my legs."

"Oh, of course. Trudy can help you find the cream you need. Why are you itching?"

"I fell into to a bush and I think it was poisonous."

"Oh, you poor thing," Isabella said sympathetically.

"I'm Isabella, the Foreman's housekeeper."

"Nice to meet you," I said as I was doing an itching dance. An old refrigeration smell greeted us as Isabella opened the door to the General Store.

"Trudy, this here is Abigail. She's new in town and she has an awful, itchy rash. What kind of cream do you think she needs?"

Trudy stood in front of me. Her face went ashen and her eyes were wild as if she'd seen a ghost. She blinked rather quickly and then looked at Isabella. "Do I look like a doctor ta ya?" Trudy hesitantly yet roughly grabbed my arm and looked it over.

"I believe I fell into some kind of poisonous bush." I said lamely.

Trudy dropped my arm like a dead fish. "That doesn't look like no poisonous rash ta me. It looks like hives frum a food allergy. But like I said, I ain't no doctor."

Food allergy—I thought back on what I had eaten in the last twenty-four hours and realized that the fruit bar Miriam gave me had strawberries in it. "Why didn't I think of that? I'm allergic to strawberries and I ate a strawberry fruit bar for breakfast."

Trudy grabbed a bottle off the shelf. "Allergic ta strawberries, huh?" She shook her head and ignored her thought and said, "Here, then this is what ya need." Trudy looked me up and down and then at Isabella. "Does the Foreman know that we have ourselves a visitor?"

"Yes. I've met the nice Foreman." I said sarcastically.

"Boy, ain't ya'll a sassy one. Keep that up and ya'll find ya'self in a whole heap of trouble."

Just then the door opened. "Good afternoon to you, Trudy," a tall, blonde-haired man said. He quickly looked my way and back at Trudy, paused and then looked back at me.

"Ya, she's new." Trudy said flatly.

In a low soft voice Isabella said, "Her name is Abigail."

The man nodded. "Trudy I need some roofing nails, please." An older lady stood next to him.

Isabella leaned over and said, "That's Lisa Marie. And that's Sheldon, they both live in the mission's house." I nodded my head to let her know I heard her. She whispered, "And Sheldon's single."

Isabella quickly covered her mouth and giggled as if she let out the world's greatest secret. "Good to know. "I said and handed Trudy a half a pack of gum for the trade.

"Seriously? That's all ya got?" I shrugged my shoulders as a response.

"Trudy, just put it on Walter's tab." Isabella said, and smiled shyly.

"Thanks." I said.

I headed to the door when the young man stepped in front of me. "Oh, here, let me get that for you." The man offered.

"Why thank you. It's nice to see that chivalry isn't dead." The poor man looked like he wanted to respond, but was struck by the mute button. All he did was stare at me as if he was drinking in the moment. By the look in his eyes, it looked like he'd never seen a red haired woman with a horrible rash.

Oh, goodness. That's it; he's looking at me as if I'm some kind of diseased freak. I could only imagine what I look like. The redness that flushed my cheeks only added to the rash.

"Sheldon, are you okay?" Lisa Marie asked as she grabbed hold of his arm to steady him in the doorway.

"Yes, I'm fine," he said as he balanced himself and then looked at me again. "I'm… I'm…"

"Sheldon is what he's trying to say. And I'm Lisa Marie." She said as she held out her hand.

"Nice to meet you both." I wanted to flee from this very awkward moment.

Lisa Marie asked, "So you're new to the town? Planning on staying long?"

"For a few days. Not really sure."

"Staying at the SunKissed Hotel?" Sheldon managed to ask.

"Actually, I haven't found a place yet. I've been on the quest for a cure to this rash."

"Didn't even notice a rash," Sheldon said as he gave a shy laugh. "It's kind of dark in here. Your skin looks great."

"Thanks, I guess," I said, feeling even more awkward.

"Well, you can stay with us over at the mission's house if you like. No charge," Lisa Marie invited.

"Thank you. That's very kind of you."

"We can walk with you to the mission's house?" Sheldon asked through flushed cheeks.

Isabella cleared her throat and said timidly, "Um, the Foreman actually wants me to take her to his office once we're done here. I would be more than happy to take her to the mission's house later."

"Then it's settled. We shall see you later, Abigail." Lisa Marie said with a smile and another hand shake.

Once outside, I drank the awful, nasty tasting medicine. While Isabella and I headed toward the mansion, I noticed Trudy lingered in the doorway watching us.

Isabella seemed very polite as she rattled on about Foreman Lovit's rules. "In spite of his controlling ways, it's truly a peaceful place to live." She concluded as if trying to convince herself.

I looked at her and said, "I don't plan on living here, just visiting for a few days."

Isabella smiled, "That's what they all say."

****

Isabella led me into the Foreman's office. "He'll be right with you," she said and left.

Upon entering the office, the rich scent of old books and the age of the home greeted me. The mahogany crown molding, carved in flowers that trimmed the window panes and walls, was breathtaking. The deep, hunter green wallpaper with black, velvet florals captivated me the most.

I walked behind the desk to look closer. It looked so silky, and smooth, I just had to touch it. I'd never seen wallpaper like that before. I felt like I was touching a part of history. I could only imagine the stories and secrets that were soaked into the stains. As I continued to caress the velvety pattern, my hand ran across something metal. I looked closely. "Well, that's interesting." I said.

"What's interesting?" A deep, authoritative voice startled me.

I jumped. "Oh, you scared me." I pointed to the wall. "The wallpaper, I've never seen anything like it."

"That's nice. How about you tell me the real reason why you're here?"

"You make it sound like it's a crime to visit your town? Am I being arrested or something?"

The Foreman's face was unreadable. His arms were crossed with legs slightly apart, as if he were secret service ready to interrogate. He was only missing the dark sun glasses.

"I told you, I don't take kindly to Misfits just showing up in my town. In fact, I'm surprised to even see a Misfit traveling to a new town. So I suggest you state your business or I'll have one of my men escort you back to where you came from."

"Wow. That's hospitality." I said flatly.

The Foreman slammed both of his palms down on his desk and leaned in toward me. "For someone who believes making eye contact a gesture of respect, you sure are showing a lack of respect for authority with your mouth, young lady," he seethed.

"You're right. I'm sorry. You're only doing your job as Foreman and protecting your people." I backed off and lowered my eyes only out of respect for his position. I knew God would want me to. He straightened himself and adjusted his tie and suit jacket.

"The reason I'm here, Foreman Lovit is because I was in a plane crash and I walked in search of civilization.   So here I am."

I noticed the Foreman's eyes enlarged with nervousness and shock.   "Yes and here you are.   Any survivors other than you?"

I was just about to answer when Isabella walked in. I said sympathetically, "No, I'm afraid I'm the only one."

"Did you talk to anyone?" He asked anxiously.

"No, not really.   No, I take that back.   I talked with a woman named Meredith."

Isabella looked up at me and slanted her head in curiosity. "You were in a plane crash and survived?" Isabella asked.

The Foreman whipped around and said, "Isabella, if you don't mind, this is a private conversation.   Lunch will have to wait."

"But she said she talked with a woman named Meredith. Was it Meredith Thompson?" Isabella asked as she placed her right hand over her heart in worry.

The Foreman grabbed her arm firmly and said, "I'm sure it wasn't your mother, Isabella. Now go." He tried to push her away, but she stepped in to hear my reply.

"I didn't get her last name."

"Did she have long brown hair with a patch of gray down the center?"

I had to think.   "Yes.   I believe so."

Isabella's eyes instantly welled up with tears. "Is she...?" Isabella started to ask, but was too afraid to finish.

"Now Isabella, I'm sure it's not your mother. There could be a number of other women who look like that."

"Tell me. Is she dead?" Isabella cried.

"I'm afraid so," I said.

Isabella looked at the Foreman and cried, "What was she doing on an airplane? That explains why I haven't been able to reach her for the past couple of days." Isabella covered her face and ran out of the room.

"Great. Look what you've done. You've totally messed up my day. Not only am I going to have to make other arrangements for lunch, but I'm going to have to deal with an emotional woman, and I hate dealing with emotional women." I stood silently not saying a word.

Irritated, the Foreman sighed and asked forcefully, "So what did she say?"

The Foreman's curiosity about my conversation with Meredith seemed more than just casual talk. *But why?* I wondered. I knew my answer could possibly change the outcome of my day. Will I confess my faith or will I cower to the fear of man?

I forbiddingly looked into his dark, evil eyes and said bluntly, "I led her to Jesus Christ."

The Foreman's mouth tensed as he clenched his teeth and rolled his eyes as if repulsed by my words.

"Let me make myself very clear here. Rule number one, lower your eyes to me young lady! Rule number two, I dislike Christians and there will be no speaking of the so-called 'good news' or the mention of that name while you are here. And If I see or hear you doing otherwise, I will see to it that you never speak again."

I stood very still and said respectfully, "I understand, Sir." *So this is what it was like to act in the opposite, which certainly wasn't in my nature.* At that moment, the Lord made it very clear to me that I obviously needed to work on being more humble because it took all my restraining to hold my tongue.

I believed my soft tone surprised him. He stood aloof, blinking quickly as he said, "Good, because the last person who defied me was stoned to death."

I stood with confidence as I held my head high, but kept my eyes lowered. "I'll keep that in mind." I said, as I shook off the threat as if it were a spider crawling up my arm.

He recoiled back toward the office door. "You are free to go." When I was inches away from him he whispered in my ear, "Two days Miss Banderas. Then I want you gone."

****

Since Isabella wasn't feeling well, I walked myself to the mission's house and was greeted by a friendly face.

"Welcome, Abigail." Lisa Marie smiled as she held the door open for me.

"It's nice to know not everyone around here is as cranky as Foreman Lovit." I grumbled. Lisa Marie laughed.

"I see you're still here, and in one piece." Sheldon teased.

I gave him a quick smile as Lisa Marie walked me into the living room. Since it was lighter in the house than in the General Store, I took notice of my new companions.

Lisa Marie's welcoming eyes seemed to sooth my home sickness. Part of me wanted to call my parents, but the other part of me knew how they would react, and I wasn't sure I was up to dealing with overprotective parents.

Sheldon stood next to Lisa Marie with his head slightly down. Even though he didn't look into my eyes, I could tell he was looking at me. His staring made me feel self-conscious. He was handsome and I usually don't handle myself very well around good looking men; it's as if I turn into this dork from outer space.

"Here, let me take your backpack and show you to your room." Sheldon offered as he looked my way. The color of his eyes distracted my thinking. They were a soft cobalt blue. The kind of blue the ocean is after a storm and when our hands collided, I felt a heat wave rush to my cheeks as his warm hand lingered on mine.

I let go of the pack and said, "After you."

"It looks like your rash has gone down considerably. Do you feel better, Abigail?" Lisa Marie asked as she motioned for me to follow Sheldon around the couch to the stairs.

"Come to think of it, yes, I do feel better." I said.

When I walked around the couch, I tripped on one of its legs, which sent me flying head first into a small wastepaper basket. Sheldon and Lisa Marie immediately came to my rescue. They pulled me to my feet. I could tell that Sheldon was doing everything in his power not to laugh. Lisa Marie was wide-eyed and asked if I was okay. I looked at Sheldon and said, "Go ahead. I know you want to laugh."

"No. It would be rude of me." He tried holding back a snicker.

I, too, was trying not to laugh. I looked over at Lisa Marie who was trying not to laugh herself. They both looked like they were ready to burst, so I decided to be the first to laugh. Then we all started to laugh. Sheldon's turned into a gut wrenching belly laugh.

"Oh come on now, it wasn't really that funny?" I said. I noticed that Sheldon looked over to Lisa Marie. "What?" I said with a slight laugh.

Lisa Marie pulled out of my hair a half-eaten piece of peanut butter toast. "Great. Just great," I said. I continued to laugh to hide my embarrassment.

CHAPTER THIRTEEN
The Star

Walter tossed and turned as the night sky released bullet-sized rain that hit the window pane like hail. With the strobe-like lighting, the howling of the wind, and the crashing sounds of thunder, he finally opened his eyes.

Walter watched the shadows dance on the walls with each flash of lighting. He usually wasn't the fearful type, he loved thunder storms, but this particular storm was different. He sensed something wasn't right. He didn't feel right.

Ba-boom! Another crash of thunder echoed in the eerie night and sounded more like a bomb had gone off.

With the unsettledness of the storm, Walter put on his robe and tip-toed to Isabella's room. He quietly opened the door to check on her. Through the glow of the night-light, he could see her sleeping. He stood resting his head on the door frame and watched her sleep.

He smiled to himself as he lovingly admired her beauty. She looked peaceful with her blonde hair fanned out on the pillow and her soft pink lips at rest. She was his Goldilocks. He yearned to entangle his fingers in her silky, golden locks, to inhale the intoxicating aroma of it, and to touch her ivory, porcelain skin. He ached for her to look into his eyes with the same yearning as he did for her.

Hot tears welled up. He realized Isabella did not love him. He slid down to the floor and held himself tightly and allowed the tears to win. Walter flashed back to a similar time—a night much like this.

It was fiercely storming and Walter's father ordered him to go to bed. But after watching his father and his friends in a bizarre ritual that cost his mother's life, he was unable to sleep.

At thirteen, he understood the consequences of defying his father's rules and he didn't want to end up like his mother. She must have pushed him too far this time with her preaching of Jesus.

A loud thunderous boom vibrated the entire house causing a shock wave of fear shooting right down Walter's spine. Walter froze as tears fell. He wanted to run into his mother's arms to soothe his fear. He got enough courage to open his door and tip-toed to his parents room. He quietly opened the door and stood frozen in the doorway.

"Mom?" Walter whispered. "Mom are you okay?" Walter ran up to her and shook her aggressively. "Mom, wake up!" he cried, but there was no response.

He buried his head in her stomach and cried. Her white nightgown felt wet and sticky. He pulled away and saw a large circle of blood. He felt his forehead and there was blood on his hand. He quickly ran back behind his door. He slid down, held himself tight, and cried as the frightening storm raged on.

Another loud boom jolted Walter back to the present. He got up slowly and quietly shut Isabella's door. He walked back to his room feeling numb and exhausted.

He looked out the window again and the fear returned. He thought of Abigail Banderas.

****

Foreman Lovit and Sniper sat at their usual table. Marco placed their drinks in front of them and quickly left them to their business.

"It's time to start asking around if anyone has the key. Maybe Maximus didn't take the key.

"But who?"

Walter frustratingly ran his fingers through his hair and said. "I don't know, maybe Sheldon Michaels has it." He leaned back in his chair and said with an evil smile, "Sheldon Michaels is long overdue for a rough talking too anyway. I've just been biding my time to unleash my vengeance. And today is that day." Walter put down his chair and leaned in toward Sniper. "It will be like Hades releasing the Kraggin unto the world."

Sniper grew excited and said, "That sounds mighty painful, even more painful than sewing Trudy's hand together." He laughed. Walter smiled with pure pleasure.

Sniper slapped the table and said, "Well then what are we waiting for! Unleash the Kraggin!" They both got up and left the saloon.

****

"There you are. I need your help. Sheldon has been badly beaten." Lisa Marie said, anxiously out of breath as I came bouncing through the front door. I had been up early and walked through the town.

I walked up to the couch and there Sheldon lay bleeding and badly beaten. I quickly bent down on my knees. "Oh my, Sheldon are you okay?"

He didn't answer. His right eye was swollen shut. His lips were bleeding and he had a small gash above his right eye.

"Here." Lisa Marie said as she handed me the first aid kit. "I'm so glad you're back. I hope you're good at handling blood because I'm not. It looks like he's going to need stiches."

I looked up at her with petrified eyes and said, "I'm not so good at this stuff either."

"I don't care if either of you are good at it, just fix me." Sheldon mumbled. "Ow!" he said as he held his ribs.

"Who did this to you?" I asked.

"It was the Foreman and Sniper," Lisa Marie said as she squatted next to me. "I was taking out the trash and I saw Sheldon crawling home."

"He looks bad," I whispered. "I'm not a doctor, but I think he needs one."

"The only doctor we have is Dr. Blake and he's one of the Foreman's guys."

"Well, what are we going to do?" I asked.

"The nearest hospital, or doctor's office for that matter, is at least fifty miles away." Lisa Marie responded.

"Will you two stop chit-chatting and do it yourselves."

Lisa Marie and I looked at each other. "You can do it. I have faith in ya," Lisa Marie said as she nodded for me to continue.

"Okay, fine. Get me some warm water, and some towels."

There was so much blood oozing that I didn't know where to start. When Lisa Marie returned with the towels and warm water I started cleaning the most severe wound. And then, to my surprise, I sewed up the wound-without passing out. Piercing the flesh with the needle and feeling the thread pull through the skin was about all I could take.

"It looks like you have everything under control. I'm going to go make us lunch." Lisa Marie said as she patted my shoulder.

I lightly dabbed at his lip. "Ow. That hurts," he winced. I moved in closer to wipe the blood off his face. "You smell nice," he whispered.

"Well it's good to know that your nose isn't broken," I teased.

"But I think some of my ribs are."

"I'm afraid the only thing I can do is wrap them."

"Well, I guess I won't be doing any sit-ups for a while."

"I think a man in your condition shouldn't be doing anything for a while, other than rest."

"Well you just took the fun out of my day," he joked as he lightly squeezed my arm.

"Okay, you are all cleaned up. All I have to do is wrap your ribs," I said.

"Are you sure you're not a nurse?"

I gave him a coy expression. "Why?"

"Because you're doing a great job."

"Thank you," I said shyly.

"I should have stood up to them," he admitted.

I smiled and said, "Well, then, I suggest you get up, adjust your armor and take a stand. The battle isn't yours anyway; it's God's and He'll do the fighting. By the way, can you stand and lift up your shirt so I can wrap your ribs?"

Sheldon painfully stood up and was struggling to take off his shirt. "I need your help here. I can't lift it."

It was another one of those uncomfortable moments. "This feels really inappropriate," I said timidly.

"Oh come on, you're just being my nurse. It's not like..."

"Yeah, I'm glad you didn't finish your sentence."

"Don't tell me you've never seen a guy with his shirt off?"

"Let just say I don't go around making it a habit."

It was very uncomfortable and embarrassing for me to see Sheldon with his shirt off. I felt like I shouldn't be looking at him, but it was hard not to notice his tight abs and tan body.

"I believe the lady is blushing," he teased as he dramatized looking at me with his good eye.

Irritated by his boyish play, I said, "Okay, can you just hold still so I can wrap you up and be done."

Because he squirmed so much I had to adjust the bandage four times. I personally thought he did it on purpose. "Could you please hold still? You're making the bandage slip and fall off."

"Your hands are cold."

"My goodness, you sure are being a baby," I said as I held my cold hand flatly against the end of the bandage and his side to keep it from falling.

He felt so warm. I almost wanted to leave my hand there just to keep it warm.

"Why did the Foreman and Sniper do this to you anyway?" I asked trying to divert my mind off of his warm body.

"I don't know. Walter kept insisting that I have his key."

"His key?"

"Yeah, some key he needs to open a door. I told him that I didn't know anything about a key and I told him that I didn't know what he was talking about. He refused to believe that I didn't have the key and the more I said I didn't have it the more he and Sniper used me for their punching bag. When they finally left me, I told myself this has to stop. I've had enough, Abigail. It is time to take a stand. I just don't know how to go about doing it."

"All done," I said as I helped with putting his shirt back on.

"What if I said I had the key?"

"What? What do you mean? How would you have his key?"

I quickly ran upstairs to grab the rectangle box with the key. By the time I got back downstairs, Lisa Marie was sitting next to Sheldon. I opened the box and took out the key. "At the plane crash a woman gave this to me. Before she gave up her last breath, she was getting ready to tell me who to give this to." I paused. "When I was in the Foremen's office the other day, I felt a key hole in his wall. I believe this key is to that hidden door. Sheldon, I think I know a way we can start taking a stand and it just may have to do with this key."

CHAPTER FOURTEEN
The Pill Box and The Key

"Are you sure this is going to work, Sheldon?" I asked.

"Isabella assured me that as long as Marco keeps refilling the Foreman's glass, he'll be there all night. He loves to drink and brag to his men about what he can do to people."

"And how do we know that Marco will keep his glass full?"

Sheldon's face got real serious. "Because, Marco knows the repercussions if he doesn't. Do you have the key?" I held out my hand to show him.

We went around the back of the mansion just as Isabella had instructed us. We opened the back door and walked into the maid's quarters, and down a long skinny hallway. We came around the corner to the foyer where the library, parlor, and Foreman Lovit's office were.

"I've never been inside of his house before. I've always wondered what it would look like with everyone's belongings in it. And I don't know why, but being in his office is creeping me out," Sheldon said as he began to look around the room.

"Yeah, it is a dark room. Although, I do have to say, I like the wallpaper. It's rather unique." I felt for the key hole.

"It's most likely the original wallpaper. I know that he tried very hard to keep most of the original design after the remodeling. I give the man credit for having taste—expensive taste, I might add." He looked at me. "Where is this key hole?"

"On this wall behind his desk. The hole is in between the edges of two flower leaves." I quickly looked up at Sheldon and noticed he kept shifting his weight from side to side.

"Why are you so nervous? If the Foreman is going to be there for a while, there shouldn't be any reason to be nervous. If Isabella's right, we have plenty of time, right?"

"I know, I know. It's just being in here, in this room that is making me nervous. I feel like I'm doing something wrong. It's just that..."

"It's just, what?" I asked.

But he didn't want to answer. He shook his head and dismissed me like a child. "Just hurry up. I'd rather be on the other side of that door."

It took me a few moments to find the key hole. I stuck the skeleton key in the door, turned it and the door popped open.

A wave of musty air punched at our faces. I pulled the key out and followed behind Sheldon. I was hearing Sheldon say something but with the creaking of the door I was unable to make out what he said.

"Make sure you leave the key in the door just in case the door automatically locks us in."

The door closed behind me.

"Please tell me that the key is still in the door?" Sheldon asked as he froze halfway down the steps.

I shrugged my shoulders and turned down the corner of my lips as I held up the key.

"Are you serious? You took the key out and we're locked in here?"

Sheldon trotted up the few steps and slightly pushed me aside to check the door. Sure enough we were locked in. The back side of the door had no handle. Angrily Sheldon snapped, "Great! Just great! How are we going to get out of here? If the Foreman finds us down here, we're dead!"

"I'm sorry! I didn't hear you say to leave the key in the lock. Besides, he can't come down here anyway, remember?   He needs the key to get in," I snapped back as I held the key close to Sheldon's face.

Do to the soreness of the ribs, Sheldon carefully walked down the steps. I jogged down after him and said, "Look at it this way; maybe it will turn out to be a blessing in disguise."

He turned around and glared at me. I gave him a confident smile, which seemed to aggravate him even more. He quickly looked to the floor, grunted and shook his head.

"If we had left the key in the door, what would happen if the Foremen did come home early? He would have seen it and yeah, then we would be dead meat!"

Sheldon stopped me at the last step and whispered, "At this point, I don't care what you think."

"Well okay then," I said as I pushed my way past him. "I THINK!" I turned around and said right into his face, "You need to chill out and have faith in God!"

I must have hit a bruise with him because his forehead scrunched tightly together and he narrowed his eyes. I softened my tone and said, "Look Sheldon, I'm sure there has to be some kind of access door down here. People don't build a secret room and not have an exit."

The eight steps led us down to a small room. It smelled like mold as if it had once been a cellar, but now was set up like an office. The office desk was close to the end of the wall as you came down the eight shallow steps. The left wall was lined with bookshelves, with at least two hundred books. Old artifacts and beautiful oil paintings decorated the walls and floors. The room had a high ceiling and was crowded with furniture. To one's eyes, it looked like there was no exit door to be found.

Sheldon wiped some sweat off his eye brow and sarcastically said, "I hope you're right, Nancy Drew."

"What did you say?"

"Nothing," he mumbled. "Let's just get to work on why we are down here. What is it exactly that we are looking for, anyway?"

We both began to look around. "I'm not sure. Look for anything that could tell us what he's up to. Or anything you think might be suspicious."

Sheldon stopped looking through the stack of papers from on top of the desk. "Suspicious?" he laughed. "The man is nothing but suspicious and mysterious. No one can figure out what this man is up to, let alone why he does what he does. He does what he does because he can!" He wiped his brow again. "Man, it's warm down here."

I rolled my eyes at him and said, "This sort of stuff takes time. Have patience."

"Did you just roll your eyes at me?" Sheldon asked.

I decided not to look at him this time and kept to my work. "Yes, I did."

"And why is that?"

"Do you really want me to answer that question?" I could tell that he was looking at me, so I gave him a challenging smile in hopes he would want me to give him the answer.

He only kept his stare for five seconds before he looked down again. The Idealist rules sure had a mind-control on not wanting people to look at each other in the eyes.

He slightly tossed the papers he had in his hand onto the desk. "We're never going to find anything. He covers his tracks well. What makes you so sure we'll find anything anyway?"

"Because, God sent me here to help. And I..." I paused and sat down at the desk and asked, "What is it that you miss before the Foreman came and the locusts' hit?"

Sheldon looked far off as if trying to find that one important file in his brain.

"Normalcy." he finally said.

"Normalcy?" I inquired.

Sheldon spoke softly, "I miss the freedom we had." He paused and then asked, "What were you doing when the locust came?"

"Believe it or not, my family and I were watching the news. When the warning came about the coming of the locusts, my dad had us grab food, a radio, water, and bedding and we settled into the basement. My dad locked the door, placed an old dresser and a workout bench against it and we remained down there for three years. It wasn't any fun, needless to say. We almost died of starvation. And you?"

Again, Sheldon looked far off. This time I saw pain emerge in his eyes. "I came to the mission house when I was eighteen. It had been two years since I had seen my parents and thought it was time for a visit. I had only been there one day when they hit. We had no warning. They broke through the glass, ate through the wood siding and into the house. Right away my parents got stung. I ran as fast as I could to the basement while whacking the locusts with a frying pan and ran into my dad's secret room that he built into the cement wall. His 'man cave', he called it. It's where my dad would go when he wanted to be alone.

"One locust followed me. I fought long and finally smashed it with the frying pan." Sheldon paused and barely looked up at me. "I hate to admit this but, I hid under my dad's desk for hours covering my ears to my parent's horrible screams. I wanted so badly to help them but, I could hear the horrific sound of the locust's wings and their crunching as they were trying to eat their way through the house.

"Several weeks later I was able to creep out of the room. When I did come out, I wished I hadn't. The house was destroyed. My parent's eyes and face were sunken in; their skin was greyish-yellow and they were in excruciating pain. Their skin was so sensitive, I couldn't even touch them. I tried making them as comfortable as I could, but nothing helped. They had no appetite and yet I forced them to eat soup. Through the pain, my dad was able to describe what he was feeling."

"And what did it feel like?" I interrupted.

"He said it was like having the shingles, but more intense and with paralysis. They were unable to move. They were only able to lie there and suffer. It lasted about six months and then they just stopped breathing."

"I'm so sorry, Sheldon." I said softly as I stared at the few papers that were in my hands. "It must have been awful for you. I never saw what they looked like other than a fiberglass type of wing that I found stabbed into a tree."

"Oh believe me; you wouldn't want to see those hideous things..." Sheldon's voice trailed off and he went quiet. His eyes widen and darted back and forth.

"What? What's wrong? You're scaring me." I said as I quickly looked around.

"Oh my goodness..." Sheldon began as if a revelation came over him. "They reminded me of how the book of Revelation describes them and yet they were different. The sizes of those things were as big as a baby bird. The front half comprised of a real insect with metal wiry-like hair. Its shell was really tough, equivalent to body armor. It had sharp teeth, like a lions', its black eyes bulged out and its facial features resembled a human's. The other half of its body was like a robot. And like you said about the wings, they seemed to have been made out of clear fiberglass. When they flew, I saw red lighting glowing through the wings veins. And they had a tail like a scorpion."

My eyes grew big. Sheldon was right, I was glad I didn't see them. They sounded like something from a bad horror flick.

"I actually dissected one of them and found some interesting things about it."

"Really!" I said excitedly. "Like what?"

Just when Sheldon was about to speak, we jumped at a loud noise, which we quickly realized was the water pipes. "I think we better get back to work before the Foreman returns." I nodded in agreement.

I could tell that Sheldon was getting more irritated by the minute, so I prayed. I knew I was given the key for a purpose, and that purpose was to find something. I didn't want to leave the room empty-handed. It was time to bring all of what the Foreman was doing to an end. Whatever that end was, only God knows.

I began looking intently at the oil paintings on the wall, looking behind them to see if there were any signs of hidden envelopes on the backs.

"What are you doing?"

"I'm looking for a safe."

"A safe?"

"Yes. It occurred to me that maybe he could have a hidden safe." I said.

"Well, I suppose that would be a good way to cover your tracks. Oh, I know!" Sheldon paused and moved in front of the bookcase. "What if I removed one certain book that unlocked this whole bookcase and it magically shifted to the left and wha-la! There you have it, one giant safe," he said sarcastically as he swung his arms high up in the air to the left.

I put my hands on my hips. "You're mocking me aren't you?"

He smiled really big and teasingly said, "Yep! I have decided you are truly a Nancy Drew."

By the expression on my face, I could tell that Sheldon wasn't quite sure what to expect from me. I wasn't about to take offense to his little inside joke. So instead, I surprised him and said, "You know, that is a really good idea. Start pulling out books and let's see if the bookcase moves."

"I was only kidding. You do realize that there are over two hundred books on this shelf?"

"All I'm asking you to do is slightly pull them out one by one. Not strip the whole bookcase."

Sheldon sighed heavily as we slightly pulled each book out as quickly as we could. "Lord, please help us find something. Guide us to it." I whispered under my breath.

After several moments of silence, I saw Sheldon reading a few of the book titles. "Sheldon, we don't have time for you to be checking out a book here."

"No. I'm just realizing something. He has five of the same books on philosophy. Why would anyone want five copies of the same book? He must really like reading about philosophy. And right in the middle of the five he has a book called basic principles of this world. He certainly is a strange man."

I smacked Sheldon's arm and squealed, "The Bible page!"

"Hey! Ow! The ribs, remember. What are you talking about? What Bible page?"

I pulled out the crinkled Bible page from the pill box that was in my pocket. "I wasn't sure where this would fit in, but this has to mean something. Look here." I said as I pointed to Sheldon the highlighted words in the verse. "The words philosophy and basic principles are highlighted. Grab those books."

Sheldon opened the "Basic Principles of This World" book to find a small remote in a hollowed-out space. "Great, a TV remote. Obviously he doesn't want anyone watching his TV." Sheldon teased as he pointed the remote at a wall with no TV.

"Very funny. Give me that." I said playfully, as I grabbed the remote out of his hand.

Sheldon teasingly reached for the remote, but the soreness of his ribs prevented him. "Well, I don't know if I can trust you with it."

Playfully, I tapped him on the arm with the remote and said, "It's getting late and we need to keep working. I'm going to go see about a painting. When I was looking at the paintings on the wall, this picture over his desk seemed to be built right into the wall or screwed in tightly. Maybe there's something behind it."

"You can tell all that by a picture being screwed to the wall?"

"Well, all the other paintings come off the wall. This is the only one that doesn't move. That's got to be significant. Don't you think?"

"Yeah, maybe. Even if there is a safe behind it, how would we know the code?"

"I don't know. Maybe that remote has something to do with the safe?" Sheldon shrugged his shoulders.

"I need to think and pray." I said, squatting to the floor.

Suddenly, Sheldon's mood switched. "You think God is going to answer your prayers?"

Why was it that every time I talked about faith or praying, a completely different man came over him? A man I wasn't sure I wanted to be around. "He has so far." I said.

Sheldon kept his head down and his mouth twisted as if he wanted to say something, while randomly pushing buttons.

I closed my eyes to pray, "Lord, I feel that we have found this remote for a reason. Please continue to guide us the rest of the way. What is the code? What could it be?" I prayed.

I heard the Lord whisper, "Look closer at the Bible page." My eyes popped open and I looked at the Bible page. "Sheldon, I think I've got it. Try punching in c-o-l-2-8-1-3."

"Wait a minute. How do you know that's the code?"

I showed him the Bible page again. "The C-o-l is highlighted; the two, eight, one and three are also highlighted. It's worth a try. Do you have any other ideas?"

Sheldon punched in the code and the big oil painting on the wall above the desk popped open. "Well, I'll be." Sheldon laughed. The picture frame was heavy, so Sheldon had to finish opening it. "Great, we ran into another problem."

I crossed my eyes and sighed heavily with disappointment. "What's the problem?"

"There's a safe alright, but what's the code for the safe?" Sheldon opened the frame wide to expose the safe. It had a key pad on the door.

"I don't know. I don't always have the answers you know. Why don't you try the code again?"

"Fine." Sheldon quickly punched in the code and the door unlatched. Neatly folded was a beautiful quilt. Underneath the quilt was a jagged, golf-ball sized crystal. Sheldon pulled out the quilt and handed me the jagged crystal.

Disappointed, I said, "That's it? There's nothing else? Just the quilt and this stupid rock or crystal or whatever this is?"

"That's it."

I plopped down into the office chair defeated. *Why God? Why? I thought quietly to myself. You brought me all this way just to find a silly quilt and a rock. What does this have to do with anything? Now what?*

While I fingered the beautiful quilt I asked, "Since you know the Foreman and his, so called kooky ways, tell me, why on earth would he keep a quilt and a crystal in a safe?"

Sheldon stared at the quilt that lay on the desk top and shook his head in frustration.

I picked up the quilt. It was heavy and bulky. "Help me spread it out. I want to look at it." The quilt was at least as large as a king-sized bed.

"I know that the Foreman enjoys taking people's prize possessions. He can sense a priceless item a mile away and can sense when the item is of special value to the person. Probably because of their expression when he looks at it." Sheldon sighed heavily and then continued. "They were obviously someone's prize possessions. It may have no real value to him, just the satisfaction of taking it away from its owner. It all could mean nothing."

"But that doesn't make sense to me. Why not just keep the quilt draped on the back of this small love seat then? Why not use the crystal as a paper weight if it doesn't matter? Hiding this stuff in a safe tells me that these items do have more meaning to the Foreman than you think."

"Perhaps." Sheldon shrugged. "Are you sure you're not a detective of some sort?

I looked up to see Sheldon's soft eyes gleaming down at me with a gentle smile across his face. He looked as if he were enjoying the view. I, of course, started to blush again. Heat rose up in my already hot-streaked face. I turned back to the quilt. I got up and walked around it. I had to admit, it was the most beautiful quilt I had ever seen.

"It looks like the town." Sheldon casually said. He bent down beside me and pointed to each object. "To the north are the mountains..."

"Looks like the direction from which I came," I quickly added.

He smiled. "Over here to the left appears to be the Lazy Days Saloon, the Trading Post and Sunkissed Hotel. To the south end is the Foreman's mansion. Wrapping around to the right is the ole' mission house, a few homes, and the gift shop. Next to that, is Trudy's General Store. Behind the General Store is the old train station. It's now the home of the orphans."

I pointed to the top far right corner of the quilt and asked, "I don't recall seeing an apple orchard or a church. There's a church?"

After I had posed my question to Sheldon, the same dark expression came over him like once before. We sat in silence for a while as Sheldon just stared at the apple orchard and church.

"Shortly after Foreman Lovit came, he had the orchard and the church burned down. That's when everything really started to go evil. Not that those buildings are our "God", but it was as if he took the heart of God right out of this town. Where once was a beautiful, apple orchard is now a ghostly, grave yard. And instead of a church, there's a stake, waiting for the next person to either be crucified or burned."

Sheldon's voice seemed to be filled with much pain and sorrow as he choked out the words to me. And yet, I heard the voice of a very bitter man. I sighed and continued to study the quilt.

"I just love the texture of the fabrics the person used, corduroy and leather to represent woods, and mountains; pretty solid colors for siding. This art work was very well thought out. I mean, look at the little apples that are on the apple trees. They're movable but yet sown in between a see-through fabric so they don't fall out, they look and feel like little tiny red rubies."

In a dry tone Sheldon replied, "Yeah, real cute."

I intently looked over the mansion and was amazed at the detail in the accuracy of the house. Then I noticed down at the far right corner the initials of T.C.

"Sheldon, who is T.C.?"

"The only person that I know of with those initials would be Trudy Capone. It would make sense if this was hers. She is an excellent seamstress. She takes great pride in her work. I remember her bragging one time that she doesn't use a sewing machine. She does everything by hand, just like her mother and grandmother had done."

"Wow, that's amazing. Something like this could actually be worth a fortune. I've known of quilts being sold at craft shows for five hundred dollars or more."

Sheldon gave me a quizzical look. "Seriously?" I smiled and nodded a yes.

"Well, I know that the Foreman has a tendency to acquire items of great value from people on collection day, but why would he want a quilt Trudy made?"

"And want to keep it in a safe no less?" I added. I held up the jagged crystal. "And why would he want a jagged crystal? Where did you come from?" I whispered loud enough for Sheldon to hear.

"Perhaps the ground?" he said in a silly voice as if it were the crystal talking. His silly voice made us both laugh. Then we heard voices. Neither of us moved. We barely even breathed.

A loud boom echoed all the way down to our ears followed by a couple of loud voices. "I need my key! I need to have it and I need it now! I needed it several months ago!" Walter yelled as he slammed his fist on the secret door.

"Foreman, I've searched high and low for it. I can't find it. Have you asked Isabella if she has it?" Sniper asked.

"I told you, she claims to have never heard of a key for this STUPID door! If Maximus did take the key then I'm…" Walter pounded again on the door. "Errr!" he hissed and grunted out of frustration.

"Foreman, I know how upset you are right now, but don't you think we should see to finding this Abigail woman and Sheldon. I have a bad feeling that those two are up to something."

"You're right. I sensed it too. I don't like how she's been poking around here as if the rules don't apply to her. Once we find them, I want you to deal with her."

"Yeah, sure boss. What would you like me to do?"

I looked at Sheldon who looked at me and said, "We really need to find a way out of here and fast."

Walter's and Sniper's conversation became mumbled, making it hard to understand what they were saying except one statement. "Start asking around, and if they don't talk… well, you know what to do."

"If we don't find a way out of here soon, a lot of people could end up hurt on account of us. Sniper is capable of doing some really cruel acts." Sheldon said as he began folding up the quilt.

As I hurriedly grabbed the other end of the quilt, I noticed strange zig-zag stitching on the back of the quilt. I whispered, "Wait. Turn it over."

Through clenched teeth, Sheldon whispered, "We don't have time to waste looking at a meaningless quilt. We have to go. If anyone gets hurt, I'll never be able to forgive myself. Now move it!"

I knew that I was really pushing his buttons when I told him again to turn it over, but I needed to look at the back.

Sheldon dropped the quilt and walked up to me, rather rudely. "I don't think you fully understand the seriousness of this situation. The Foreman and Sniper will harm anyone who does not produce answers."

"Yes. Okay. I understand. Just give me two seconds."

"I don't believe you! What can possible be on the other side of this quilt that you would risk people getting hurt?" He angrily grabbed the quilt and said, "Look, the only thing on this side is the double stitching from the other side. Now let's go!"

"Sheldon, I'm really not trying to anger you, but I feel the Lord wants us to look at the back side. Can you just turn it over for two seconds? Please!"

"You know what? I am getting really sick of this 'God stuff' with you; God telling you this and God telling you that. As if he's standing right here with us telling you step by step what to do, and you being the only one hearing from the Lord. Meanwhile, innocent people are in danger of getting hurt." Sheldon moved closer to me, so close in fact that I could feel the anger permeating off of his body.

"Who do you think you are, some kind of super-hero working with Jesus? You know Abigail, you are unbelievable, and ever since you came to this town you've come across as if you're better than us. What, our prayers weren't good enough so he had to send you to help? You have no idea what this town has been through. Many of us have lain awake wondering if we were going to live to see another sunrise, or make our next payment so we would have a place to call home, or wondering if our loved ones would be the next in line to be burned at the stake. Wondering..."

"Okay, okay. I get the point. I'm not heartless you know. Miriam told me a lot about what the Foreman and Sniper have done to this town. Why do you think I'm so driven to find out his need to control the town and for holding it in captivity? Because that's what you all are—captives. In fact, you're his prisoners of war, and if you ask me..."

"Well, I'm not asking you. And you don't have to tell me about being a prisoner. I feel it every day."

I softened my voice. "I'm sure you do." I placed my hand gently on his arm. It twitched a little as I felt the heat rise through his shirt. "Sheldon, God did hear your cries. He's answering your prayers in his way and his timing. Why He chose me to help, I don't fully know. But nonetheless, God answered. It's time to put an end to all of the Foreman's wicked ways. God wants to set this town free. And from what I'm figuring, it has to do with this quilt, this jagged crystal and this pill box and key.

"I've been taught that in most situations, God is always working around us and it's our choice to join him in what he's doing. And right now, God is working to set the captives free and he wants us to be his vessels, like he did with Moses."

"I guess I didn't see it that way. It's just..."

"What?"

Sheldon rubbed his face with both hands vigorously as if trying to prevent tears from coming. "For four years I have cried out to God to help this town and I've heard nothing but silence in return. Day after day, I would plead my case asking why so many of our loved ones have to die, asking Him for his provision, begging for His mercy. You know, I came to this town as a missionary to serve God in any way I could. For a while, I could see the work of the Holy Spirit exploding through the town, until one man shows up and rips the faith rug out from under all of us. So forgive me if I don't show an exuberant amount of faith here!"

Sheldon walked away and vigorously looked for a way out while I examined the back side of the quilt. To my amazement, the stitching resembled that of a drawing. "Sheldon, take a look at this." I said excitedly.

"Can't, I'm too busy trying to save our hides and others."

"Well, okay then. I guess you're too busy to see how we can get out of here. 'Cuz, according to this here map, there is a hidden door right next to the bookshelf."

"What? Where? Let me see." Sheldon slightly pushed me out of the way to examine the quilt himself. It was a map of an underground tunnel leading to a cavern.

"Was this house originally an underground railroad for slaves?" I asked.

"It could have been, but I've never heard of any of those types of houses out here in these parts of Idaho or Montana." Suddenly Sheldon's eyes grew big, as if a light bulb turned on. "Or maybe it's an underground mining facility."

"Oh, that would make perfect sense. Oh my goodness..." I held up the golf ball size jagged crystal. "Could this crystal be a diamond? Is that what he's been up to, mining diamonds?"

"And this quilt is the treasure map."

Vanessa Matheny

CHAPTER FIFTEEN
"The Ruby"

To our amazement, the skeleton key also unlocked the secret door next to the bookcase. I found a large bag and stuffed the quilt into it. I took in a deep breath and was ready to face whatever was on the other side of the door.

A strong stench of mildew and decay filled our noses as Sheldon pried open the door. The long, skinny corridor was dark and musty. He flicked on the light and the corridor slowly lit up revealing a narrow, dirty path. Old electrical wires hung low with every other light bulb missing. Cobwebs and spider webs coated much of the rotting ceiling. The floor boards were covered with falling, dirty, white paint chips, dirt, old forgotten hardware and animal feces.

Underneath my breath I whispered, "Here we go again, heading into a dark, damp, musty, enclosed place that would possibly have mice."

My heart pounded as my eyes darted everywhere in search of any signs of small creatures that would want to chew on my feet. I inhaled and grabbed hold of Sheldon's shirt.   I felt as if we were two blind people trying to guide each other.

The path seemed to get narrower and narrower and the stench of old rotting wood and dust intensified.   I could hear the echo of my heartbeat in my ears, which caused a headache.

"Oh, God, you know how I hate places like this.   Please give me the peace and the courage that I need to get to the end." I whispered into the dry, musty air.

Together we shuffled our feet forward in silence and that is where God met me, in the silence of my mind. It was as if a movie began to play and I was the star of the show. I started to see myself back at the cave dealing with the overwhelming fear of small, damp, musty places with mice.

It was then that I felt a revelation sweep through. It didn't come like the usual still small voice or even an audio one; it was as if God placed a "knowing" in me. The knowledge that God healed my soul back at the cave because He knew I would be facing another moment like that.

I had to marvel at the goodness of God and the depth of His love for me—that He cared about the intricate parts of my life.

My thoughts quickly diverted into a rabbit hole as I imagined how God would talk to me. "Hey kiddo, I see that you have a fear of damp, musty places that mice like to play in, so I figured you would appreciate me taking time out of my busy schedule to heal your soul. That way you don't freak out the next time you're in a place like that."

I chuckled and relaxed with the peace that came with the revelation. I felt free to let go of Sheldon's shirt. I stood tall and brave. With each step, I felt more confident and I was even proud of myself for overcoming the fear of small, damp and musty places where mice might live.   My faith felt strong and I felt like I was ready to conquer the world, until...

Sheldon's hand quickly covered my mouth. "Whatever you do, do not scream. Let's just keep walking. They will not harm you."

I stood very still nodding my compliance as a mouse scurried across my foot.

"I'm going to let my hand go now. Promise me, you're not going to scream?"

Again, I slowly nodded.   Believe me, I wanted to scream as I watched the mouse sniff my foot.

We heard low, muffled voices coming from the other side of the wall. We figured it must be the Foreman and Sniper.   They hadn't left yet. They were still talking. We drew closer to the wall to listen.

"I need that key!   If I don't get it, my Boss is going to..." Walter's voice was cut off by a hard thud.

"I know you are upset, but is there something else that is bothering you?" Sniper asked.

"Why do you ask?" He snapped.

"Because when something is really upsetting you, you run your fingers through your hair and you sigh a lot, like you're doing now."

Sheldon leaned over and whispered, "I'm amazed at how thin these walls are. You can hear everything perfectly."

I leaned in closer. "Yeah, so we need to keep quiet or they'll hear us." I said as I shushed him.

"Sniper..." Walter said. "Something has been bothering me. It's been bothering me since the day I arrived."

"What's that?"

"While I was on the train I had a dream. It started out exciting. I found myself in the middle of a desert field at the opening to a mining cave. I saw something shiny and I dug it up. It was a ruby. It was the most beautiful and flawless ruby I had ever seen. I held it up to the sun and admired its clarity and color. The color was deep, velvet, red like that of blood. The excitement rose up within me as I thought I hit the jackpot and was going to be filthy rich, because the size of that thing was the size of an orange.

"Then the dream shifted and it wasn't so exciting any more. As I was holding the ruby, it got very hot in my hands, so hot in fact that it caught on fire. I threw the ruby up in the air and then..."

Sheldon and I pressed harder to the wall.

"And then?" Sniper prodded.

"The ruby turned into an eagle. It first sprouted wings and then it became an enormous eagle swooping down from heaven snatching me off of my feet. The eagle wasn't like that of an average eagle. I had never seen an eagle like this before. Its wings were massive, its claws were like human hands, and the head was the size of a dog."

"Wow. It sounds cool. Kind of prehistoric, don't you think?"

"Sniper!" Walter yelled. "It wasn't cool. That thing, that eagle, took me to its nest high in the tress where its babies were and they tried to eat me. I was trapped and helpless."

"Well thank goodness it was only a dream. So what's the problem? Why are you freaking out over a dream? It's just a dream, right?"

There was a brief moment of silence and Walter said, "I think it has something to do with that Abigail woman."

I felt something crawl up my pant leg. Sheldon noticed my panic and whacked the mouse off of my leg as I muffled my scream into my hands. We heard rapid shuffling sounds and the voices grew silent. We both froze.

I whispered, "We'd better move on." Sheldon agreed.

After a few feet of silence Sheldon finally spoke, "That dream does mean something." He paused and faced me. "God told me that the Ruby is you."

CHAPTER SIXTEEN
One Wild Ride

After a short while, we came to a 'T'. "So now what?" Sheldon asked.

"Well, I don't know. Maybe we should do what the famous saying says." I said sarcastically.

"And that would be?"

"When in flight take a right."

Sheldon shook his head as he quietly laughed. He bowed at mid-waist and gracefully swept out his hand for me to lead the way. I mockingly gave him a curtsy, turned on my heels and took a right.

It wasn't long before we found ourselves at a dead end. "Oh, you've got to be kidding me!" Sheldon snapped angrily.

When in flight, take a right!" he said in a girly tone.

"Well, it's always worked before." I shrugged.

Sheldon rubbed his forehead and sighed heavily. "Well, I guess we're going to have to turn back."

An unusual metal shape in one of the wooden panels of the wall caught my eye. I felt the wall and I knew what the metal shape reminded me of—a key hole. "No way." The whispered words flew out of my mouth as if they could free us. "Sheldon, wait! Look it's another secret passage."

Sheldon turned around like a reluctant child throwing a tantrum. "For real? I mean, why on earth would a house have so many secret doors? Why not just have doors with a knob?"

"I am beginning to understand why this key is so important to the Foreman. I bet this key opens this door too." Sure enough, the key fit perfectly like a glove to a hand.

The door opened to a mining cave which looked ready to cave in. An old mining cart was locked in its place as if it was ready to be shipped down to another end. The cart from a distance had appeared to be bigger than it really was. A small child would even be cramped in it. All I could think of was how we both needed to fit into it.

"After you," Sheldon said rather too politely.

"You know, we're both not going to fit in this thing."

"Well, we don't have a choice. We need to get out of here. I feel like we've been down here way too long as is."

"Why is it that I should be in front and not you?" I asked, having my suspicions of why he would want me in front.

A coy expression came over his face. "Well, the way I see it, if a band of spider webs happens to show itself, you'll be the first to move it out of our way. Or if a low beam comes up, you'll hit it first and then I'll know to duck." My jaw dropped. "I'm just joking."

"Yeah, right."

"Look, Abigail, I really am just joking. I'm not this cruel guy that you think I am. I promise I'll behave. I'll get in first and you'll have to sit on my lap. I think that's the only way we'll fit. We'll need to keep our heads low in case there are any low beams. We just never know what we'll be heading into."

"Fine, Texas Ranger, let's do this." I teased back. We squished into the cart like two sardines. I felt uncomfortable sitting on his lap so I placed the quilt in between us.

"Are you ready?" he asked.

"Ready as I'll ever be." I said giving him an apprehensive smile.

Next to the cart was a lever. Sheldon pulled the lever and we slowly started to move. The cart picked up the pace and zigzagged to the right, and then zigzagged to the left. It raced down and chugged up. The metal wheels screamed and whistled as we soared through various tunnels. It felt like a long rollercoaster ride, but then again, how would I know, I'd never ridden one.

"Shouldn't we be there by now?" I yelled.

"I can't hear you!"

When I tried to repeat myself, something flew in my mouth. "Yuk. Oh gross!" I frantically wiped my tongue off with my hands. The combination of bug and motion sickness made the bottom of my stomach started to churn. I kept swallowing and breathing back the urge to vomit.

The urge quickly left me as a wave of panic hit when we felt the cart dive over a hill. We both screamed as the cart zoomed down. That was all it took, I had lost my stomach.

I lifted my head slightly only to be greeted by a huge spider's web. "Ahh!" I screamed as I anxiously removed the spider's web from my face. And I think there was even a spider on it. Without realizing it, I had elbowed Sheldon in the face while trying to remove the spider.   I could hear a low, muffled holler from him.

Many times we hit our heads together.   I was beginning to feel like a weeble-wobble toy that was wedged in its car by a two-year-old. The cart took a sharp, hard right, almost tipping us; then came to a crashing halt in a heaping pile of sand. The instant stop launched us both, head first into the sand, along with the quilt.

"Are you okay, Abigail?" Sheldon asked as he helped dig me out.

I slowly stood and shook the sand out of my hair.   "Wow! That was painful."

Sheldon looked me up and down.

Worried, I asked. "What?"

Holding his nose, he asked, "Did you throw up?"

"I'm afraid so." I looked down and saw vomit and sand sticking to me in clumps.

"Are you okay, though?   Are you hurt?"

"Not really. Just a little scratched up from the sand. You?" I blinked a couple of times and noticed that his lip was bleeding.

"I think I hit my lip on your arm or something."

"Oh, that might explain the scratch on my arm. I thought it was from the sand." I took my one clean sleeve and wiped the blood from his lip.

It was definitely another one of those awkward moments. *Why? Was something happening between us? It doesn't matter,* I told myself, *because I'm not looking to have a relationship. I made up my mind about that a few years ago.*

"I suppose we should get moving." Sheldon said as he headed toward the opening of the cave.

The mention of the word move made my eyes grow big. I stood very still and looked up at Sheldon.

"What's wrong? You're looking kind of funny."

I tried to speak, but instead I vomited all over Sheldon's shoes.

"Nice. Now that you got that out of your system, do you feel better?" I wiped my mouth with my sleeve and just nodded a yes.

"Don't forget the quilt." Sheldon said over his shoulder as we headed out of the cave. Once we were out, Sheldon found a clump of grass to wipe off his shoes. Never in my life have I had more embarrassing moments with a guy.

I looked up at the evening sky and thought, *God what are you doing?*

The butterflies in my stomach were hard to discern. *Was this the beginning of feeling something for Sheldon, or the feeling of having to vomit again?* I, of course, chose the latter.

"Your shoes look a lot better now that they're clean." I teased.

"Yes they do, and I would prefer to keep them that way, thank you. That's of course; if you're all done throwing up."

"Yes, I am. I'm beginning to feel better now."

Sheldon took a small step away from me and looked me over. He offered one of his shoes to me and harassed, "Are you sure. Because to me, you look like you could do another round of hurling."

I suddenly felt self-conscious as to what I must really look like. *Oh, no.* I thought. *Here we go again; not only the dork was unleashed, but the lunatic from Alcatraz is metamorphosing again. Oh, I bet I'm just a picturesque Mona Lisa!*

"No, thanks, I'm fine," I said as I tried smoothing out my hair, straightening my shirt, and dusting off the clumps of sand and vomit.

"Good, because I didn't want to walk around in a squishy shoe soaked in puke. But being the gentleman that I am, I thought I'd offer."

I gave him a small punch on the arm.

CHAPTER SEVENTEEN
The Plan

After a long, invigorating shower, I went downstairs to say good night to Lisa Marie and Sheldon. Sheldon had the quilt spread out in front of them. "You know how we saw the quilt as being a map?"

"Yeah." I answered.

"Look carefully at the layout of the town and where the mining cave is and tell me; doesn't this look like the stitching on the backside of the quilt?"

I stood in astonishment. "It sure does."

"Abigail, I think I know what the Foreman is up too."

"You do?"

"What I was getting ready to tell you; down in the office, is that when I dissected the locusts, I discovered not only the green venom in the tail, but that it was being fueled by a diamond."

"Whoa." I said.

"I think you're right. That crystal is a diamond and the Foreman and Sniper are looking for diamonds in the cave. What if that key unlocks a door to where the diamonds are hidden?"

I stood wide eyed. "Don't tell me that Damion Callaway wants the diamonds to build another army of them?"

"Oh dear God help us if he does."

"What do you think we should do?"

Sheldon gave me an encouraging smile and said, "Well, I guess you better ask God. After all He did send you. I also know of another person we could talk to—Trudy." Sheldon didn't say anything else. He stood and went upstairs to shower.

I sat next to Lisa Marie on the couch and asked, "What's with Sheldon?"

"What do you mean?"

"One moment we seem to be getting along and the next we're like cats and dogs trying to eat each other."

Lisa Marie laughed, "Oh that. That's Sheldon's way of showing he likes you."

"What?"

"Oh, don't tell me you hadn't noticed. That day he met you?" Puzzled, I shook my head.

"He practically hyperventilated himself into a non-speaking fool. He swooned back and thankfully caught himself in the door frame.

We both laughed. "I've also discerned your zealousness for the Lord is convicting him. He hasn't said anything to me, but I know Sheldon pretty well. I think he's ashamed of where he is with the Lord and wishing he were zealous again, like you. These past few days, I can see the power struggle that's going on within him. His bouts with anger are his way of battling his convictions. Especially when you hit a bruise on closely related topics, like God." Lisa Marie added.

"Why does Sheldon look so forlorn when he looks at the burned stake?" I think I surprised Lisa Marie with my question. She jolted upright from her sitting position and bounced her legs over the edge of the couch. "I'm sorry if I was to forward with my question. I don't mean any disrespect."

"Oh, no you're fine. Yeah… um…"

"If it's too painful to talk about, I'll understand."

Lisa Marie grabbed a pillow to her midsection and crossed her legs again. "It was shortly after the Foreman came to the town and banned all Bibles and told us 'Christians' that we were no longer to evangelize or speak the name of Jesus anymore. Well, that made Katie, his fiancé, and Sheldon even more zealous. They thought of themselves fearless like the apostles in Rome.

"One day, Sheldon walked near the mountains. Katie went to share the gospel with a woman. The Foreman found out that she talked to someone about Jesus, and he was angry. He walked right up to her in the middle of the street and grabbed hold of her. They were walking fast together as he made their way to the hill where a big wooden cross stood in the place where the apple orchard and the church use to be.

Sniper was already waiting for them with rope in hand, wood around the cross, and lighter fluid.

My eyes grew big with shock. "You mean that he burned her to the cross?"

"Yes. The way Sniper gathered the town's people to watch made us all feel like we're going to a circus sideshow. Before I walked up the hill, I anxiously looked everywhere for Sheldon, but he was nowhere to be found. When Sniper lit the wood and it immediately caught on fire, I noticed Sheldon standing on the huge hill to my left. She began to scream. I couldn't bear to watch. I turned away and watched Sheldon run as fast as he could to where we were, but by the time he got there, it was too late. There was nothing left of her. They had been engaged for a year and were to be married that fall."

I was speechless. After hearing the story, I began to understand Sheldon more.

"After it was over, the Foreman announced that anyone who disobeyed the Idealist's rules would pay just like Katie did. He used her as an example of what type of punishment he was capable of doing. It was after that, fear moved in and the Holy Spirit moved out. I don't know if what I saw was really in my imagination or God's way of showing me in the natural what had taken place in the spiritual, but a dark cloud moved in and seemed to have never moved out."

We both sat in silence until Lisa Marie looked at me with a small curve across her face. "On a much lighter note, would you like to hear a God story?"

"Sure." I said.

"Three days later, Miriam gave the Foreman a word from the Lord. Well, obviously he didn't appreciate it nor accept it. Instead, he got mad and scheduled her to be burned at the stake. I was mortified to find out he wanted to burn another person, especially someone so dear to me. He gathered us around, again. Sniper tied her up and soaked the wood in lighter fluid. The Foreman gave some kind of speech that she was a practicing witch sent by God. That clearly was not biblical 'nor' the truth. After he was done, he nodded to Sniper and he lit the wood, but nothing happened. The wood would not catch on fire. They both spent at least twenty minutes trying to set the wood on fire. No matter what they did or how much lighter fluid they put on the wood, it would not catch on fire.

"First they started to argue that Sniper put on too much lighter fluid causing the wood to be wet. Then, he said it wasn't enough, that the wood was to dry.

"Miriam laughed and her laughter became contagious. The Foreman grew angrier and angrier until he commanded us all to stop and told Sniper to cut her down. He blamed it on the wood being wet with rain.

"She and I both knew it was the act of God saving her life. And her laughter, I believe, was the outpouring of the Holy Spirit comforting us.

Once she stepped off the wood, the Foreman told Sniper to escort her out to Bitterroot Forest, never to be seen by the town's people again. "I think the Foreman was so embarrassed, he, himself didn't know what to do."

"Wow. Miriam told me only a little of the story, but I like your version better." Lisa Marie giggled.

"You know the sad thing is the Foreman found other ways to punish those who disobeyed, and would always incorporate the Bible and twist it."

"I'm so sorry for the pain and suffering all of you had to endure. I have been praying and asking God what he wants us to do. All I know is that something has to be done to stop his cruelty."

"You know, I was reading in Deuteronomy this morning and I got stuck on a scripture. For whatever reason, I just couldn't move on. I believe God was trying to tell me something because the scripture reminds me of us. Hold that thought." Lisa Marie said as she held up one finger for me to wait as she ran to retrieve something. She came back with her Bible.

"Whoa. You have a Bible?"

She gave me a smile like that of Cheshire cat and said, "And I hide it well."

"Oh, you go, girl," I teased as I snapped my fingers in a quick 'Z' formation.

She opened the Bible and read Deuteronomy chapter thirteen verse twelve. "If you hear it said about one of the towns the Lord your God is giving you to live in that wicked men have arisen among you and have led the people of their town astray, saying, 'Let us go and worship other gods' —gods you have not known— then you must inquire, probe and investigate it thoroughly. And if it is true and it has been proved that this detestable thing has been done among you, you must certainly put to the sword all who live in that town.' So what do you think God might be saying?"

"I think I know, but I feel I need to first tell you what Sheldon and I heard in the tunnel about a dream the Foreman had and then I think we should pray to confirm what I believe God is saying."

"Sounds good," she said.

After I shared the dream, a short prayer and a long time of listening, I felt the Lord answered. "Before I tell you what I believe the Lord is saying, I want to ask a question. By asking this question, it will help me receive confirmation if what I heard is from the Lord or not."

"Okay, shoot."

"Have all the believers gotten together for a prayer meeting to seek the will of God on this matter?"

"Oh good heavens no, It's too risky. I know a lot of us pray on our own, but we've never heard God tell us what to do."

"I understand that we are dealing with a higher up leader who is slowly taking control of our communities, towns, and some states but do you feel there is something wrong with this picture? You guys are a small town and there are just four men up against, how many are in the town?" I asked.

"I believe we have about a hundred and fifty, give or take. But only about twenty-five of us still quietly keep the faith. Why? You're not thinking of holding a prayer meeting are you, because if we get caught we'll all end up dead."

"Here's what the Lord is telling us to do. This land was given to all of you by Him and when the Foreman moved in, he was the wicked man to arise. As he placed fear in the town, it caused most of you to worship him instead of God. Like you say, only twenty-five have kept the faith. God wants us to join forces and use our sword to put him to death."

Lisa Marie clapped her hands excitedly and said, "Wow that's awesome! How do we do that?"

"Our answer lies in Matthew."

Lisa Marie's eyes grew wild with anticipation and the letter 'o' formed her mouth. At that point, I knew we were on the same page.

"That if two of you on earth agree about anything you ask for, it will be done for you by my Father in heaven. For where two or three come together in my name, there am I with them." Lisa Marie read as she squealed with delight and bounced up and down on the couch.

"I'm going to need your help to get everyone together." I said. It appeared that my statement was a kill joy. Her shoulders hung low and her eyes looked worried. "What?"

"If one word is released that I'm trying to get a prayer circle together, I am as good as dead. Not to mention that fear might keep them from coming," Lisa Marie said worriedly.

"You do know that prayer is a very powerful weapon," I said to encourage her.

"Yes I know," she said trying to encourage herself.

"Well, let's do our part, pray and leave that problem to the Lord. It's really late and Sheldon and I are going to Trudy's first thing in the morning."

I started up the stairs when she called after me.

"Abigail, I just want you to know that I believe God is here working on our behalf through you. If Paul and Peter could go out and spread the gospel and not fear being flogged, then I too can go out and get the people for the prayer meeting."

I smiled and said good-night.

CHAPTER EIGHTEEN
Map Quest

Isabella rushed to the General Store.   She wanted to get there before many of the towns people woke, including Walter. The closed sign dangled in the window when she arrived.   Bound and determined to get her item, she faced Trudy's wrath for waking her so early.

Trudy angrily swung the door open to see Isabella's flushed and frantic face. "What on earth is so important that ya need ta wake me up three hours before I open?"

"I haven't been feeling well and I need something for it."

"Well fer petes-sake, can't it wait til' I open?   Why so early?"

Isabella started to cry and Trudy hated Isabella's crying spurts. "Come in. What's all the blubberin' about?" Trudy said annoyed. Isabella stood before Trudy with her body trembling with sobs. Trudy rolled her eyes and said, "What'd he do this time?"

Isabella looked at Trudy with a red, wet face and said, "I think I might be pregnant. I don't want to have his baby. I don't know what to do?"

Trudy sighed hard. "Well, I'm sure ya ain't the first."

Isabella looked at Trudy and an awkward silence fell between them. Isabella thought for a moment and then asked, "Did he? Were you?"

The awkwardness was too much for Trudy. She looked away and scolded, "I don't want ta talk about it. Why don't ya jes pray ya have a miscarriage?"

"Is that what happened?" Isabella said sympathetically.

Heat rose up in Trudy's face. She placed her hands on her hips and said, "Like I said, I don't want ta talk about it. Give the baby up fer adoption then, I don't care."

"But that's the point; I don't want to have it at all. But I'm against abortion. The thought of killing an innocent baby who never asked to be in this situation is sickening to my soul." Isabella whined.

"Well, I don't know what ta tell ya." Trudy said coldly. Trudy walked down an aisle, grabbed the item and said, "Here, go take care of ya'self and leave me be. I'll just put it on Walter's account."

Isabella tucked the item in her purse. Her hand was on the door when she looked back and asked, "Could you please not tell anyone, especially Walter. I will tell him in my own time, when I feel ready. I'm only asking because I know how hard it is for you to keep secrets."

Trudy's mouth twisted in anger and her eyes grew wild. She pointed to the door for her to leave.

****

As Sheldon and I headed to the General Store, I grew tired of his inquisitive stare. I said, "Okay, you clearly have something on your mind. So let me have it."

Sheldon looked at me and said, "In spite of me being exhausted last night, I couldn't get you out of my mind, Abigail."

The heat rose quickly to my cheeks. I didn't realize just how quickly I could blush. "I beg your pardon?"

Sheldon realized how he sounded and started to stumble over his words. He nervously looked around in search for words that made more sense. He cleared his throat and tried again.

"Oh look, here comes Simona," I said, as I saw her running toward us full speed. I was glad for her interruption. "Hey, Simona, how's it going?"

Simona was out of breath by the time she reached us. "I'm okay, but the little ones ain't."

"What's wrong with them?" Sheldon asked as he knelt down on one knee to soothe her.

"I tried reaching you at the mission's house, but Lisa Marie said you'd gone walking to the General Store. I don't mean to keep pestering you for help but..."

Sheldon rested his hand on her sweaty head and said, "Oh, Sweetheart it's okay. You know you've always been like a little sister to me. It's never been a burden to help you and the others."

He lifted her chin up and looked her in the eyes. "I love to help. Are they ill or is someone hurt?" I could tell it was uncomfortable for her to look him right in the eyes. She looked so skinny and unsure of herself.

Big bullet tears gushed out as she sobbed her way through the story of how the Foreman took away all of their food yesterday because she didn't know where Sheldon and Abigail were. "And he warned us that if we were caught in the General Store getting any food, he'd..." Her hard moans muffled her voice to an unintelligent dialect.

"He'd do what Sweetie?" I asked softly.

"He'd make sure our next meal was poisoned," she wailed.

The story was heart wrenching to hear. I choked back tears. The young girl that stood sheepishly before us reminded me of me. I knew what it was like to go hungry, to be threatened and beaten.

"Anna and Billy's tummies hurt something awful 'cuz they're so hungry. Lily's been dry-heaving. I can't get Zack out of bed. He's been complaining of a headache and Carry's in her own little world of make-believe, pretending she's a princess eating at a banquet. The past few days we haven't had much to eat. I'm afraid, Sheldon that they'll die soon if they don't get food. I don't know what to do. I was looking for you all day yesterday so I could tell the Foreman where you were."

"I'm so sorry, Simona that I wasn't here for you, but I am now. You run home so the Foreman doesn't see us talking together and I'll drop by real soon with a bag of groceries. Now listen closely. I want you to hide the food as well as you can for me, okay? We don't want anyone to get hurt." She nodded and hugged him tight before she ran behind the General Store to the barn.

"Lord." I prayed, "Please swiftly help us. I don't know how much more these people can take."

I remember one of my professors shared with me that sometimes situations will get worse before they get better; the greater the battle, the greater the victory. So, I knew great things were coming to the towns' people that Satan had stopped for such a long time. Well, it's high time he returns all that he's stolen!

A haze of humidity wrapped around our bodies as we walked into the General Store. The stale old refrigeration smell seemed worse than the last time I visited and the floor boards creaked as I walked up to the counter.

"Where do you think Trudy is?" I asked Sheldon, as he was looking around for her too.

"Ring the bell that's on the counter." I playfully tapped the bell sending a sharp loud ting through the quiet air.

From behind the curtain came a loud, shrill voice. "Comin'! Oh, it's ya'll." Trudy said disappointedly as she looked at me with scornful eyes. "Ya mean the Foreman hasn't chopped off a piece of ya yet?"

"Trudy, we came to talk to you." Sheldon said as he peaked around the corner of an aisle.

Trudy pointed at Sheldon and said, "Ya'll I'll talk ta. Her, well, she can move that little behind of hers right outta here before I use it as a human dart board."

"Trudy, please this is really important. We must speak with you." Sheldon pleaded.

Trudy gave a condescending laughed, "Huh! Important!" She whipped around, pointed to me and said through clenched teeth, "Do ya know what important thin' that girl cost me yesterday?"

"I'm sorry for whatever the Foreman did to you, but I'm hoping that through our talk you'll come to understand that we are actually on the same side here, and we're here to put an end to all of this," I said as politely as I could.

Trudy put her hand up to her ear like an immature school girl and said, "I'm sorry, did ya hear somethin' Sheldon? Or was that the sound of an annoyin' bee buzzin' around my head." She paused and then continued, "He's been lookin' fer ya's. And if he found out that ya'lls been here, he'll have my hide. I want ya's both ta leave. I don't want any more trouble ya hear. Now skit!"

Sheldon moved closer to Trudy, "Please, you must hear us out. I believe we're on to something big and we need to stop him before another world catastrophe happens. We just need to confirm a few things with you."

I suddenly noticed a forlorn shadow cast over Trudy's eyes. She looked to the floor as she ran her fingers through her short hair. Her left hand started to tremor. My heart softened toward her. The woman was obviously in great fear of this man. I couldn't imagine what scars he had left on her soul.

"Oh, all right, I'll bite. Ya'll come in."

"Before we do Trudy, I need to purchase some food for the children." Sheldon said, as he started grabbing items off the shelves.

"Those poor youngen's have been whinnin' at my back door fer the past few days. My heart breaks fer em'. I would like ta do more, but I've jes been ta afraid ta feed em'. I seemed ta find myself in enough trouble with Walter lately."

Sheldon put the groceries on the counter and pulled out a few dollar bills. "Will this be enough for a trade?"

Trudy looked to me. "I would help, but I lost most of my stuff in the plane crash."

"Oh fer pete-sakes, jes take em'. But don't either of ya breathe a word of this ta the Foreman or I'll, I'll put snakes in ya'lls boots."

While I followed Trudy, Sheldon delivered the food to the children. Her home adjacent to the store was small, somewhat cozy and filled with the same clamminess as the store. I noticed, after I sat, that the furniture was old and tattered with a spring poking through a cushion. Trudy sat down hard on her overstuffed chair with an even deeper forlorn expression. I discerned that she really must know something and is contemplating whether or not to share. Her gaze was fixed on the shabby curtain that separated the store from her home. I noticed her breathing became shallow and her forehead was perspiring. I wasn't sure if it was the heat or the spirit of fear I was facing.

I wasn't taking any chances. I thought, *Lord, let the battle begin.* I casually looked away and under my breath I whispered, "In the name of Jesus Christ, I bind the spirit of fear. You cannot manifest in my presence."

I was a bit startled when she started to speak. "What is it that ya think ya found? Is that why Walter is lookin' fer ya two? Does he know that ya found somethin'?" Her eyes enlarged. "Do ya have it with ya?

"No, we don't have anything with us and he doesn't know anything. He doesn't even know where we've been."

Trudy swallowed and wiped her forehead. Her breathing intensified. I hoped she wasn't going to hyperventilate and pass out. "Are you okay, Trudy?"

"I'm fine. So where've ya guys been?" She snapped.

"Well, we got locked in the Foreman's secret office and managed to find our way out through a mining cave."

It took a few moments for Trudy to respond as she rubbed her hand nervously over her face. I could tell she was trying to control her breathing and was careful not to let on that she knew anything. Instead, she fished for answers before she gave them.

"How did ya find his secret office?"

The Lord warned me not to give too much detail, so I went straight to the point. "Trudy, we found the quilt you made. It's a map to the mines isn't it? Is the Foreman looking for diamonds?"

Trudy anxiously started to shake her leg, crossed her arms and talked fast. "How did ya find the quilt? Where was it? And what makes ya think he's lookin' fer diamonds?"

"Because sitting on the bottom of the quilt was a jagged, golf-ball sized diamond. We believe he might be here to get diamonds for Damion."

Trudy stood up, shook her head and began pacing. "Whatevea fer?"

"We think Damion might be recreating another army of locusts."

Trudy laughed nervously and said, "How on earth did ya come up with that stupid idea?"

I swallowed back a few mean words and replied, "Well, years ago, Sheldon happen to dissect one and learned that one single diamond fueled a locust. Why else would the Foreman be looking for them?"

"What makes ya think he's lookin' fer diamonds?"

"Why are you so nervous talking about this?"

Trudy quickly sat back down and leaned forward and said harshly, "Neither of ya don't have a clue of what's he's up ta. He can't be stopped. Callaway can't be stopped. We're all doomed."

We both jumped as we heard Sheldon entering from the back door.

"Sorry it took me so long. So what've I missed?" He asked.

"I'm not sure you missed anything. I'm asking her questions, but she in turn is asking them to me. We're getting nowhere." I said quietly over my shoulder.

Sheldon placed his hands on Trudy's arms and said, "Trudy, won't you please help us? Help us get control back of the town and possibly save us all from another attack. Aren't you tired of the Elite bullying us around? I mean just take a good look around you. It's time we stood up to the Foreman and take back our lives."

Hot streaming tears flowed down her sweaty face as she choked out her words. "I can't help ya. I'm in this ta deep. It's time fer ya's ta leave."

That was it. We couldn't get her to share anything. *Now what Lord?*

The children had told Sheldon that the Foreman was walking around the town looking for us, so we thought it best to leave the back way.

"Sheldon, did you hear what she said? She's in this too deep. I knew it. She knows a lot more than we thought. Why do I feel we've entered a deep rabbit hole here?"

"I think I may know of another person who could help us." Sheldon said.

****

Trudy went into the bathroom and splashed cold water on her face. Staring at herself in the mirror watching the water drip from her face, Trudy's mind flashed back.

"So Trudy, tell me about this beautiful quilt?" Walter said in a silky voice as he gingerly picked the quilt off her bed.

She couldn't resist the handsome man that stood in front of her. The several days they had spent together, he seemed to be a decent man. A man she could love. Even though she had feelings for her fiancé Frank, there was something about Walter that stirred the wild side in her. He intrigued her. And she wanted to spend more time with him and if that meant telling her family secrets, then so be it.

She unfolded the quilt and spread it out for him. Trudy ran her fingers over the stitching and said with pride, "I made this here quilt fer my daddy. It's become a family heirloom. It holds a family secret that has been kept fer four generations."

Walter gave her a dreamy smile and in a soft tone asked, "And what family secret is that?"

She smiled back and went slightly weak at the knees. Her heart melted each time he talked. Frank never made her feel that way. She turned the quilt over and said, "If ya look closely ya'll see that it's a map."

Walter's eyes lit up like the Fourth-of-July. His smile broadened and his heart pounded with excitement. He had to remain calm so as not to show too much excitement and give away his plan. He casually asked, "A map of what?"

Trudy delicately placed her pointer finger on his lips and made him promise that her family secret would be safe with him. He kissed her finger and nodded.

Trudy walked over into the store, grabbed a step ladder and reached high on a shelf for an object that was hidden behind the sugar jar.

"For a second, I thought you left me." Walter teased.

"I left ta git this." Trudy held in her hand a rectangular, decorative pill box. She held it out for him to take.

Walter examined the pill box closely. It looked just like the one he had. Again, excitement rose up in his chest like a child opening his first gift on Christmas. He opened the box and a wicked smile crossed his face. He thought to himself, *jack pot!* "And there's more where these came from?"

"Yeah, and the quilt will show ya the way, but there's a downside ta this equation."

"Oh, and what's that?" he asked.

"There's another pill box that contains a key. Ya'll need the key ta git in. Without it, what ya see in the box is unreachable."

Walter worked hard not to let on that he had the key. He pulled her close and teasingly sniffed her neck and whispered tenderly, "And where may I find this key?"

She softened like putty in his hands as she affectionately spoke back, "That's the downer. It's been missin' fer ova thirty years. No one's been able ta find it."

With him being so close, she thought he had plans to kiss her, but to her surprise… He released her and said coldly, "Then I'll have to improvise." His release made her unsteady on her feet. She grabbed the back of her chair to keep herself from falling.

He grabbed the quilt and started to head out the door.

"Wait, I'll let ya take the quilt, of course, but ya can't take the pill box. That belongs ta me. And if people were ta see what's in it, ya'll have a riot on ya hands."

He looked at the box in his hand and grabbed her arm firmly and said, "I'll let you keep your pill box under one condition, that you don't breathe a word of this to anyone. It will be our little secret." He roughly pulled her closer and said through gritted teeth, "I will be keeping you close. After all, you are my insurance to my investment."

Trudy blinked her way back to the present and spoke into the mirror, "And so it's been that way fer eight long years. Maybe it's time ta git a different investment."

The bell on the counter dinged obnoxiously followed by an all too familiar voice. "Trudy!" Walter yelled.

Trudy quickly dried her face, straightened her sticky blouse and entered the store to face her on-going investment. "Yes, Walter, I mean Foreman. What can I do fer ya?"

"Marco said he saw Sheldon and that Banderas woman coming in here. Is that true?" He moved quickly over to her and gripped her arm. "Is that true? You know how I feel about liars."

She sure did, and she'd paid a hefty price each and every time for it. Her stomach ached and she felt light-headed. She didn't know how much more she could take from this man before she would end up dead.

"They only came ta buy food fer themselves." She said in a weary voice. He pulled her to her knees. "Ouch!" She wailed.

"I find it hard to believe that it was just food they were shopping for." He grabbed hold of her short hair and pulled her head back. "What did you tell them?"

"Nothin'," she cried. "I said nothin'. I promised ya I would never tell anyone of our little secret. And I haven't gone back on my word."

"So it was just food they were after?"

"Yeah."

He roughly let go, flinging her head forward. He quickly looked around and said, "They better not have gotten food for those varmints!"

She knew better to quickly look away. "Just food fer themselves, Sir."

"Good, then my work here is done. Where did they go from here?"

As much as she hated to rat them out, she pointed in the direction of her back door.

****

While Walter was out looking for Sheldon and Abigail, Isabella grabbed the pregnancy test she'd gotten from Trudy and ran to the bathroom. While waiting for the results, she went to Walter's office and apprehensively reached for his black Bible.

She thought it best to stay in his office to read where she could watch out the window for his return. She sat in his chair, flipped to the back of the Bible and continued to read all the scriptures on love. She had been looking forward to reading it all morning.

Walter always told her that the God of this Bible was a vengeful god who lashes out his wrath on his people who disobey his rules. And that he, Walter, was his disciple in helping him carry out his wrath. She knew she wasn't the sharpest crayon in the box, but that just didn't make sense to her.

She picked up where she left off. She was amazed at the contrast of beliefs Walter always spewed out. It read, "...The Lord, the Lord, compassionate and gracious God, slow to anger, abounding in love and faithfulness, maintaining love to thousands, and forgiving wickedness, rebellion and sin."

Isabella quickly looked under the word disciple and again she was astonished at the contrast she'd been told. In John 13: 34 it read, "A new command I give you: Love one another. As I have loved you, so you must love one another. By this all men will know that you are my disciples, if you love one another."

Isabella slammed her fist on his desk and said, "He is so not a disciple of God. There is absolutely no love in that man."

Outside of knowing that Walter was not a disciple of God, she needed help to understand the truth. She wanted to know more about God and His love and why Walter would think such the opposite.

She put the Bible away and looked out the window, still no Walter. She knew the only person she could trust with these questions would be over at the mission's house. Was she willing to sacrifice everything in search of her answers?

Before she left, she quickly looked at the pregnancy test. Her heart dropped. Tears welled up in her eyes as she whispered, "God, what do I do now?" She hurriedly tucked the test into the bathroom trash and headed for the mission's house.

****

"Oh, Sheldon, Abigail, just the two I wanted to see." Isabella said nervously.

"Us as well. We would like to talk with you if that's okay?" Sheldon asked.

"Yes, of course. Let's talk at the mission's house. I know Walter will be back soon. You do know he's been looking for you both again?"

"Yes. And we are trying to avoid meeting up with him. We have business to discuss and we need to get some answers before he finds us." I said.

We reached the mission's house and I immediately started to ask questions. "Isabella, do you know anything about this key?" I said as I pulled out the skeleton key from my pocket.

"I've never seen it, although, Walter has been carrying on about a missing key."

"Do you know what the key goes too?"

"No. I think I know where you're heading with these questions. Look, I don't know what he's been doing. I could care less. I serve the man and do what I need to do and then I leave the man be. I cannot stand being in his presence. So whenever I'm done serving him, I find something else to do. But I will tell you what I do know and that's he's been talking to Sniper about some mining cave, needing a key that's missing. That's all I know."

"What about a quilt that is made up like the town? Have you seen it?" Sheldon prodded.

"Now that you mentioned it, Maximus, the Foreman's butler, showed me a beautiful quilt he needed to put in the Foreman's safe."

"Do you know where the safe is?" I asked.

"No. Maximus didn't show me or tell me where the safe was, just that he needed to put it in."

"Do you know that the quilt is a map to the mines?" Sheldon inquired.

"Like I said, I don't really know anything. I'm sorry. These questions are a waste of time. But I have some important questions of my own."

"Okay, what do you want to know?" Sheldon asked impatiently.

Isabella drew in a deep breath and let it out fast as she spoke, "I want Jesus to be my friend like He is to Maximus and you, Sheldon."

Sheldon was surprised. "Wow! Isabella, that's awesome that you want to receive Christ. May I ask how you came to this decision?"

Isabella smiled big and said with excitement, "Maximus, when he was here, talked to me about Jesus. I liked hearing how wonderful Jesus is." She looked down sheepishly and continued, "I've been sneaking into Walter's office and reading the Bible."

"Isabella, that's so brave of you." I said. I was so elated for her.

"I can't explain it but, when I read the words that are written in that book, something happens to my heart."

Sheldon and I both grinned and simultaneously said, "Oh, we know what you mean." Sheldon quickly reached for Lisa Marie's Bible. "Isabella, I want you to understand that not only do we need Jesus to be our friend, we need Him first to be our Savior." Sheldon said.

Isabella tilted her head and scrunched up her forehead in confusion. "What do you mean, Savior?" She giggled shyly and continued, "Do I need to be saved from something?"

I kind of chuckled. Isabella's innocence was so sweet and endearing which made leading her to Christ that much more special. I said, "Yes, Isabella, there is something to be saved from— eternal death."

Isabella's face turned serious. "Oh um, yeah, that would be something."

Sheldon opened the Bible and said, "For the wages of sin is death, but the gift of God is eternal life in Christ Jesus our Lord. For all have sinned and fall short of the glory of God. But to all who did receive him, who believed in his name, He gave the right to become children of God."

Isabella blinked repetitiously to hold back tears. "I have sinned greatly." She covered her mouth and began to sob.

I got up and sat next to her. I put my arm around her and said, "Oh Sweetie, it's going to be okay."

"No! You don't understand. I've been in an inappropriate relationship with Walter and now I'm pregnant. And I can't stomach the thought that I helped killed Henry." She plopped her head on my shoulder and wept. Her body violently shook as she squeezed my arm.

Sheldon scooted to the edge of the couch and gingerly placed his hand on hers and said, "Isabella, God created man in His own image because He wanted to have a relationship with His creation. He loves us that much. When Adam and Eve ate of the tree of the knowledge of good and evil, they sinned against God. At that moment, man's relationship with God was separated. Man was in threat of eternal death. Now that's sinning greatly.

"But God put a plan together to bridge that gap between Him and His creation. Jesus said, 'I am the way, and the truth, and the life. No one comes to the Father except through me.'

That is when God chose to leave His Heavenly throne and came to earth as the ultimate sacrifice in building that bridge. The Bible says, 'In the beginning was the Word, and the Word was with God, and the Word was God. He was with God in the beginning. The Word became flesh and made his dwelling among us. We have seen his glory, the glory of the One and Only, who came from the Father, full of grace and truth.' Jesus became the ultimate sacrifice when he died on the cross for our sins. But Jesus overcame death when He rose from the dead."

I grabbed a hold of her face and looked intently into her eyes and said lovingly, "I want you to know that Jesus carried that cross with you on His mind, Isabella, because He loves you. He doesn't want anyone to perish. He wants you to be with Him for all eternity.   And He is standing here waiting with open arms to receive you."

"Jesus still loves me after everything I've done and will allow me to have Him as my Savior?" Isabella cried.

"Absolutely, all you have to do is ask for forgiveness of your sins and confess with your mouth that Jesus Christ is Lord; and believe in your heart that God raised him from the dead, and you will be saved." Sheldon said, as he patted her hand for comfort.

"Okay, I want to confess, Jesus is my Savior."

"We'll lead you in a prayer." Sheldon said.

I held her hand and wrapped my arm around her.   Sheldon scooted even closer.

Isabella cleared her throat and repeated what Sheldon said, "Dear Lord Jesus, I know that I am a sinner, and I ask for your forgiveness. I believe You to be the Son of God who rose from the dead. I turn from my sins and invite you into my heart. Have Your way in my life and I will trust in You.   I chose to follow You all the days of my life. In Your Name, Jesus Christ, amen."

Isabella looked up and smiled as she wiped her eyes. "Thank you both so much. I feel so much better inside. I can't explain it, but I feel free. I finally feel like I can breathe easier."

We all three hugged.

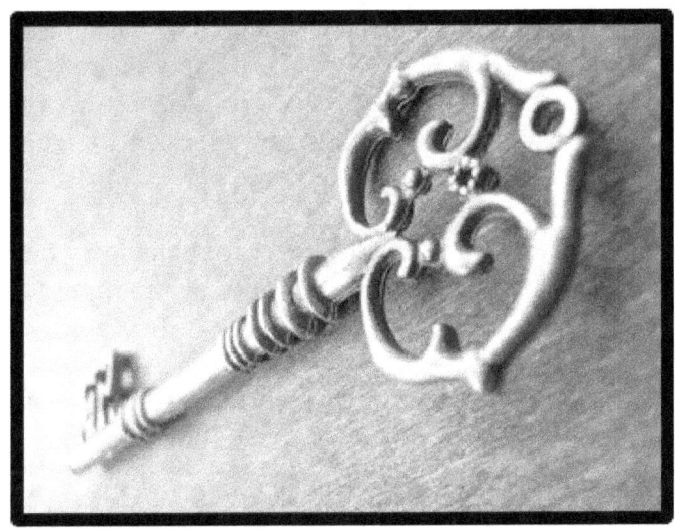

CHAPTER NINETEEN
The Prayer Meeting

Walter didn't sleep well. He had tossed and turned all night rehashing the dream he had when he first came to Chesterville. He roughly threw back the covers and quickly got ready. He learned through a source that some of the town's people where having a prayer meeting in the morning and he wanted to be ready to shut them down.

While he was dressing, his hands trembled. He didn't feel like his confident self. His heart was beating faster than usual. His throat tightened and his mind raced.

I've really messed up this business deal. If I don't get that key back today, I'm a dead man. I've always been able to get the job done. Why is this one any different? I feel so incompetent and every time I turn around something goes wrong. Why? Walter fixed his tie in front of the mirror.

"Your people are turning against you." A raspy voice said from behind.

Walter looked past his tie and saw a silhouette figure leaning in his doorway. "Boss, I didn't hear you come in."

"I'm disappointed in you Walter. I thought you would have had the diamonds by now? Callaway is getting impatient. And why are you allowing this Abigail Banderas to be a thorn in our sides?"

"I... I... I'm not sure. She's been complicating things and it's been taking extra time." Walter stuttered out of fear.

"I thought you made it clear to the people who they were dealing with?"

"Yes, I have."

"Then what's the problem?"

Walter swallowed hard and couldn't answer the question.

The Boss took a step forward into the bathroom and met Walter's eyes. It was the first time Walter really saw what his boss looked like. The Boss' eyes were pale, cold and empty. His face was so sunken in that his cheek bones were protruding out.

"Don't they know we are doing this for them and for you as well? You see, it's always been about them. They needed a shepherd to guide them. To help put them on the right path. You are that shepherd. And once again, they are going astray. They are following the Banderas woman instead of you. You need to know that once Damion gets the diamonds, things will be better for us all." the Boss said.

The Boss moved in. His eyes grew angry. "You incompetent fool. I will put an end to this today if you don't produce the goods. I will do to you what I did to your mother."

Walter was stricken with fear. "I won't let you down, Boss. I'm on my way to take care of the problem now."

"Yesss. Yesss you are." The raspy voice hissed like a snake.

Walter looked down at the sink and then into the mirror at the door. The Boss was gone. He quickly went to look for Isabella to see who called and to contact Sniper and his Elite team to intervene in the prayer meeting.

Walter came rushing down the stairs and around the corner. He noticed the main bathroom light was on. He peeked in to see if Isabella was in there, but found it empty. His eyes darted around and just as he was getting ready to turn off the light, he saw something sticking out of the garbage.

He knelt down and pulled it out. "She's pregnant." He whispered. A noise coming from down the hall startled him. He left the bathroom to investigate.

****

After she heard the front door slam, Isabella snuck into the library to read the Bible again. Several Psalms she read said God is her helper in time of need. Her eyes fell on one particular Psalm and she wondered if God was talking to her like Sheldon had told her he does through his word. It was Psalm 55: 22-23. "Cast your cares on the Lord and He will sustain you; He will never let the righteous fall. But you, O God, will bring down the wicked into the pit of corruption; bloodthirsty and deceitful men will not live out half their days. But as for me, I trust in you."

"There you are. What are you doing?" Walter snapped.

Isabella froze. She looked at his Bible in her hand and panicked. "I... I thought you left." Isabella said fearfully.

Walter moved into the room and ripped the Bible out of her hands. "So is this what you've been doing behind my back?"

She pointed at the Bible and yelled, "God is nothing like you say! And, and you are not His disciple! A true disciple is one who shows love, mercy, and kindness. You, Walter Lovit, are a wicked, wicked man!"

Walter pulled back his hand to slap her, but stopped. "Go ahead and hit her. She deserves to be punished." Sniper said.

Walter spun his head around to see Sniper, Blake and Jethro standing in the room. He looked back at Isabella. Her mouth was set straight and hands on her hips as if she was ready to fight.

"Has everyone gone mad?" Blake asked.

"No. They've just forgotten their place with the Foreman." Jethro said.

"So are you going to stone her?" Sniper asked.

Walter grabbed a hold of Isabella's arms and seethed, "Why did you betray me?" He shook her hard.

"Ow! Walter, you're hurting me." Isabella cried.

Walter let her go, but forced her to sit on a couch. Isabella was shocked to see a deep sorrow come over his face. He stood looking at the floor mumbling as if he didn't know what to do and then he began to pace.

"Sir, I don't mean to rush you, but we need to go." Blake said.

Walter ran his hands through his hair and roared, "Out! Everyone out!" Walter's anger was so frightening to Isabella that she ran toward the front doors.

"And just where do you think you're going Lil' Missy?" Sniper said as he stopped her from exiting the house. "I'm sure the Foreman wants you to stay put!" The three men looked at her with predator's eyes. She quickly turned and ran up the stairs.

"Ugh!" Walter yelled as he violently swept everything off his library desk. "Why? Why did she have to break the rules? I don't want to have to punish her." Walter slid down on the floor and began breathing heavily with rage as he thought of how deeply Isabella's betrayal had cut. His mind became cloudy and he could faintly hear his father's voice.

"Anyone who breaks the rules must be punished, no matter who they are or how close they are to you. You need to show them who's boss. No mercy to the weak."

Walter curled up in a fetal position and wept bitterly, "What have you done, Mom? Why did you break the rules? Mom! Oh, Isabella you've betrayed me. Mom, you've betrayed me! Isabella, how could you? I love you."

Walter sat up and held his head as the hot tears fell. Dazed with grief as to what to do, Walter kept repeating himself as he rocked back and forth. "I have no choice. I have no choice. Those who break the rules must be punished."

Jethro lightly tapped on the door and opened it slightly. The other two men followed behind. Sniper ran up to Walter and knelt down beside him. Walter's eyes were wild and swollen as he sat in a stupor, staring at nothing.

Sniper looked at Blake and Jethro and whispered, "I've never seen the Foreman like this. He gently pulled Walter to his feet. "Sir, are you all right? Why are you calling for your mother?"

"You need to pull yourself together, Foreman." Jethro said.

He straightened out his unruly hair and said wearily, "What you've just witnessed doesn't leave this room. Do I make myself clear?"

"Yes Sir." The three men agreed.

"Do you plan to punish Isabella?" Jethro asked hesitantly.

Walter stood silently staring at the black Bible that was lying on the floor. As much as he felt betrayed, he didn't want to punish her. He loved her and he didn't want anything to happen to her, especially after finding out she's pregnant. He spun on his heels and said firmly, "We have bigger business to worry about."

As they were about to leave, Isabella slowly descended the steps. Their eyes met. Isabella didn't understand why Walter was so tear struck. She almost felt sorry for him.

In a low weary voice he said, "You're coming with me today."

****

"Abigail, Sheldon, I think everyone is here. Maybe we should begin the prayer meeting?" Lisa Marie said after everyone was gathered in the Sunkissed Hotel's large banquet room.

I was surprised to see Marco. Lisa Marie said he wasn't a believer, but was interested in what we had to say and how we were going to take back the town. I also saw several people that I hadn't met yet who lived on the outskirts of town.

"I would like to begin by saying..."

The door swung open and my heart skipped a beat, afraid it was the Foreman with the Elite. I was pleased to see it was Trudy. "I'm sorry I'm late."

I went up to her and gave her a hug and said, "I'm glad you decided to come."

Trudy squirmed in my embrace a little but allowed me to hug her. "It's time," she said.

I knew what she meant. It was time for it all to be over.

"Thank you, everyone, for coming," I said as people found their seats. We called this meeting because Sheldon and I believe Callaway has sent Foreman Lovit here to find diamonds so he could recreate, possibly, another type of GMO's."

I saw Trudy's face go white with shock and fear. "Abigail, do ya know that fer a fact? Where's ya'lls proof?"

"The only evidence we have is a quilt and a golf-ball sized diamond we found in the Foreman's office safe." I said.

"What does the quilt have to do with diamonds?" Marco asked.

"The quilt is a map to an underground mining facility." Sheldon said.

"A quilt, that's a map and a diamond doesn't prove anything." Marco stated.

"Marco, Sheldon dissected a locust and discovered that diamonds are their fuel. We're afraid that's what the Foreman wants the diamonds for. And this is how we found the Foreman's office." I held up the key.

Several people in the room gasped. Trudy's eyes got big. Marco rubbed his jaw with his hand and Margo slapped Tony and said, "I told you so. She's here to help save us."

I could tell by the look in Trudy's eyes that she seemed upset. "Ya mean ta tell me that ya'lls had the key all along? Do ya know how many of us have suffered because of that key?"

"Yes, Trudy and I'm very sorry. We believe Damion has placed Foreman Lovit here to keep this town under his control so he can work on finding the diamonds. By placing you all in fear of him, he keeps all of you oppressed and distracted.

This is an example of Satan's strategies. He will use an earthly circumstance as a catalyst for spiritual gain. We all know that our fight is not against flesh and blood, but against the powers of this dark world. He's just as much after our souls as God is, but for all the wrong reasons, of course."

"Abigail, so are ya sayin', this whole charade of Damion and the Foreman holdin' us captive and busyin' himself with the diamond mines is a tactic of Satan ta steal us away from God?" Trudy asked.

"Yes. Because, if he can do that, he will not only rob you of eternal life, he will rob you of your God-given purpose." I said.

Trudy's jaw hung low as she looked down. I saw a few tear drops sprinkle onto the floor. I heard Trudy whisper, "It was all a lie. He tricked me."

Marco raised his hand to speak. "This is all speculation. You guys think they are looking for diamonds and you 'believe' they'll use them for more locusts, but where is your real evidence? Because to me, a quilt that's a map and a big diamond still doesn't prove Damion is going to make more GMO's. Does anyone have any proof of this knowledge?"

Marco addressed the group and no one said a word. Tony and Margo looked at one other, and Trudy had the look as if she was hiding something. All the others simply shook their heads 'no'.

"You can't just go up against a powerful group like this based on assumptions and spiritual feelings. You have nothing and you've wasted my time." Marco said as he stood to leave.

Sheldon stood and reached out for his arm. "Marco, this is why we called everyone, and that's to seek God's help and wisdom to know what to do. You and I both know we can't live like this anymore. Aren't you tired of him taking your liquor, bossing you around and making you do things you don't want to do? I know where you stand with God, but it wouldn't hurt to see what He has to say."

Marco's shoulders drooped down. "I am tired of being held prisoner in my own town and saloon. I'm not much of a praying man, but I will support whatever needs to be done." Marco said.

Tony, Margo, Trudy, Lisa Marie and the others stood and said, "We will too."

"Great!" Sheldon said as he clapped his hands.

"Shall we pray, then?" I asked. "I feel we should pray on our knees as a tangible way to honor God."

Everyone knelt as I led in prayer. After a few moments of meditation I heard Sheldon clear his throat and felt him touch my shoulder. "I believe the Lord has something to say." Sheldon whispered. I nodded.

Sheldon opened Lisa Marie's Bible and began to read. "If my people, who are called by My name, will humble themselves and pray and seek My face and turn from their wicked ways, then will I hear from heaven and will forgive their sin and will heal their land."

Marco took to his feet and angrily said, "What! Turn from our wicked ways? We didn't do anything wrong here! We're the victims..." Marco pointed at the door and continued. "He's the one that needs to humble himself, not us."

Sheldon, still on his knees, began to weep as the Lord continued to speak to him. "Marco..." Sheldon began. "I know you may not understand but if you would be kind enough to hear what the Lord is saying then maybe you will."

Marco crossed his arms and set his mouth straight.

"Marco, are you familiar with the story in the Bible where Moses led the Israelites out of Egypt and they wondered around in the desert for forty years?" Sheldon asked.

Marco rolled his eyes and said, "Kindof."

Sheldon flipped to a different page and read, "Remember how the Lord your God led you all the way in the desert these forty years, to humble you and to test you in order to know what was in your heart, whether or not you would keep His commands. He humbled you, causing you to hunger and then feeding you with manna which neither you nor your fathers had known, to teach you that man does not live on bread alone but on every word that comes from the mouth of the Lord. Your clothes did not wear out and your feet did not swell during these forty years. Know then in your heart that as a man disciplines his son, so the Lord your God disciplines you."

Sheldon continued, "What I feel the Lord is saying, is that through these past four years we have been tested. Prior to then, we were going strong for the Lord, sharing the gospel, allowing the Holy Spirit to flow, spending time with Him in prayer. Life seemed easy and at peace. Sure it's easy to praise God when all is well, but what happens when a storm comes? Will our house stand because we've built it on a rock or will it sink in the sand? I believe God wanted to test us to see what was in our hearts. Through test or trials, will we still love, serve and obey Him?"

Sheldon looked up at Marco with a tear streaked face and said, "Father forgive me for letting my fellow brothers and sisters down by stopping the spread of Your good news. Forgive me for being afraid of what mortal man can do to me rather than trusting in You. Forgive me, as a servant of the living God, for not gathering Your people to unite in unity to seek Your help in the power of Your Name. Forgive me heavenly Father for being complacent, for laying down my armor and not fighting the battle. Forgive us Lord for not seeking Your face. Thank you Lord, for truly showing us what was in our hearts—fear, fear of man, complacency, a lack of trust, lack of faith and pride."

Sheldon looked toward the door and wept hard. "Father, I forgive Walter A. Lovit for murdering Katie." He paused to catch his breath before he continued. "And I forgive him for all that he has done to the town's people. I ask Father that you will in some way call him into your kingdom.

Father, forgive us of our sins. Bring us back to our first love, which is You. Help us to put You first and to trust You. Make our faith strong again by tearing down the stronghold that is fighting against us. Please hear our cry and deliver us from captivity."

Margo cried, "I'm sorry for cowering under persecution instead of taking a stand and for not trusting in You. And forgive me for making my possessions more important than You. I, too, forgive Walter Lovit for all that he's done."

With my eyes still closed I could hear many voices offering up their forgiveness. But I couldn't keep them closed for long. I had to see where Marco stood with God. I tilted my head slightly and opened my eyes slowly. Marco was standing looking dazed as if seeing the reflection of his own heart.

I saw Trudy wide-eyed and limp as if she was lost in her own realization.

Sheldon wiped his face with his sleeve and closed the prayer, "Father, like Abigail said, this is a holy war. So, we, Your people who are called by Your name, ask You in the name of Jesus Christ to go before us in battle, for the battle belongs to You."

Everyone said, "Amen."

CHAPTER TWENTY
Dry Bones

I heard the front door slam and before I could move, I felt the Foreman pull me up by my hair. "I hear you have my key and I want it now! Where is it, Banderas?" Walter screamed.

Even though the pain was intense, causing me to wince, I refused to tell him where the key was, for everyone's safety.

"Maybe this will help." Walter said as he pulled out a gun and pointed it at my head.

Everyone in the room froze except Trudy. She lunged forward as if trying to protect me. I couldn't help wonder why she would place herself in danger like that.

"What? Wait. What are you doing?" Walter barked as he pointed the gun at Trudy.

"Leave her be, Walter!" Trudy yelled. She looked at me with longing and terrified eyes.

"Go sit down." Walter said as he pushed her down and placed the gun on my forehead.

"Walter, no!" Trudy shouted.

Walter looked confused and kept his eyes on Trudy. "What's wrong with you? She's a complete stranger. Why on earth would you care that I'm holding a gun to her head?" He paused and then he smiled wickedly. "The only reason you would act this way is if she is of value to you."

Trudy swallowed hard as her eyes darted around the room in shame. Walter's smile grew bigger as he said, "Don't tell me the apple doesn't fall far from the tree?"

I looked at Trudy with surprise.

She looked at me and said, "She's my daughter. Please, Walter, you've taken everythin' away from me. Don't take her ta."

The news of Trudy being my mother came at me like one getting injected with a shot. The mixture of feelings ran through my heart. I was confused, angry, dumbfounded and most of all speechless. Tears flooded my eyes. I wanted to freeze this moment and have her explain everything to me, but I had a gun to my head.

"Well, well, well, isn't this the icing on the cake." Walter said as he cocked the gun and pressed it hard into my temples.

"Foreman, please. Just leave her alone." Sheldon begged.

Walter laughed and waved his gun around. "Oh, come on here people. What? Are you her brother? Or, oh let me guess, you have a thing for her." He snorted and then placed the gun back to my temples, "Leave her alone? No! I don't think so."

My eyes met Sheldon's. I could see his genuine concern for me. I didn't want to see him hurt again, so I thought I would do what was best for all of us. "Fine, if you're so intent on having your stupid key, I'll take you to it." I said, as I tried to free myself from his vice-like grip.

"Abigail, no!" Trudy shouted.

Sheldon stood and moved toward us. "You don't have to do this, Abigail," he pleaded.

"And just where do you think you're going? Take a seat. You know, ever since the day I met you, you have gotten on my nerves. Well, today is that last nerve. I've wanted to do this for a long time. Get back down on your knees, Jesus freak."

"Please don't, Foreman. I will take you to the key, I promise. There's no need to hurt him. I'll cooperate. Let's go right now." I begged.

Walter kept his eye on Sheldon and said, "I see the table has turned. You both have feelings for one another. How cute, one trying to rescue the other; all for the sake of love. I personally think love is over rated." Walter's eyes darted over to Isabella. "But then again, love isn't love if it's not given in return, is it?" Isabella looked away.

"So what would you say, Jesus freak, if I told you the only way to save your life and the woman you love, is to renounce Christ as your Savior?"

"I would tell you to shoot," Sheldon said bravely.

"Then so be it." Walter pulled the trigger.

"Oh, dear God! No! Sheldon!" I screamed.

Everyone in the room screamed and cried out. Praise be to God. The gun didn't fire. Walter kept trying to pull the trigger, but the gun wouldn't work.

"I've got my gun, Sir." Sniper said as he pulled out his.

Trudy piped up and said, "Well, ya can't blame this one on the rain."

Walter's eyes burned with anger. "Shut up! I suggest all of you keep your mouths shut!"

Walter's outburst caused Margo to bury her head into Tony's shoulder. Tony placed his hand on her head for comfort. Lisa Marie flinched at Walter's icy cold stare as he looked around the room. Marco sat in silence with his eyes to the ground. Everyone else kept their eyes to the floor.

"Sir, do you want me to shoot Sheldon?" Sniper offered.

"No!" Walter snapped. "We'll keep him as leverage in case Miss Dreamy-eyes over here forgets her promise. Blake, Jethro, you two stay here and tie them all up and then meet up with us in the mining cave. Sniper, Isabella you come with me."

Walter gripped my left arm hard and pulled me to the door. Trudy and I met eyes. I wanted desperately to reach out to her, but the Foreman dragged me outside. "Where is the key Abigail?" Walter screamed.

I wasn't sure what to expect. I wasn't even sure what to do. "Lord, give me a plan." I prayed under my breath. "It's in your office." I said.

Walter scowled at me as if he was confused, but he pushed forward dragging me toward the mansion.

Sniper entered the house first, followed by Walter, who tossed me inside like a rag doll. He then pushed me into his office. I had to smile at God, because the moment I stepped foot in his office, I knew what He wanted me to do.

"I've looked everywhere in here. It's not in here! You're stalling," Walter seethed. "Tell me, why would you be so stupid to hide it in my office, if it's truly in here?"

I walked over to his desk ignoring his question. "Have you looked in here?" I asked as I quickly picked up the square box full of push pins and paper clips.

Walter and Sniper moved closer to the desk. Once they got close enough, I threw the box of push pins and paper clips at their faces. I grabbed the chair and rolled it hard at their knee caps causing them to lose their footing. I reached into my pocket and unlocked the hidden door and closed it behind me, with key in hand.

The door slammed shut as Walter tried grabbing it. Out of rage, he pounded his fist on the door wall and said, "She's locked in."

"Now what do we do, Sir?"

Walter laughed wickedly, "She'll make her way to the mining cave. We'll meet up with her at the other end. Bring the truck around."

"Yes, Sir."

****

Marco strained himself to reach inside his right boot. He slowly and carefully pulled out a switch blade. "Hey, Sheldon," he said as he tossed the knife over to him.

"Thanks Marco, you're a good man." Sheldon cut himself free and then cut Lisa Marie free.

"Sheldon, don't worry about us. You need to help Abigail. I'll untie everyone else. Now go!" Lisa Marie said.

Sheldon was about to head out the door when Trudy anxiously reached for him. "Sheldon ya need ta save Abigail. It's real important that ya do."

Sheldon looked deep into Trudy's eyes. She looked worried as tears ran down her face. "That's what I'm gonna go do."

Trudy pulled him in tighter and said firmly, "I mean it. Ya'll save her fer me right?"

"Yes," he said impatiently. Sheldon got the feeling that there was still more to Trudy's urgency for saving Abigail.

"Well, then I know of a quicker way ta the mines. I'll show ya."

Trudy took Sheldon to the General Store. Behind her counter, Trudy grabbed an old ice pick. "You're going ta need this ta open the doors frum the other side."

Sheldon looked at it.

"I use ta use it when I was a kid ta find out what my father was up ta. Ya can use this ice pick ta open the doors frum the other side without needin' the key. Ya have ta feel yall's way until ya hit the push button. Push it in and twist right.'

"Thanks Trudy. I owe you one."

"No. It's time I owe everyone else. Consider ya'self the first. And save Abigail." Sheldon gave Trudy a confused expression. "I'll explain later."

Trudy took Sheldon into the house and behind her curio cabinet was a secret passage way. "Once ya git down the steps ya can either take a right, which leads ta the mansion or take a left ta head toward the openin' of the cave."

"Gotcha."

"Oh and one more thin', Sheldon, be careful."

"Thanks again, Trudy."

Trudy switched the lights on and watched Sheldon reach the last step before she closed the curio cabinet. He wasn't sure which way to take. He looked to the left and to the right. He went right in hopes that Abigail would head his way.

****

"Abigail!"

I heard what sounded like Sheldon's voice yelling my name. *Great! I'm going to be rescued.* "Sheldon, I'm over here!" I yelled.

"Keep yelling and I'll follow your voice."

After a few minutes of yelling, Sheldon finally found me. "Why did you go this way?"

"I wanted to see if there was another way out."

"Well, obviously it appears to be another dead end. Or did you happen to see another hidden door?" Sheldon said sarcastically as he looked at the rock pile I was in.

"I'm not sure. What do you think?" I said, as I pointed to a small crack in the door.

Sheldon strained himself to look inside the opening. "Well I'll be." he said.

"What? What is it that you see?"

Sheldon looked at me and said, "A room full of diamonds."

"For real?"

"Yep."

"And I have the key to open the greatest treasure."

Just then we heard the Foreman and Sniper's voices echoing through the tunnel. At the moment, there was only one door separating us and it had been left open from when Sheldon and I were last down here.   It was too corroded to close. We needed to get to the bookshelf door and close it before they reached us.

"Oh man, we gotta go."

"If we go back to the office, aren't we locked in?" I yelled.

Sheldon yelled back, "We were wrong. The key can unlock it from the inside."

"You mean the whole entire time we were searching for a way out we could have gotten out through the office door!"

"Yeah."

I was frustrated to hear that. By the time we reached the bookshelf door, the Foreman and Sniper were hot on our tails. Sheldon pushed the ice pick in the door and twisted right.   We barely squeezed through when the Foreman reached out for me.

I pinned his arm in the door sending him screaming. It made him clench onto the door even tighter. Sheldon and I hurried up the stairs to the Foreman's office.

"When I get my hands on you, Sheldon, you're a dead man!" Walter yelled from the bottom of the steps.

I quickly unlocked the door with the key and we both scrambled out. Within a fraction of a second, we heard a gunshot go off. The Foreman fell into the door face down.

"Foreman, I'm so sorry," Sniper said as he knelt down beside him.

Walter moaned, "You're a fool, Sniper."

Sniper looked up at the two of us. "It was an accident. I swear it. I tripped coming up the steps and I accidently shot him in the back."

I was glad of it. What Sniper had done reminded me of the stories in the Bible where God had thrown confusion into the camp of the Israelites' enemies and they, in turn, killed one another.

Sniper dragged the Foreman further into the office and propped him up against a wall.

"Come on, Sheldon, let's go," I said. I was afraid Sniper would shoot us. We turned to leave.

"Oh, man, he's losing a lot of blood. I think he's dying." Sniper said sadly.

"Won't Blake and Jethro be here shortly? Maybe they can offer you some help?" Sheldon asked.

"No. There was a tunnel cave-in. I believe them to be dead.

"Come on, Sheldon. Let's go. He got what he deserved," I said as I tried getting Sheldon to walk away.

Sheldon looked firmly into my eyes and said, "Everyone deserves a chance."

I mouthed, "What?" And then I voiced, "After everything he's done to you. You want to help him?"

Sheldon took off his top shirt and put pressure on the Foreman's back to help stop the bleeding. Despite how I felt, I knelt down beside Sheldon and was ready to help.

I saw a glimmer of surprise on Sniper's face as we knelt beside the Foreman. "Why are you helping us?" Sniper asked.

Sheldon looked a little toward my way and said, "Because it's the right thing to do."

The Foreman's eyes grew wild as he grabbed hold of my arm. "The Ruby, the eagle-it's you. You're the one in my dream and what's happening to me right now is the eagle feeding me to the..." Walter buried his face in my side. "Hideous looking creatures are coming for me. Make them go away. Make them stop gnashing their teeth at me!" he screamed.

"Who, Sir?" Sniper asked. "I don't see anybody."

Walter tried harder to hide his face with my body. "They're coming for me, just like in my dream."

Sniper whispered, "Who's he talking about? Do you see anybody?"

Sheldon looked at me and asked, "Is it possible that he could be seeing demons?"

"I believe so."

"Demons?" Sniper squealed.

"Yes, Sniper, demons. Do you know what demons are?"

"Fallen angels, aren't they?"

"Yes," I said.

"I thought they were only made-up stories."

"Oh, they're real alright." Sheldon added.

Sheldon leaned over and whispered in my ear, "Abigail, you know what's going on here. You can't just let a man..."

"I know, I know," I said sympathetically.

Walter moaned a deep raspy sigh and coughed. "Ow!" He jolted upright and yelled, "They're coming closer and they have chains." He covered his ears. "They're here to take me, they said. No, go away! Leave me alone!" He gasped for breath and continued, "It's the Boss! I've disappointed him and now he said he's here for payment."

"Abigail, we don't have much time. Do something." Sheldon pleaded.

"Walter..." I began; "...the reason you are seeing demons is..."

In a low, gurgle, weak voice Walter said, "Because of all the bad things I've done?"

"We've all done bad things. We sin every day. It's because you haven't given your life over to Jesus Christ, which has made you a child of the devil. This means you don't have eternal life. Accepting Jesus Christ gives you that. It's free. All you have to do is repent and ask Jesus into your heart, and through the power and blood of Jesus Christ we can command those demons to leave you. We have the authority to take them down. What do you say?" I asked.

Walter's eyes welled up with tears. "I think it's too late for me. My father was a warlock. When I was thirteen, my father took my mother, who was a devout Christian, and sacrificed her to Satan. I saw the demons take her. From what my mother told me, God is a powerful God and He could do anything. I just couldn't understand why He didn't save her. So I got angry at God for allowing it to happen, and I believed that Satan was the real god."

"It's never too late, Walter. God is a God of forgiveness."

"It's worth a try. But I don't know how to pray," he said as he gasped for more air.

"I'll lead you, but in order to get rid of these demons, you're going to have to repent for pride. It was pride that opened the door to a principality." I said.

Walter whispered, "You mean the Boss?"

"Yes. Once you take down the king, then all the others must follow and no longer have authority to stay."

Walter closed his eyes and said, "God, please forgive me for pride and while I'm at it, please forgive me of all the hurtful things I've done to people, for murdering, lying, stealing..."

Once Walter repented from all that he did, I continued to lead him. By commanding the spirit of pride, control and all the other things he confessed to, to leave him. I noticed Walter's countenance changed. Walter opened his eyes and looked in the direction of where he had seen the demons. "They're gone," he said and looked up at me.

I gave him a victorious smile. "That's because you belong to Christ now and He removed those demons from your life, and it's all for the sake of love." I gave him a wink.

I could tell the last words I spoke moved Walter. Despite the pain he was in, Walter wept heavily.

He lightly grabbed hold of Sheldon's arm and said, "Sheldon, I know saying sorry isn't good enough for all what I've done to you. But, I am truly sorry for the pain I've caused you. I'm sorry for murdering your Katie. Will you please forgive me?"

I could tell Sheldon was overtaken by his apology. His eyes instantly welled up with tears. It took Sheldon a few moments to find his voice. "I've already forgiven you."

Walter's breathing became shallower by the minute. Walter made sure to look Sheldon in the eyes and slowly said, "I know that must have been difficult. I want you to know, I appreciate your forgiveness. My anger toward you was only out of jealousy for your faith." Sheldon nodded.

"It's important that I talk with Isabella and Trudy. Could you please get them?" Walter asked as he coughed up some blood.

Sheldon found Isabella and Trudy at the mission's house. Out of breath he said, "Walter is dying and he's asking for both of you."

"What do ya mean 'Walter is dyin'? What happen'?" Trudy asked as she was confused by Sheldon's request.

"I'll explain on the way. I need you to hurry. He doesn't have much time. He gave his life over to the Lord and now he's asking people's forgiveness."

Isabella looked at Trudy and then at Sheldon. "I don't think I can forgive him for what he's done. He's the devil's spawn and I don't want anything more to do with that man," she said in a cold, dry tone.

"I'm glad he's dyin'. He got what he deserved," Trudy laughed heartlessly.

"Well, then, I'm certainly glad the fate of my salvation isn't in either of your hands," Sheldon said dryly.

Trudy stopped laughing and sighed out of irritation and conviction. "Fine. But I can't guarantee I'll fergive the man."

Trudy nodded to Isabella to join her. Sheldon led the way and explained how Sniper accidently shot him. When they got there, Walter was barely hanging on.

"He keeps losing consciousness. I don't know how much longer he's going to hold on." Sniper said to Trudy and Isabella.

Isabella knelt down beside Walter. With a weak hand, Walter grabbed Isabella's hand and said, "I know about the baby." Everyone in the room went completely silent. Isabella looked around and then straight to the floor in humiliation.

"Isabella, I'm so sorry I forced my love on you. I only wanted you to love me back. I want you to know I really do love you. Please forgive me for what I've done to you. I have something else to confess." Walter paused, caught his breath and then continued. "I had Maximus killed. The plane crash; he was on it."

Isabella looked at me and said, "The same one Abigail was on?"

Wearily, Walter looked my way and said, "I'm afraid so."

Isabella stood and cried, "My mother was on that plane."

"I'm so sorry Isabella. I didn't know, I swear."

"How could you!" Isabella screamed and ran out.

Trudy looked down into Walter's eyes with contempt. She hated everything about him. She looked at Sniper and said, "Thanks Snipe, fer doin' somethin' I've wanted ta do fer years."

"Come on Trudy; give the man a chance, will you?" Sheldon scolded.

Trudy rolled her eyes and reluctantly squatted down next to Walter. "Could you give us a moment alone, please?" Walter asked. Everyone left the room.

"Out of everyone, I know I've hurt you the most. And you're right, I do deserve to die. But doesn't everyone get a chance to ask for forgiveness?" Trudy didn't respond. "Please. I need to hear that you forgive me."

"Why?"

"Because it's important to me. You never deserved the things I've done. I wish I could take it all back. Tell me what can I do to deserve your forgiveness?"

"Answer me this... Why did ya do it?"

"You were the only way for me to get close to the diamonds." Walter said as he slowly put his hand in his coat pocket to touch the yellow piece of paper he had been carrying around for years.

"So ya used me. Ya never did love me?"

"Yes, I used you. I'm sorry I never really loved you."

Trudy held back her tears. She was good at burying her tears. She had Walter to thank for that. "And now look at ya, ya dyin' because of it. Was it worth it?"

"I'm not sure how to answer that."

Trudy waved her hand in the air and said, "Aw, fewy! Somehow I knew this was all about the diamonds. Is Damion going to build another army of locusts?"

Walter coughed and then whispered, "Yes. He's going to use the blueprints your dad designed. I haven't given them to Damion yet, there still in the quilt. I was waiting to find the diamonds."

"And that's why ya wanted the quilt; ta git ya'lls hands on the design. He hid the blueprints in the quilt so no one would find it. How did ya know it was in the quilt? And where on earth did ya git the key?"

"Apparently my Boss is cousins with your dad."

"That lying thief. So he's the one that stole the key frum my dad all those years ago."

"After I took the quilt from you, I opened up a seam where the Boss told me to and found the blue prints for the locusts."

"My dad only created those locusts ta help farmers with their crops. It was ta provide a future way ta pollinate organic matter ta the seeds. This was what Frank was trying ta warn me about. The Secretary of Defense hired a team of science ta come up with a toxin that could be used as a bio-warfare weapon ta use against our enemies—Korea being one of them."

"I'm afraid our surrounding countries are in danger. Damion has found a way to navigate the locusts to their precise targets. He wants to take over the world. And I was trying to help him. He needs the diamonds and the blueprints to finish the details on the locusts."

"Well, he can't have them."

Walter clutched his chest and with a raspy voice asked, "Are they down in the mines?"

"It's been a family secret all these years. I want ta keep it that way."

"I beg of you, as a dying man's last request, I need to know and then maybe I'll know if it was worth all of this."

Trudy leaned over him and whispered into his ear. Walter coughed up more blood.

Trudy came around the corner and said, "He's askin' fer everyone." And under her breath she whispered, "I certainly hope he takes the secret ta his grave."

All of us gathered around Walter. Walter was slouched over and barely breathing. He looked up slightly and said, "Sniper look, it's Jesus. He really does exist. He has his hand out for me." Sniper looked to where Walter was looking and saw nothing. Walter held out his shaky hand and it dropped as he gave up his last breath.

Sniper's eyes widened with both fear and excitement. "Sheldon," Sniper said as he fixed his eyes on where Walter saw Jesus. "With Walter being the man that he was, I believe him to have seen Jesus. I too want to ask Jesus into my heart and I'm sorry for all the things I've done. Trudy, I'm sorry for all the cruel acts I've done to you. I don't want to be a man who goes with the demons. I want to be a man who goes with Jesus when I die."

Sheldon and Sniper knelt down.

"Sniper, repeat after me, Father God, please forgive me of all my sins. I believe you died on the cross for my sins and I ask you, Jesus Christ into my heart. I give you my life and I ask that you shape and mold me into the person You want me to be. I thank you for Your forgiveness and for giving me eternal life. Amen!"

As I sat there listening I felt ashamed of myself. I knew it wasn't the place to break out in tears, so I got up to go sit out on the porch. I had to deal with my own prideful feelings along with knowing I would have left Walter to die. Sheldon's example of a strong Christian man showed me I still have much to learn.

Suddenly my mind shifted to Trudy—my mom. "Trudy, I feel we need to talk." I said, as I rested my hand on her arm.

"How about we go ta the General Store ta talk, it would be more private."

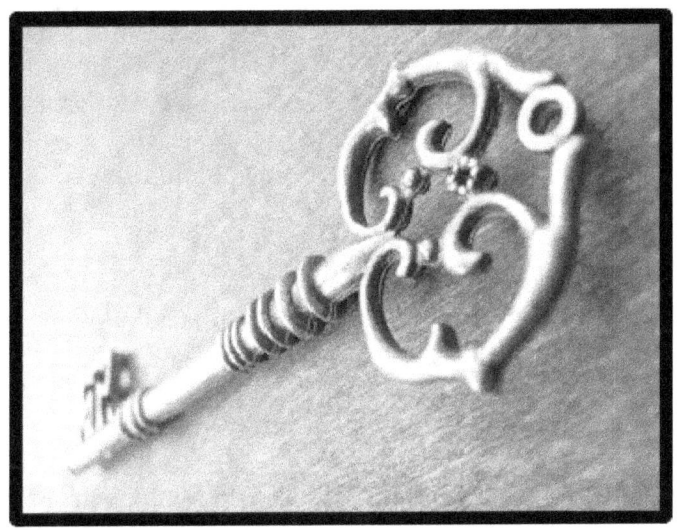

CHAPTER TWENTY-ONE
True Identity

We walked in silence. Yet my mind was loud with many thoughts.

"I know I have a lot of explainin' ta do." Trudy said, as she held the curtain open for me and I went and sat on the couch. And we both sat in silence. Finally, Trudy spoke. "So, did ya see it?"

"See what?"

"The diamonds?"

I paused to think. And then I smiled and said, "Sheldon and I both did."

"Well, I guess it's time fer me ta tell ya somethin', and ya'll be needin' this." Trudy said, as she took off her necklace. She held it up to the light for me to see. It was a beautiful cameo locket with a gold chain. "This was my great, great grandmother's."

"Oh Trudy, I don't think I could take such a keepsake."

"Yeah, ya can, because it rightfully belongs ta ya."

Puzzled, I asked. "What do you mean?"

Trudy blew out a deep, heavy sigh and said, "What Walter said back at the prayer meetin' is true."

"About the apple not falling far from the tree?"

"Yeah. I'm ya'lls mother." Trudy said as she blinked heavily with anticipation and yet was reserved. Her voice grew with excitement as she began to speak. "I had a feelin' it was ya when we first met. I thought I was lookin' right at ya daddy. Ya look so much like him. Abigail, your father's name is Ted Studder."

I sat and listened. "We were high-school sweethearts. We planned on getting' married, but he died in a car accident. We both were jes barely out of our teens when he died."

My mind was reeling with so many thoughts and questions that my heart was beating so fast. I looked at Trudy, my mother, with bewilderment. "Is that why I ended up in an orphanage? You were too young to take care of me?"

"No. My sister stole ya frum me. When she came fer Ted's funeral she told me that she had jes lost her baby. I felt fer her and didn't think ta much about ya bein' in danger. Until one mornin' I woke up ta ya both bein' gone. I tried searchin' fer ya, but I wasn't able ta find ya. I'm so sorry fer everythin' ya went through."

My voice was still quivering as tears started to well up. "God had a way of taking care of me with some really good parents."

"Glad ta hear of that." She patted my hand and threw out her next words so casually as if it weren't life changing. "Ya'll also a princess."

"What!" I said.

"Silas Muir Stedman was my great-great-granddad, son of the King of Africa, which makes you a princess. Unfortunately, his wicked brother killed him and sold Silas ta the Coalition Rebel ta become a slave in the diamond mines.

Anyway, buried deep in the catacombs of the palace, in Africa, is a hidden sacred tomb that contains our family secrets, wealth and in the wrong hands, destruction. That key opens the catacomb doors, as well as ta the doors ta the diamonds below the mansion. Ya already know that the quilt is a map ta the diamonds, but what ya need ta know is that hidden securely inside the quilt is the blue prints ta a more sophisticated, GMO. We have ta keep the quilt, the blue prints, and the key out of Damion's hands."

"How?"

"By separatin' the lock frum the key. I will be givin' the quilt ta Isabella. It should be safe with her and I'm givin' ya'll the locket ta store the key in ta keep it safe."

I opened up the locket, placed the key inside and said, "I will do my best to keep it safe."

"I'm bound and determined ta keep those family secrets buried and safe. Abigail, now that ya know who ya are, I think it's time fer ya ta reclaim the throne and figure out how ta take Damion down."

"Oh Boy!" I said, as I was overwhelmed with shock. I sat for a moment contemplating what to do next. "Trudy, do you have a way I can make a phone call. It's time for me to call my parents."

Trudy looked down and said, "Nobody is ta have a phone. Foreman's rules, but yeah, I secretly have a way ta contact people."

Trudy took me into one of her bedrooms and pulled a light fixture down like a lever and a bookshelf slid open. Inside the room was a switch board on the wall. It looked very old. She sat down, placed an old fashioned headset on and cranked a gold handle around multiple times. She looked at me and asked, "What's the number?"

"555-745-2010." I said, hoping my parents were near the phone.

"It's ringing." Trudy handed me the headset and had me set at the switchboard. "I'll give you some privacy."

"Hello?"

"Mom, it's me, Abigail."

"Oh thank God. Your father and I have been worried about you. So how is it going with you and your friends?"

"I didn't make it to my friends. I was in a plane crash."

The phone went silent. "Mom can you hear me?"

"Oh dear God, are you hurt? Where are you?"

"I'm fine. I'm in a small town called Chesterville. I've met some really nice people and..." I paused. I wasn't sure how to tell my mom that I met my real mom.

"Sweetie are you there?"

"Yeah, Mom."

"Well, will you be making your way home?"

"Mom…"

"Yeah Dear?"

"I found my real mother." I said apprehensively.

Again the phone went silent. "Hello? Did you hear me, Mom?"

"Yes. Is that the real reason you left home, to find your real mother?" The tone in my mom's voice sounded worried and sad.

"No. It just so happens she lives right here in Chesterville, Idaho."

I could hear my mom sniffling and chocking back some emotions. "So I guess this means you'll be staying there?"

"For a little while, at least. I would like to get to know her. But I want you and Dad to know that I love you very much and finding my real mom doesn't change that. You will always be my mother."

My mom was slightly crying. "That's good to hear. And it is certainly good to hear that you're all right."

"Tell Dad I love him and I'll try calling another time. It's getting harder to hear you, so I think I'll let you go for now."

"I love you very much too, Sweetie. Good-bye."

"Good-bye."

Trudy came into the room and asked, "Everythin' alright?"

I smiled and said, "Yeah."

"There's somethin' goin' on up on the hill. Wanna come with and see what's all the fuss?"

"Sure."

Trudy nervously wrapped her arm around me and said, "Thanks fer acceptin' the news.   And fer me."

"It's going to take time, but you're welcome."

****

After the men of the town helped Sniper take down the stake, they placed a lamppost in its place to signify that Chesterville was now a light in the world, a city on a hill that cannot be hidden.

Sniper cleared his throat and addressed the crowd, "Before Walter died he wanted me to ask all of you for his forgiveness for everything he had done. I hope in time you can forgive him. I, too, am asking for your forgiveness for everything I've done. Toward the end, Walter found Jesus. I know for some of you that may be hard to believe, but he did see Him. Knowing that he saw Jesus, I too believed and received Jesus. Secondly, I wanted to show you how sorrowful I am by taking down the stake." he waved his hand in the direction of the lamppost.

"I hereby reinstate your reading of the Bible and the preaching of the gospel. No longer will this town be in terror of me. I also want to give back what all Walter took. Margo, you may take back all your possessions that are in the mansion."

"Why thank you, Sniper. That means a lot to me, but the Lord showed me through this that I held my possessions as an idol before the Him. So for now, they may stay there until He tells me otherwise."

Tony rested his lips on her cheek and whispered, "I'm proud of you honey."

"Trudy, I would like you to move back into your home."

Trudy looked over at Isabella who looked lost. "I'm perfectly content where I'm at. Isabella is more than welcome ta continue livin' in the mansion." Trudy said as she gave her a sympathetic smile.

Isabella's eyes ran with tears. "Thank you Trudy."

"And Marco..." Sniper began. "No longer will we take advantage of your liquor. I would like to use the Saloon in a more respectful manner. Also, I will pay you back the revenue that Walter stole."

"Thank you, sir." He paused and held up his pointer finger to initiate a comment of his own.

"Yes, Marco you have something to add?" Sniper asked.

"In light of the situation, I feel now is a good time to bring this up. Since you will be paying me back the revenue, I will be turning the saloon into a restaurant, one of my life long dreams. There will be no alcohol."

At first the crowd went silent. Everyone was looking to each other to see their response. Then all eyes were on Sniper.

"Very well, Marco. You're a good man. Excellent choice, if I do say so myself," Sniper said.

Many of the town's people cheered. Several of them congratulated him.

Again, Sniper cleared his throat loudly for everyone's attention. "Excuse me; there are just a few more things I would like to say. Sheldon, Lisa Marie, I would like for you to reopen the missions house to use as you wish. I want to build a new home for the orphans and a new church."

The crowd cheered with laughter and hooting and hollering. It proved to be a very exciting day for everyone. Several of the town's people asked Sniper more about his experience and asked him to share Jesus with them.

A man who stood in the far distance yelled out, "Nice speech! I think Sniper-Eyed Jones should be appointed as the new Foreman!" All heads turned to see the person who yelled out.

Isabella gasped, "Maximus? Is that you?"

Standing next to a tree was Maximus and another man named, Luke. They were both wearing Elite uniforms. The two men approached the crowd.

"If this funeral is over, we have business to discuss with you, Sniper." Maximus said.

"It is finished." Sniper said.

"Good. Care to join us?" Luke, the Elite, asked. Luke started to walk Sniper down the hill when Isabella stopped Maximus.

"You're alive and you're a part of the Elite group, not a Misfit?"

"I know I have a lot of explaining to do. If you would give me a few moments, I'll come see you."

Bewildered, Isabella said, "Okay, I guess."

Isabella walked away stunned and numb as lies unraveled all around her. She found herself walking toward the mission house instead of the mansion. She thought at least there she would find light at the end of the tunnel.

****

"Sniper, Luke and I should take you into custody for betraying your leader like that. Damion would be disappointed to hear that announcement you've just made." Maximus initiated.

Sniper hung his head low and pleaded, "I understand. But I'm a changed man and I'm done doing a wicked man's biding."

"I see." Maximus walked around Sniper and questioned, "Were you able to retrieve the diamonds?"

"No. And being the changed-man that I am, I would tell you." Sniper looked into Maximus' eyes and asked, "I thought you were dead?"

Maximus looked nervous as he glanced over at Luke. "Luke, why don't you go and ask some of the town's people if anyone knows anything about the hidden diamonds?" Maximus offered.

"You should start with Trudy. Walter believed she knew all about the diamonds." Sniper added. Luke headed toward the General Store.

"Listen to me carefully, Sniper, since you just gave your life to Christ, I feel I can trust you. I am really a Misfit. I went undercover to help a man by the name of Sawyer Traxton. He was a dear friend of John Callaway and he's been secretly putting a group of people together to stop Damion. You know then, that we're all in some serious trouble. We have to stop Damion from building those locusts.

I was the one that stole the key for Sawyer. I was on my way back to Washington, DC to give the key to him when I saw Jethro and Blake. I knew when I left Isabella that Walter was close to finding out what I was up to and he had threatened to kill me and Isabella if I didn't leave. It was a perfect plan anyway for me to just leave so I did.

Blake and Jethro were closing in on me and I had to get rid of the key so it wouldn't end up back into Walter's hands. I faked getting on the plane and used Isabella's mother to take the key back to me in Washington, but the plane never made it.

"Walter had Blake and Jethro plant a bomb on the plane because he knew you would be on it."

"And now the key is lost with her." Maximus said sadly. "I shouldn't have gotten Isabella's mother involved, but she wanted to help."

"It's not lost. Somehow this Abigail Banderas woman has it. Walter and I have been searching everywhere for that stupid key. That's why we haven't been able to find the diamonds. It wasn't until today that we found out Abigail has it."

"Who is this Abigail person? Does she know anything about the blood diamonds and the locusts?" Maximus asked.

"I don't really know. She just showed up one day and then everything Walter and I worked hard for collapsed. Of course I believe it took a nose dive shortly after the key went missing."

"And you believe Trudy knows more than what she's telling?"

"Yes. I saw her whispering something to Walter as he was dying, but I couldn't make it out."

Maximus sighed heavily and said, "Hopefully, Luke will be able to get some information out of her."

"You know Trudy; she's always been a tough nut to crack."

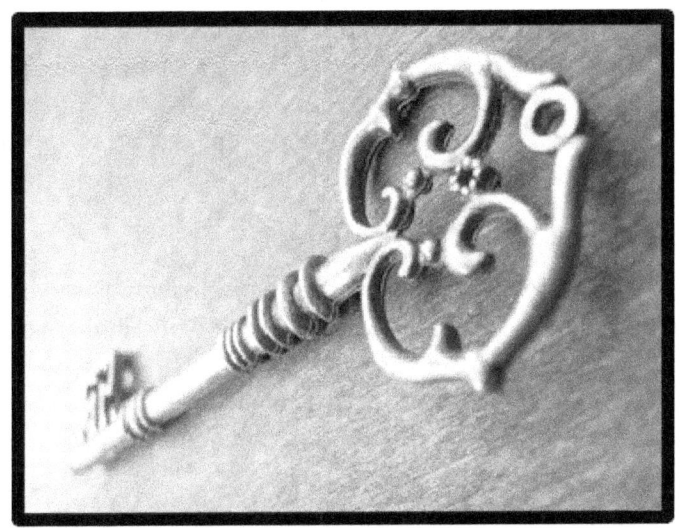

CHAPTER TWENTY-TWO
Priesthood of All Believers

Maximus headed straight for the mission's house to see Isabella and to hopefully retrieve a very valuable key.

For Isabella, seeing Maximus alive thrilled her heart and yet she was in such shock she didn't know what to think. A small part of her felt betrayed and abandoned.

Maximus got part way up the steps when Isabella met him. Her heart was telling her to run into his arms, but her flesh made her cross her arms and asked, "Where have you been? Why didn't you say good-bye? I thought you were dead, you know."

"I know I'm sorry about that. I..."

"You're an Elite?" Isabella said with disappointment.

"I can explain."

"I'm all ears," Isabella snapped as she tightened her arms around her.

Maximus walked up the last two steps, escorted her to a chair, and sat next to her holding her hands as he looked lovingly into her eyes.

"I'm not a real Elite. I'm undercover. However, Luke, my partner, is a true Elite. I need you to trust me and I will eventually tell you everything. Do you trust me?"

Isabella nodded her head as she whispered, "Yes."

****

As the front door to the mission's house swung open, we all turned to see Isabella with a tall, dark and handsome young man. The young man came right up to the edge of the couch and stood next to me. "You must be Abigail?" he asked.

"Yes." I said as I stood and held out my hand.

"I'm Maximus. Um, Isabella told me a lot about you."

I tried looking Maximus right in the eyes, but he reached out for Sheldon's hand to shake. "Good to see you again, Sheldon."

"Maximus, good to see you're alive."

He pulled me aside and whispered in my ear, "Where's the key, Abigail? I know you have it."

I whispered back, "How do I know that I can trust you? You're an Elite."

When I looked into Maximus's eyes, a flash of remembrance came to my mind. He was the one that had the key at one time, knew the safe code, and placed the quilt in there. I bet he was in cahoots with the Foreman and Damion.

Maximus ran his fingers through his black, thick hair and exhaled a deep, irritated breath. "You don't."

He was about to grab hold of my arm when Sheldon quieted everyone down and cleared his throat to make an announcement. Sheldon grinned. "Could I have everyone move outside? Lisa Marie and I have something very important to say."

While everyone was corralled outside, Maximus kept me inside for further interrogation. "You need the key to get to the quilt, don't you?" I said not letting on that I knew Trudy planned to give Isabella the quilt.

"So you know about the quilt, which means you got into the safe." He paused and then said, "The pill box. Did Meredith, Isabella's mother, give it to you?"

"Yes."

"How involved are you in this?" he asked.

"Enough to know that I don't want anyone to have the key's power to build something."

"What do you think I'm trying to do here? Abigail, I don't think you realize that this goes beyond, Foreman Lovit."

"So it does involve Damion?"

"Well, obviously you're a smart woman. That's why I would appreciate you handing over that key. Do you have it on you right now?"

I raised an eyebrow and said, "Do I look dumb to you? It's hidden in a safe place."

Sheldon waved for me to join him, but Maximus held me tight. I smiled and politely waved. I quietly whispered through tightly closed lips, "Not until you prove you're not a true Elite."

"I'm working with a man named Sawyer Traxton, who is trying to stop Damion before the world meets a new form of GMO's."

"I knew it."

"Then help me by giving me the key."

"Fine. I'll get it." I said.

"I'm going with you. I'm making sure I get the key." We jogged up the stairs and went into my room. "I didn't want to leave Isabela with Walter, but I thought trying to save the world was a little more important at the time. I knew that if I didn't get the key to Sawyer to stop Damion from getting his dirty hands on those diamonds, there wouldn't be a world to save. When I left, a storm blew in and I took refuge in a cavern. It was in there that God showed me the spiritual battle that's going on." Maximus shared as he entered my room.

"A cavern? I took refuge in a cavern. It had a lantern and drawings all over the walls. Was that from you?"

"Yeah. I hoped that after Sawyer got the key and hid the diamonds that the world would be safe and I could come back for Isabella. Now I feel really bad that I used her mother and now she's dead."

I saw Maximus trying to keep his composure as he wiped at his eyes. He choked out, "She struggled with her relationship with the Lord. I don't even know if she truly accepted Him as her Savior."

I gave Maximus a smile full of compassion and said, "God has a unique way of working things out. Just before she died, she not only gave me the pill box, but gave her life to Jesus."

He looked up at me and smiled. I opened my top dresser drawer and pulled out my little ceramic music box. "The key! It's gone." I said frantically. "After the funeral, I placed the key in the music box on top of my dresser. I didn't tell anyone where I hid the key."

Maximus rubbed his forehead and exhaled worryingly. "Abigail, seriously I need that key, and if you're lying to me."

"Maximus, I promise, I'm not lying. I can see know how important that key is."

"Who do you think could have taken it?"

"I don't know. I'm beginning to think I can't trust anyone around here."

"Sheldon or Lisa Marie maybe?"

"I honestly don't know."

We went back downstairs so Maximus could find the person who took the key. With his Bible in his hand, Sheldon raised it high into the air to silence the chattering crowd. "I just want to say thank you all for coming. As you all know, things have changed around here since the passing of the Foreman. And one of those changes is..."

Simona held her breath as her eyes grew wide with anticipation.

"Instead of building a new home for the orphans, Lisa Marie and I want to make the mission house the new home."

The crowd cheered and yelled. Sheldon nodded his excitement. Lisa Marie smiled wide as she lifted up Anna, the three-year-old, so she could see the excitement of the people. Simona jumped up and down as she clapped her hands.

Sheldon again held up his Bible to quiet the crowd. "I would like to read a scripture that the Lord gave me as confirmation that this is what we are to do. So by the word of God I decree it to be established. 'Religion that God our Father accepts as pure and faultless is this: to look after orphans and widows in their distress and to keep oneself from being polluted by the world.'"

The sea of people went wild again. Many of the town's people started to praise the Lord by lifting up their hands.

"The Lord..." Sheldon continued as he held his head high and gave me a sly smile, "...showed me two things from that scripture in James 1:27. One was the confirmation of using the mission's house for the orphans and secondly, the spiritual battle of us being polluted by the world." Sheldon paused.

"I don't know about all of you, but I certainly feel that these past four years, I have been polluted by the fear of man. And by having had that fear, I feel I have been in darkness. It has caused me to show a lack of faith and distrust in God. But even so, I believe that through our crying out to the Lord to set our town free from the clutches of that fear, God has answered our prayers. He has answered them through sending us a willing vessel to help, not only to challenge our faith, but to act upon it. I would like all of us to give God the glory for sending us Abigail. God has used her mightily to help us."

My face suddenly went flushed when the crowd cheered and yelled my name. I raised my hand to silence them and said, "I just want to say that it was all God and a group effort." I looked at Sheldon and winked.

"Victory belongs to our God!" Sheldon yelled. Everyone shouted and raised a fist to the sky in victory.

After the crowd died down Sheldon turned to 1Peter 2:9. "The Lord also led me to this scripture to share with all of you as a reminder of what He has done for us. 'But you are a chosen people, a royal priesthood, a holy nation, a people belonging to God, that you may declare the praises of Him who called you out of darkness into His wonderful light.'"

The crowd once again clapped and cheered as Sheldon closed his Bible. After everyone stopped clapping, Sheldon pulled me aside and asked, "I don't know your plans, but I feel God wants me to ask you if you would be willing to stay and help us with the orphanage?"

I smiled and thought to myself how awesome God is. To me, this was my moment of redemption. *This is just like God to use my experience to bring Him glory!* "I would love to." I said. I saw excitement rise up in Sheldon like a jack-in-the-box as he quickly hugged me and headed out into the crowd.

****

Trudy was just about to leave when a puff of warm air blew in. "May I help ya?" Trudy asked.

"I certainly hope so because I'm tired of going place to place and not getting any of my questions answered."

"Well, then I suggest ya keep movin', because I'm all out of 'em."

The man slapped the counter top hard three times and said, "No, no, no. You see, I will get my answers even if it takes me all day."

Trudy looked at his perfectly pressed Elite uniform. His hair was closely shaven to his scalp and topped off with a black beret. Trudy then looked to his face. The way the man was chewing on his gum reminded her of the way ole' Betsy, a cow she used to have, chewed its cud.

"Enjoyin' ya gum I see."

The man didn't answer. He drew down his bottom jaw and moved his gum to the other side with his tongue and said, "The name is Luke."

Trudy casually said, "I don't care that ya name is Luke. I have nothin' ta say ta ya. Now if ya excuse me, I have somewhere ta be."

Luke blocked Trudy's path as she went to leave. He placed one hand on the door and closed her in with his body. "I believe we have much to talk about. How about we have ourselves a chat, in there?" Luke nodded in the direction of the worn curtain that led into her home.

"Fine."

They both sat quietly. Luke looked around and Trudy sat with her hands in her lap to keep them from shaking.

Luke scooted his bottom all the way to the edge of the couch and leaned over and said, "Silas Stedman. Does that name ring a bell?"

Trudy kept quiet.

"I know that Silas Stedman is your great-great- grandfather. You see it was my great-great-granddad, a watch guard, that tried cutting your great-great-grandfather a deal, but he reneged on that deal by stealing the diamonds for himself—that no good, lying thief."

"I don't think my great-great-granddad was the thief."

"No?" Luke said as he faked a surprised look.

"We both know who the real thief was." Trudy said through clenched teeth.

"Those diamonds belonged to my great-great granddad. They had a deal." Luke seethed. Trudy remained expressionless and sat very still while her heart raced.

Luke smiled wickedly and shook his head. "Silas Munir Stedman, a small African boy, taken from his family to become a blood diamond mining slave under the Coalition Rebel." Luke pulled out of his pocket a decorative rectangle shaped pill box and showed it to Trudy. "Recognize this?"

Trudy's mouth contorted even more.

"Silas was too smart for his britches. Once my great-great-granddad figured out how Silas was smuggling the diamonds out for his own greedy hands, my great-great-granddad had no choice, but to put a bounty on his head.

"It was quite ingenious, actually, how Silas smuggled those diamonds. Who'd thought that by mixing the chiseled gravel from the cavern walls, a little white cement powder, and placing a few diamonds into the mixture, shaping it into a pill, and putting them in a container like this one, would get no attention from any of the guards?

According to the story that was passed down from generation to generation, once a month the younger children would be able to see their families. Silas would pass the pill box to his mother and she would give him an empty one. By the age of twenty-five, when his mother had passed away, he had escaped, taken the diamonds and headed toward the mountains.

But Silas didn't count on my great-great-granddad being on his trail. So Silas got smarter. To throw him off track, Silas hid himself up in the mountains, and married a Caucasian woman and took her last name. Apparently he had his children do the same.

Eventually, through the generations it got harder to find the African American lineage of Silas Munir Stedman. Am I telling the story right, Trudy?"

Trudy burned with anger.

Luke continued, "It wasn't until fifteen years ago when the pill box and it's so called pills showed up again under the name Capone, Jacob Capone, that we got back on track. Oh let's say, he started a very lucrative pharmaceutical company right out of Chesterville, Idaho. I'm guessing he decided to continue his great-great-grandfather's work and falsified so-called 'prescription pills' to smuggle blood diamonds for the black market."

Trudy licked her lips and said, "So now ya know. And I'm guessin' ya're continuin' ya's great-great-granddad's business, by bein' a dirty, thievin' cop... an Elite."

Luke stood, towered over Trudy and said, "I'm here to collect what is rightfully mine. Now give me the key and tell me where the diamonds are hidden!"

Trudy stood up and spat in his face and said, "I don't have the key and besides, ya need a certain quilt ta figure out where the diamonds are hidden. My great-great-granddad worked hard ta mine those diamonds and he had every right ta keep some fer himself."

Luke grabbed her arm tightly and said, "By law the diamonds belong to the Coalition Rebel and my great-great-granddad was a member of that."

"Trudy, is everything okay?" Sniper asked as he walked into her living room.

Luke turned and said, "This is none of your business, unless you have decided to get on board with Damion."

Sniper walked up to Luke, released Trudy from his grip and grabbed hold of Luke's throat. Through clenched teeth he said, "Remember, I am a highly trained killer and I won't lose any sleep tonight if I squeezed the life out of you. I may have changed, but I will do some serious damage unless you leave right now and never bother this woman again. Now she says she doesn't have the key."

Luke wiggled in Sniper's grip and choked out, "Okay. Just tell me where the diamonds are. Did Walter find them?"

Sniper let go and said, "If you want to know where the diamonds are, find Evette Lorrenzo. She's Walter's sister. A few weeks ago he mailed her a small black book that would tell her where to find the diamonds. All they needed was the key and the blueprints from the quilt."

Trudy's eyes widened as she looked at Sniper. *How could he tell Luke such important information that would lead to the findings of my family's inheritance?* Her jaw dropped with devastation. *So Walter knew all along where the diamonds were? Why did he want her to tell him on his death bed where the diamonds were if he had already known?*

"And where would I find Walter's sister?" Luke inquired.

"Washington, D.C."

Luke froze with shock. He lowered his head so they wouldn't see his facial expression on knowing the name. He couldn't believe that Evette Lorrenzo was Walter's sister, which meant Secretary of Defense, Carl Lorrenzo was her husband. He had been working very hard as to not let anyone know he was secretly in search of the diamonds for himself. After all, he believed the diamonds rightfully belonged to him. He had his own agenda for the diamonds—leverage to become the new leader.

Luke knew he had to get that black book from Evette and stop anyone from getting their hands on the diamonds. "You know this would be so much easier if you would cooperate with me Trudy, and just tell me where they're hidden." Luke seethed.

Trudy got in his face and said, "Ova my dead body."

"That could be arranged." Luke said as lunged toward her, but Sniper was quicker. "I could have you arrested for treason against Damion."

"It's time for you to go home." Sniper said as he roughly escorted Luke out of the store.

Trudy locked the door behind Luke and rested her head on the door. "Why did ya tell him how ta find the diamonds through the black book? I didn't know Walter knew where the diamonds were. That was the very last thin' he asked fer me ta tell him. If he knew already why did he ask me?"

"He didn't know where the diamonds were. I lied. I know I shouldn't have, but it was the only way to get him off your back. Searching for Walter's sister and the black book will take him a long time."

"Why is that?"

"Because he never mailed the black book to her. He lost it."

"What's in the black book?"

"It's more of a journal on the mapping of the mining cave and his thoughts of where the diamonds are hidden."

Trudy hesitantly smiled at Sniper knowing she needed to find the little black book.

****

Luke waltzed up the steps to the mission house. "There you are Maximus. I've been looking for you."

Luke glared at me as if I had just committed a major crime and said, "Did you get the key from Abigail yet?"

Maximus sighed heavily and said, "No. It is missing again."

"How convenient," Luke said sarcastically. "Maybe we'll have to put finding the key on hold for a few days. I have a new lead on the subject. Let's get out of here. I'll debrief you on the train."

Maximus' eyes glazed over as he whispered, "We can't afford to put it off."

****

Isabella replayed all of what Maximus shared. He came to Chesterville as an undercover Elite in search of the legendary blood diamonds. To her surprise, he admitted that he hadn't planned on falling in love with her, but he did and still wanted to be with her.

He also apologized for her mother's death. He told her how her mother missed her and wanted to find a way to bring her home.

Feeling exhausted with an array of emotions, she decided to head up the stairs to lie down. Casually, she looked to her left toward the dining hall. Near the baseboard, something black caught her attention.

"Hmm. I wonder what that is?"

At first glance, Isabella thought it was Walter's black Bible, but she remembered she had purposely put it back in his office, desk drawer. Wedged between the china cabinet and the wall was a little, black, leather-bound book.

She gave it a hardy tug and pulled it out from behind the cabinet. On the front was the word 'Journal' in gold letters. She opened it and saw several pages that had strange maze-like drawings. One page caught her attention and she began to read. She looked up from the page and said, "Trudy's a real princess."

The doorbell rang. She quickly hid the little black book in a linen drawer of the curio cabinet.

"Maximus?"

Maximus stood at the door and smiled sweetly. "May I come in?"

"Oh, of course."

"It's time for me to leave. Luke and I have a plane to catch tomorrow. But I wanted to see you before we left."

Isabella stood there with her shoulders slouched and head low. "I don't mean to come across rude, but you look worn out."

She looked up into his eyes and snapped, "The past four years have been very difficult on me. So yes, I am worn out!"

"I understand. And I've never intended to add to that. I had hoped to have come back for you. I've never stopped thinking of you. I love you Isabella and my wish is that you would leave with me. I would like to pick up where we left off..." Maximus lowered his head. "...if that is still a possibility?"

Isabella's heart swooned. She wanted nothing more than to be with him. Her eyes darted past him as she rubbed her belly. *What will he think of me now that I'm pregnant with someone else's child? Will he still love me? Would he want to be a part of mine and the baby's life?*

As she continued to look past Maximus at the town, she decided that whether he would want to still be with her or not, this was her ticket out of Chesterville. She decided not to tell him about the baby just yet. She wanted to wait until she was settled into a new place, a place that was far from the pain of Chesterville.

"Yes. I would like that very much. It shouldn't take me long to pack. Walter never allowed me to own many personal items."

"Speaking of items, do you know where the key is?"

"Haven't a clue. Last I heard Abigail had it."

"Well, apparently it's missing again. Hey, do you know anything about Walter having a little black book of notes? It could help us tell where the diamonds are hidden. Have you seen it around by any chance?"

Isabella stopped walking and looked to the floor, turned her head slightly back at Maximus and said, "No. The only black book I'm aware of is his Bible and that's in his desk drawer."

****

Isabella was anxious to leave, but Trudy, Lisa Marie, Margo and Abigail insisted on saying their good-byes. Trudy purposely waited to be last and handed Isabella a big box.

"Why Trudy, I do believe this is the first and only gift you've ever given me. Or is something going to jump out at me as a way of revenge?"

Trudy hugged Isabella and said, "I know I've been awful ta ya. Please fergive me fer all the mean things I've done. And I hope ya accept this gift fer ya and the baby." Isabella pulled out the quilt that Walter had taken from Trudy. "This here quilt has been in my family fer years. And I wanted ta give it ta ya and the baby."

Isabella hugged Trudy tightly. Tears welled up in both of their eyes. Trudy cupped Isabella's tired face in her hands and looked deep into her eyes and said, "Remember this, if we don't grow weary in doin' good, ya'll will reap a harvest. Fer the fruit on the apple trees is ripe fer the pickin'." Isabella squinted in confusion. Trudy smiled and played with the ruby-like apples.

Isabella's confusion suddenly left as a big broad smile came over her. "I understand." She said and thought of what she read in the little black book about who Trudy really was, what was inside the quilt and what was in the mining cave, that was still yet to be found.

CHAPTER TWENTY-THREE
The White Lamb on The Hill

"Just the man I was looking for."

Being caught off guard, Marco jumped. He turned to see Sniper walking through the door. Marco quickly looked to the floor.

Sniper walked up to him and placed his hand on his shoulder. "Marco you don't have to be afraid anymore." Sniper said as he lifted Marco's face to meet his eyes. "You are free to look me or anyone else in the eyes. I know it's going to take everyone a while to get used to doing it again."

Marco tried to relax his shoulders.

Sniper gave Marco a strong pat on his shoulder and said, "I know you're planning to start remodeling, so I came to offer some help. Where can I start?"

"You can count me in too." Sheldon's voice came from the open door as he held up his tool belt. "Now that the orphanage is taken care of, it's time for our next project."

Marco smiled and was taken aback by their kindness, so much in fact, he felt faint. "Marco, are you feeling okay? Your face looks pale and clammy. Maybe you should sit for a bit. I'll grab us something to drink."

"Good idea, Sheldon. Here Marco, let me take down some chairs for us to sit." Sniper offered.

Marco sat and worked on controlling his breathing. Sheldon had quickly returned with three colas in his hand. "I wasn't sure if you were in need of a stiff drink or a cola, but cola was all that I could find back there," Sheldon said.

Marco looked up at Sheldon. Marco's eyes were glossy and tired. "I traded all the liquor for cola. I don't want to have anything to do with booze." Marco rested his head in his hands as he rummaged through his salt and peppered hair.

Sniper placed his hand on Marco's back and asked, "How are you holding up? Are you doing okay? I know that Walter and I put you through a lot of stress."

He slowly lifted his head and in a weary voice said, "Ever since the stoning of Henry, I've been doing a lot of thinking. I keep replaying what Walter had said to me that night. 'If any one of you is without sin let him be the first to throw a stone. I know you to be an honorable man. You're definitely a man without sin.'"

Marco broke down and cried. "If I was an honorable man I should have laid down my life for Henry. I'm not a good man, Sheldon. I'm a selfish man who only looked out for himself so he wouldn't die. I care too much about my own life and not the precious life of others." Sheldon tried to speak, but Marco held up his hand for him to wait.

"Every night since Henry's stoning, I have laid awake thinking back to before the locusts came when the town was thriving financially, when the people were happy, and even when the people talked about Jesus. Yeah, I thought I was living amongst nuts and flakes, and even though some of them appeared to be fake, I admired how everyone helped each other. And then the locusts came, followed by the Foreman and the Elites. We, as a people, went to a place of darkness where nobody was happy, nobody talked about Jesus or had enough to trade. We all struggled to help each other..." Marco paused and looked at the two men who sat quietly.

"It's true what people say. You don't truly miss something until it's gone. I hadn't realized just how joyous life was in Chesterville until it was taken away. And now that life has been brought back to the town, I see a deeper picture here."

"And what's that Marco?" Sheldon asked quietly.

Tears pooled up in Marco's eyes. He swallowed back emotions. "I've learned that being a good person isn't good enough, it's about having a relationship with the One who is good."

The three men sat in silence for a moment until they heard the high pitch, chattering voices of women. "Trudy, let me help you with the door," I offered.

"I thank ya Abigail, but I can manage," Trudy said as she kicked her way through the door carrying an armful of groceries. Lisa Marie, Margo and I followed behind with meals in our hands.

Trudy set down the grocery bag and said, "Marco, us ladies figured since ya'll are in the process of remodelin', ya stove may not be up and runnin' so we took the liberty ta bring dinner fer everyone."

All four of us stood there with big smiles on our faces holding hot dishes and looking at the three somber-looking men.

Marco choked out, "I want what they have."

"Of course, we have chicken casserole, sweet potato pie, creamed corn..." Trudy sang.

Sheldon playfully cleared his throat and chuckled lightly. "Trudy, I believe he's talking about giving his life over to Jesus Christ."

Trudy looked embarrassed. We put down the dishes and gathered around the men.

"Sniper would you like to pray for Marco?" Sheldon asked.

"Could we do it together since I'm still new at this stuff?"

We all bowed our heads. After the prayer, we shared the wonderful meal and enjoyed talking about Jesus and sharing how freeing it felt to talk about Him again openly.

I looked across the table at Trudy. Her eyes were glazed over as she stared far off. She slowly got up and headed out the door.

"Trudy, where are you going?" I asked as I started to follow her. She didn't answer. She kept walking toward the hill. Directly under the lamppost was Walter's grave. Trudy was staring at it while playing with her necklace. "May I join you?" I asked.

Trudy simply nodded. I stood by her side and said nothing. Suddenly, she fell to her knees and sobbed. She was sobbing so hard that her whole body shook. I knelt down beside her and rubbed her back to let her know I was there for her. Minutes had gone by as she continually to sob uncontrollably.

Finally, Trudy wiped her face on her sleeve and said, "I haven't been able ta cry like that in years. I had built a wall ta keep my emotions at bay. Walter would always punish me fer showin' a lack of control of my emotions. He hated ta see women cryin' and carryin' on. So I learned ta shove them deep inside."

"I guess the dam finally broke," I said softly.

Trudy giggled and sniffed. "Yeah, I guess it did. Ya know I had once truly loved that man. Of course, that was before I knew what kind a man he really was. The sad thin' is I pretty much gave up everythin' fer Walter, even my walk with the Lord. I guess ya could say I sold my soul ta the devil. I feel as if I let the Lord down. I know he'll fergive me, but I jes can't get past these awful feelins'."

"Well, if you would like, I'll pray with you?"

"I would like that very much. But before we do, I have some thin's ta git off my chest."

"Okay." I said and sat down to listen.

"I'm not tryin' ta be mean but, I'm glad he's gone. Glad that he gave his life ta the Lord though. But with him bein' gone..." Trudy broke down and sobbed again. "...so is the agonizin' days of his tormentin'. Abigail, I didn't know how much more I could take of his brutal words, his cruelty and his unmerciful acts. I was gittin' ta the point where I thought I would be better off dead than alive. Why not? I was already dead spiritually. He took that away frum me a long time ago. But then I saw ya and it gave me hope."

Suddenly Trudy began to violently beat the ground. She repeatedly screamed out, "I hate him. I hate what he done ta me, and I hate who he made me ta be."

I wasn't sure what to do so I began to pray. Her screaming sobs tore at my heart. To hear the pain in her screams deeply troubled me. I knew it would take God to heal her many soul wounds.

Trudy quieted down and whimpered, "I know I need ta fergive the man." She looked up at me. "Walter must have been pretty wounded ta have done those awful thin's."

"And it's unfortunate—the enemy likes to keep a person in bondage so they will act out of those soul wounds to hurt others. It's one of Satan's ways to keep someone from living their life to the fullest." I said.

"Why didn't I ever see this? I should've known. Growin' up in the church I should've seen the signs of the enemy at work here. I think I was blinded by what I thought was love. Oh my!"

"What's wrong?"

"Well, according ta what ya tell'en me, I ta have been actin' out of my soul wounds. I've treated Isabella so poorly. It was out of jealously. I took my anger out on her because Walter chose her instead of me. I hated how he would fawn over her and punish me. Of course, I didn't treat ya very nicely when we first met either. So when I think about it, I am no better than Walter."

"I wouldn't quite put it that way. We all have soul wounds and we all react out of them. That's why it's so important to sit before the Lord daily like David. David said to the Lord, 'Search me, O God and know my heart; test me and know my anxious thoughts. See if there is any offensive way in me, and lead me in the way everlasting. Create in me a pure heart, O God, and renew a steadfast spirit within me.' It's a daily journey to ask God to heal our soul wounds, to repent of our sins and to change our ways. Don't beat yourself up. Continue to ask God for forgiveness and He will forgive."

Trudy nodded her head in agreement and whispered a prayer of forgiveness.

After she was done repenting I said, "Now we need to have God heal your soul and then we'll tell those demons to flee from you. We don't want them to enter into your heart again because they will try, by stirring up the memories, and the old feelings of hurt."

"Okay."

I laid my hand on her and said, "Father, God, I ask that You would pour into Trudy's soul Your Glory and Your Light to heal her wound."

I paused a moment to listen to the Lord to see when her soul was healed and then I commanded anger, hatred and rage to go in the Name of Jesus Christ.

After we were done praying, we held each other for a long while. She pulled me arm's length and took off her necklace and handed it to me.

I looked up at her and said, "It's the locket, but how? I hid it in my drawer and it was gone."

"I saw that Maximus was in town. I'm not sure I can trust him or anyone fer that matter, so I had Simona go and fetch it fer me. Abigail, don't trust no one with it and don't give it ta no one."

"Okay." I whispered.

****

Maximus grabbed ahold of Isabella's hand while driving with the other. "I'm glad you decided to come back with me. I've missed you."

Isabella smiled shyly and said, "Me too."

"I've found a place for you to stay until we decide to get married."

"That's great.   Thank you." She said as she cautiously rubbed her belly.

He quickly glanced her way and said, "They're really nice people, great friends of mine." Maximus pulled into a driveway and escorted Isabella up to the door of her new home.

"Evette, Secretary Carl Lorrenzo this is Isabella." Maximus said with pride.

Evette held out her hand and said, "It's so nice to finally meet you.   Maximus has told us a lot about you."

Isabella looked at Maximus with confusion.   "I thought you died, Secretary?"

Carl grinned and said, "Maximus saved me." Isabella smiled at Maximus.

"The Secretary told me that he is going to help stop Damion and advise a plan to keep things in order and in peace." Maximus said with hope in his eyes.

Evette and her husband gave each other a cunning smirk.

"Oh look honey, what a beautiful quilt." Evette said as she fingered the quilt in Isabella's hand.

"It was a gift." Isabella said.

Evette beamed as she nodded to her husband. "Why don't I show you to your room, Isabella?" Evette offered.

Carl pulled Maximus aside and asked, "Did you find the key and the diamonds?"

"Not exactly.   But I can't believe our luck. You know I have the quilt. The blue-prints should still be in there."

"What about Walter's black book?"

"Can't find that either, but now that you have the quilt, all you need is the key—the diamonds."

"Yes." Carl said with a slight irritation. "If you'll excuse me, I have some work to do in my office."

"Of course. Maybe later we could discuss what to do next."

"Yes." Carl went into his office and dialed the phone.

Damion picked up, "Do you have my diamonds?"

"No. Maximus failed to retrieve the key."

"Does he suspect that you are working for me?"

"No. He still believes that I'm trying to stop you. Damion, we may not have the key, but you'll be pleased to know, that the quilt arrived with his girlfriend."

"Great, then the plan is still in motion."

"Yes."

"And Abigail?"

"It's already being taken care of."

"Good. I knew I could count on you."

****

"Would you like to go for a walk with me? There's something I would like to talk to you about." Sheldon asked as he escorted me out of the mission's house.

I smiled, "I would love to. Are we going for another mine ride?" I teased.

Sheldon gave me a boyish grin and nervously laughed. "No. I've learned my lesson. I think we should stay clear of anything that moves." We both giggled.

"Are you okay, Sheldon?"

"Um... Yeah... I... Um..."

"You want to ask me something?"

Sheldon swallowed, placed his hands in his pockets and looked at his feet. "Abigail, now that you will be staying, I was wondering if you would give me the honor of courting you."

Courting? I thought. *Was I ready for marriage?* I was speechless. I think Sheldon saw the shock on my face because he grabbed my hands.

"Abigail, it's no secret that I'm falling in love with you. Now, I can't promise I'll never hurt you, because I'm human. But I can promise you this; I will never cheat on you, and I will work hard at being the godly man God has called me to be. I will love you as Christ loved the church." He sweetly smiled and then shook his head.

"What?" I asked.

"I remember telling God I never wanted to fall in love again and here I am."

"That's funny, because I told God that very same thing."

Sheldon grinned and said, "I guess God had other plans."

I squeezed his hand said, "And I certainly would love to be a part of that plan."

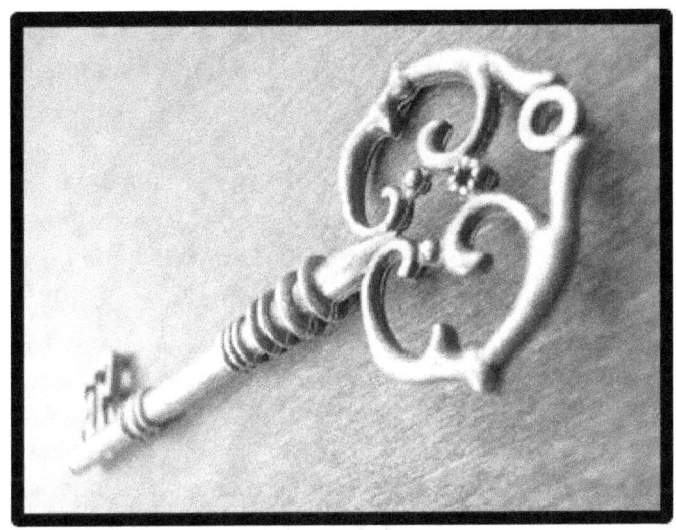

MY TESTIMONY OF FORGIVENESS

May I get personal with you? What you are about to read, I mean with all of my heart! So I would like for you to pretend I am sitting across from you looking into to your sweet eyes. The very joy of my heart is to see people get set free from the wounds in their soul. I want YOU to be set free!

As we're looking intently into each other's eyes, I want you to know that Jesus loves you. You are highly valued. You are the apple of God's eyes. You are highly favored. God has engraved you on the palms of His hands! You are the prince or princess of the Great High King!

You need to remember that Jesus carried the cross for YOU! Every time He stumbled and picked the cross back up, He had you on his mind. He dragged it to that hill for you. When the nails were driven in, He took your sins with Him. He took all those sins that were done to you, for you.

He died not only to give you eternal life, but to give you freedom! And to give your life more abundantly! And by His wounds you have been healed!

You may be thinking, Lady, you have no clue what I've been through. You don't know all the wrong choices I've made. You don't know what this person has done to me, what they'd said to me. You're right, but guess what? God knows and He still loves you!

I am asking that you don't let Christ's death and resurrection be in vain by believing the lies of the enemy. Don't believe the lie that you are worthless, not loved, that no one cares, because I care and God cares. After all, God the Father paid the ultimate price for you-Jesus! Don't allow the enemy to continue to hold you captive, because my friend, God wants to fulfill His perfect and pleasing will for your life. He can't do that if you're all stuffed up with hurts.

So I'm asking, in the face of tragedy or the aftermath of circumstance, would you be able to forgive the person who has hurt you? We've all been hurt by someone. We all carry offense, anger, shame, rejection and so on.

God's word says, "When you stand praying, if you hold anything against anyone, forgive him, so that your Father in heaven may forgive you your sins." It may require you to go to the beginning of that pain. To that situation, to a certain person or persons, or maybe it was the words unfairly spoken. Those were the moments you were wounded. That is when Satan gained legal access to your heart and planted anger, offense, rage and bitterness. The list can go on and on.

I know what I'm asking could be very painful to do. Through my own experience, I've learned what it's like to live on the other side of that darkness. The light of freedom makes life a beautiful place to be. Once I gave up the sin and forgave, God began a good work in me. This published novel is a testament to His deliverance and forgiveness!

But what if you have forgiven them? I want to let you in on a little secret the Lord gave me. You may have forgiven them, but the wound is still there. If you wrinkle up your nose when the name of the person whom you forgave comes up in a conversation—then you need to be healed from what that person has done. If you constantly share the same story about the offense-then you haven't truly forgave-the wound needs to be healed. If you can't stop thinking ill thoughts about the person, then guess what? You need that wound to be healed.

I want you to know that by holding onto those hurts, you aren't hurting that person—it's hurting you. You will not be able to move forward with God until you surrender your wounds. Don't allow Satan to rob you of your destiny any more. For where the Spirit of the Lord is there is freedom! Cry out to God and get set free today! Here is how you can begin your journey to freedom.

- Repent—ask God to forgive you for holding onto the hurts. (Name them specifically.)

- Forgive the people who offended you.

- Ask the Lord to release into your soul His Glory and His Light. Listen and wait upon the Lord until He tells you that your wound is completely healed.

- Then, command, in the name of Jesus Christ those spirits (demons) to leave you. (Anger, rage, addiction, control, bitterness, etc.)

- Do the battle—stop doing the very things that have held you captive.

When they try to tempt you to feel hurt again, tell the demons to flee, for you are set free!

Here is a prayer you can say:

Lord Jesus, please forgive me for entertaining offense (whatever it is). I forgive (whomever) and I lay them at your feet. I ask that you bathe my soul in Your blood and release Your Glory and Your Light. I thank You for forgiving my sins and ask that You give me the strength to not entertain the hurts any longer. Lord, please give me confirmation of when the soul wound is healed. I will wait upon You.

In the name of Jesus Christ, I command the spirit of anger (whatever it is) to leave me right now. It no longer has authority over me and I shut the door. Father God, I release into my soul peace, love, (and whatever else you want to release of God's goodness). Thank You, Jesus, for setting me free. Amen.

I have been involved in a women's inner-healing ministry for about fifteen years and I've seen some amazing healing take place with each woman I have sat with. I know that allowing God to heal your soul is the key to freedom. In John 3:2 it says, "Beloved, I wish above all things that thou mayest prosper and be in health, even as thy soul prospereth."

I've learned a phenomenal teaching of how to get your soul healed by Katie Souza. God has given her an amazing ministry. If you feel like your life is stuck, spiraling out of control or you can't seem to get over that addiction, then I strongly suggest ordering her teachings.

The web site is: www.expectedendministries.com. The teaching is called, *The Healing School by Katie Souza.*

If you have any comments or questions you'd like to share, you can find me on Facebook at www.facebook.com/vanessa.matheny.5. You can also e-mail me at booksbyvanessa@gmail.com. I would love to hear from you.

I pray, my friend, that all goes well with your soul!

Vanessa Matheny

Vanessa lives in Michigan with her husband of twenty-three years and together they have raised three beautiful children. She is a devout follower of Jesus Christ and loves to serve Him. She enjoys serving in her church and working with women through an inner healing ministry.

"Never in my wildest dreams did I think I would become a writer. In high school, I hated to write. In fact, I was horrible at it. It wasn't until the Lord healed my heart from many wounds of the past that He gave me the desire to write. He has taken my victories and turned them into stories. My heart's desire is to touch heaven and change Earth for the Kingdom of God one story at a time."

www.ingramcontent.com/pod-product-compliance
Lightning Source LLC
Chambersburg PA
CBHW071055250626

47159CB00002B/476